PON

8/08

JUST TOO GOOD TO BE TRUE

This Large Print Book carries the
Seal of Approval of N.A.V.H.

JUST TOO GOOD TO BE TRUE

E. LYNN HARRIS

THORNDIKE PRESS
A part of Gale, Cengage Learning

Detroit • New York • San Francisco • New Haven, Conn • Waterville, Maine • London

GALE
CENGAGE Learning™

LIBRARY OF CONGRESS CATALOGING-IN-PUBLICATION DATA

Harris, E. Lynn.
    Just too good to be true / by E. Lynn Harris.
      p. cm. — (Thorndike Press large print African-American)
    ISBN-13: 978-1-4104-0641-5 (hardcover : alk. paper)
    ISBN-10: 1-4104-0641-5 (hardcover : alk. paper)
    1. African American college athletes — Fiction. 2. Family
secrets — Fiction. 3. Celibacy — Fiction. 4. Football stories.
5. Large type books. I. Title.
PS3558.A64438J88 2008b
813'.54—dc22

                                    2008001101

Published in 2008 in arrangement with Doubleday, a division of Random House, Inc.

Dedicated to
Sean Lewis James

Thanks for being the inspiration for Brady
and for a love and friendship that for most
of my life I only dreamed of.

In Loving Memory of My First Cousin
and Big Brother
Kennie L. Phillips
Sunrise: 6/21/1952 Sunset: 4/21/2008

In Memory

Emma Bolton
Bebe Moore Campbell
Margaret "Meg" Ingram
August Wilson
Michael Stewart

ACKNOWLEDGMENTS

I must start by giving thanks to God for His many daily blessings, and for being the center of my joy. Every day I realize that it's a blessing to be able to do something you love doing, and for this I will always be grateful.

I'm thankful for this opportunity to publicly thank the people and organizations who support me every step of the way. Without them I wouldn't be able to use my time and my life to tell the stories that are really gifts from God.

I'm thankful to have a family that loves and supports me no matter what. Thank you to each and every niece, nephew, cousin, uncle, aunt, brother and sister, but most especially my mother, Etta W. Harris, and my Aunt, Jessie L. Phillips.

God has seen fit to put two special young men in my life: my son, Brandon, and godson, Sean. I don't know how I managed to live before they came into my life. Brandon and Sean keep me on my toes and have shown me a love I never knew. I must send out a special shout of real love to my little brother and trainer, Tywan Freeney, and his lovely wife, Nicole, and also to my lil bro, Lloyd Boston, for his support and for holding down the fashion scene.

I have a family of friends who are a lifeline to me with their enduring love and support. I know I don't have to mention them in every book I write, but it's a privilege to know and love these people and it's the very least I can do. So thanks for being there, Vanessa Gilmore, Cindy and Steve Barnes, Lencola Sullivan, Robin Walters, Pamela Frazier, Laura Gilmore, Sybil Wilkes, Yolanda Starks, Anthony Bell, Ken Hatten, Terry McMillan, Roy Johnson, Christopher Martin, Pamela Simpson, Reggie Van Lee, Gordon Chambers, Keith Boykin, Brenda and Tony Van Putten, Derrick and Sanya Gragg, Tracy and David Huntley, Kimberla and Will Roby, Dyanna Williams, Troy Danato, Blanche Richardson and Victoria Christopher Murray.

I can't go on without mentioning Sean Lewis James, to whom this book is dedicated because of the love and friendship he gives me every single day of my life.

Then there is my family at the University

of Arkansas-Fayetteville who have always given me more than I could ever repay. Being a Razorback has always been a great source of pride for me. Even though I'm not teaching there anymore, there are ties to folks I can't leave behind because they mean so much to me and I love each and every person dearly. The spirit programs at the U of A are among the best in the country, and that's not my prejudice — but just "Real Talk," as the young people say. The person behind the spirit programs for the last twenty-five years is a lovely woman who in the last five years has proven to be one of the people I love and trust the most. Big thanks to Jean Nail for your friendship and allowing me to play a small part in a great Arkansas tradition.

Then there is my publishing family. It's hard to believe but I'm entering my sixteenth year as a member of the Doubleday family. The support I receive from them is second to none and I'm grateful to be published by such a classy and wonderful organization. I can use these adjectives to describe this company because of one man, Stephen Rubin, our leader. Stephen is not only a leader who can relate to almost anybody, but he does so with such grace and class. It's heartwarming and humbling to be linked with this man and this company.

On a day-to-day basis, the face of the company for me has become one of my best and most trusted friends. Janet Hill holds the title of Vice President and Executive Editor, but she is so much more. Because of her brilliant editing skills, I'm able to produce novels to the best of my abilities. There is a touch of Janet's class and lovely spirit on every page of my novels.

There are many other people at Doubleday who I feel go that extra step to make me feel special. Maybe they treat other authors the way they treat me, but I don't think so. So, a million thanks to: Alison Rich, Meredith McGinnis, Michael Palgon, Bill Thomas, Pauline James, Gerry Triano, John Fontana, Christian Nwachukwu Jr., and Dorothy Boyajy. I couldn't do what I do without you and I'm forever in your debt for the way you do your jobs with such ease.

There are several other people whom I depend on more than they will ever know. Again, I've been blessed that these folks are not only smart and the best at what they do, but just great friends, as well. I have the same agents that I was lucky to start this business with, and I can't imagine publishing without John Hawkins and Moses Cardona.

My lawyer, Amy Goldson and accountant Bob Braunschweig are among the best in their respective fields and try very hard to make every area of my life run smoothly. It's a dirty job, but somebody has to do it. Chandra Sparks Taylor and Victoria Christopher Murray provided much needed editing skills and friendship.

My assistant for over twelve years, Anthony Bell, is also a great friend. He knows me better than most people and really keeps my life in order. This year Anthony decided it was time to pursue his dream of opening his own design firm, and as much as I will miss him on a daily basis I know he will always be only a phone call away. We'll see big things on the design front from Anthony real soon. Stay tuned.

Anyone who has ever met me knows of my love for college football and especially the Arkansas Razorbacks. This novel grew out of that love. In the fall of 2003, I returned to my beloved alma mater, the U of A, to teach writing. There were lots of student athletes in my classes and I wanted to write a book they would enjoy reading. It took me more than four years to write this book, because it had to be just right. All of my students contributed to this novel, but four of my favorites, Angel Beasley, George Wilson, Celia

Anderson, and Ben Beaumont, went the extra mile and deserve special mention. I couldn't have completed this novel without them.

I want to offer special thanks to all the bookstores, book clubs, black radio stations, and African American Greek organizations for their continued support.

Some of my readers might view this book as a departure from what I normally write, but I think if you read closely you will recognize familiar themes. This book is still about family, friendship, and faith that any dream is possible.

Finally, I would like to personally thank my many readers, old and new. Many of you have been with me from the beginning, and your support continues to bless my soul and spirit in ways few people experience. I can never adequately thank you for changing the course of my life. You're one of the big reasons I have such joy in my life. And for that I'm truly grateful.

LETTERS FROM THE PAST

January 18, 1987

Niecey,

I can hardly stand to write your name.

How could you do this to me?

If what you did last night is love, then I want no fucking part of it. Or you. Believe that shit. How could I fall in love with a girl who is a whore and a slut?

You make me sick.

I'm tired of you "ladies" talking about what dogs we jocks can be, when it's really you "got-to-find-me-an-NFL-husband" women who are the dogs. Female dogs. Bitches. You use that magic between your legs to lure men into your web and call it love.

What would your wannabe-high-class parents have to say about what you did? Do you think "the Rev," your dear old daddy, would still call you his princess? Hell no!

17

What about all that stuff you told me about wanting us to have three children and live happily ever after? Well, let me tell you, now there is no ever after, Niecey. Not now. Not ever.

I wanted to throw up when I saw you lying in that bed, drunk and naked. And then I had to listen to those high school boys tell me that you took such good care of them.

Niecey, you're nothing but a whore. I thought when you saved yourself for me that I would be the only man you ever made love to. Fuck that. I feel like such a fool. This shit is going to hit campus and I'm going to be the laughingstock of the locker room.

How could you do this to me?

Because of you I'm left with a heart that can no longer hold love.

My mother was right: Any woman who lays down with a man without the benefit of marriage ain't shit. I should have believed her. I should have known better, because after the first time you and I had sex, all you could think about was sex . . . sex . . . sex, SEX, as if you were a nympho. I thought you couldn't keep your hands off me because you liked the way I got down. Now I know that I fell in love with a freak.

Well, baby, the joke's on you. One day you may have children, though definitely not with me, and eventually they'll learn when you least expect it that their mother was the campus ho. When that happens, I hope you hurt as much as I hurt now.

I wish I could say it's been wonderful calling you my girl. I wish I could say that we'll get over this and become stronger, but I can't. Niecey, what you did is unforgivable and I regret the day I met you. I left a good girl for you. But from now on, whenever you see me, keep stepping. Don't look my way. When I'm a big superstar in the NFL, don't tell anybody that you ever knew me. Don't tell people that you fucked me (I now know that's all it was to you). I suggest you do what I'm gonna do: Forget you ever knew me, because I've already forgotten that I ever knew or loved you.

I hate you.

W.

January 20, 1987

Daphne,

I give up. You win. Woodson is all yours. I hope you're happy now.

I love Woodson dearly, but I made a big mistake. Deep down I think Woodson still loves me, but right now the pain is too much for him. You made him happy once and maybe you can make him happy now.

One final thing, Daphne. I know that you're spreading my business all over campus, but I have some advice for you: concentrate on your own life, and don't let my name cross your lips again. Take your fake grief-counselor act somewhere else. I'm out of your life for good. I guess things turned out the way you always wanted.

Niecey

May 20, 1987

Dear Daughter,

It pains me to write this letter, Niecey, but I feel I must. What on earth were you thinking and how could you bring such shame on our family? Your father and I have worked so hard to establish ourselves in this community and this city. I'm writing this letter because I can't even bring myself to look at you, let alone speak to you.

After all your father and I have done for you. You never wanted for anything! And now you go out and do this. How in the name of Jesus could you let something like this happen? Didn't we raise you to know right from wrong? What about all the talks we had about your future? Think about all the money we spent on your debutante ball. All our dreams ruined in one night.

What will I tell my sorors and Links sisters if they ever find out what you've done? Have you thought of the shame you brought on me personally? I used to brag about you all the time. Those ladies wanted their daughters to be like you. How can I look those jealous women in the face now? You were an honor student at the University making good grades. You were going to pledge my sorority and come back home and be a shining example for the young women of our church. Now, your father and I look like total fools.

Thank God there is a solution. Take the enclosed check and deposit it immediately into your checking account. Then call Ms. Alberta Hinson at 404-388-6367, she's expecting to hear from you. She'll handle everything from there. Follow her instructions, Niecey, and do what you're told. This is the only way to handle this situation and not bring shame to our family name.

When everything is taken care of, Ms. Hinson will get in contact with me and we'll decide what to do next. Hopefully, your father will be over his shame and we can accept you back into our family. But only if you do what we're telling you to do.

This doesn't mean that we don't love you. We do. But we have high standards that we learned from our parents and we are not going to let one night ruin them.

Your mother,
Clarice B. Johnson

▪ ▪ ▪ ▪
PRIVATE THOUGHTS
▪ ▪ ▪ ▪

March 11, 1994

Dear Diary:

I met a man today. A wonderful man who I believe is going to change my life. I know it's not unusual for me to meet men because they have been after me since I was fourteen, but this one is different. I knew it the moment I saw him.

He's tall, good-looking, and was well-dressed in a suit that looked like it was made just for him. He looked like money. Big money. He came to see my mother Lita (that's what I call her behind her back), but she and her friend May were at the bar in the middle of the day — what lushes. But Lita's loss became my gain. I offered to let him wait in the living room, like Lita tells me to do with all her male *friends*, but he wanted to wait in the kitchen with me as I finished up my housekeeping duties.

One of the first things he said to me as

he sipped the sweet tea I made for him was, "Do you realize how beautiful you are?" I'm almost eighteen years old, but I don't think anyone, not even my mother, has ever told me I was beautiful. I wanted to cry. I felt like I was in a movie starring me.

He asked me what I wanted to do with my life, and when I told him I always dreamed of moving to Hollywood to star in movies, he said that he could help. He told me he knew all kinds of famous actors, producers, and directors who could help me when I was ready. I told him that my main concern was to figure out how to make lots of money so that I could take better care of my little brother Wade since my mother Lita was so irresponsible. Wade's just always been different. He lives in his own little world. He needs care and he needs it badly. Sometimes I think my only mission in life is to be Wade's angel here on earth.

Growing up with Lita as a "hostess" (even though she's never carried a tray in her life), I was very familiar with what women had to do for work, so I thought I already knew what the man would say when I asked him what I'd have to do. But he surprised me when he said, "All you have to do is believe in yourself and always remember that your beauty can change your life for good."

I told him I was ready for anything. (Diary, you know that I've already done a few things I'd like to forget, just to survive.) He told me not to sell myself short and that the whole world could be mine if I wanted it badly enough.

Then he took my face in his big, strong hands and looked at me like he cared and said, "I will do everything in my power to make your dreams come true."

It felt like a dream, but it was real.

He said he'd speak to some people and then come back for me in two weeks. People bullshit me all the time, but I believe him. I know he will come back.

As soon as I put this pen down I'm gonna go pack my bags and get ready to meet my destiny. It's funny how life can go from shit to sugar in a split second.

Raquel

■ ■ ■ ■

A Star is Born

■ ■ ■ ■

SPORTS
THE MAGAZINE

TOO GOOD TO BE TRUE
(But Maybe Not for the
Central Georgia University Star)

August 7, 2006
By Ben Beaumont

For a college football star, Brady Jamal Bledsoe seems too good to be true. On the field, this Central Georgia University (CGU) running back is a true Heisman Trophy frontrunner, belittling opposing defenses with the rarest combination of size and speed. Off the field, Bledsoe is an excellent student, a loving son, devoted Christian, and self-described role model.

Physically, you couldn't design a more perfect tailback. At 6'2", 210 pounds, and with a swift stiff arm and powerful legs that easily churn out 4.3 forty-yard dashes and blaze past linebackers and defensive backs, Bledsoe is the force behind a Jaguar team that's defied odds to become a contender for the conference title in the mighty Southeastern Conference (SEC).

Heading into a season where Central Georgia is poised to break out after only ten years as a Division I program, the Jaguars have a trump card in Bledsoe. Coming off a junior year where he rushed for more than 1,500 yards and 21 touchdowns, caught 15 passes for three scores, and even threw a pass for a touchdown, Bledsoe's versatility, which includes a humble, team-first attitude, is the strength of the high-powered Jaguar offense.

"I don't make individual goals," says Bledsoe. "It's all about the team — winning an SEC championship and finally beating up on some of the teams that have licked us the past three years like Georgia, Arkansas, and Florida."

While his "team-first" words are sincere, it's obvious that wherever Bledsoe goes, so goes the Jaguar offense. Knowing that fact, Central Georgia offensive coaches are designing new ways to get the football into his hands. Plans include lining him up not only at tailback, but as a wide receiver and even at quarterback in the new "Wildhog" formation they took from the playbook of Arkansas offensive coordinator Gus

Malazah after visiting the Razorbacks during spring practice.

"I believe Brady's the best running back in America, and we want to showcase that," says Jaguar head coach Houston Hale. "We're going to find any way we can to get him the football, because when we do, good things happen."

Bledsoe's game and attitude on the field are rivaled only by his unbelievably gracious and squeaky-clean demeanor off the field. To say Bledsoe, a straight-A student who is already working on a second college degree, is well-rounded would be an understatement.

"I just try and work hard and remember what my mom told me: 'Stay focused and take things one game at a time'," says Bledsoe, a self-proclaimed "Mama's Boy."

Mom is Carmyn Bledsoe, a young single mother who managed to keep Brady on the right path despite the distractions of an urban Atlanta upbringing and the temptations that face young, African American athletes.

"She's not only my mother, but also my best friend," says Brady Bledsoe. "Even though I grew up without a father, I didn't miss out, because she played so many roles in my life and has never missed a game — home or away."

So squeaky clean is Bledsoe that, as a young teenager, with the encouragement of his mother, he took a vow of celibacy at his home church, opting to wait for marriage, and he's kept that pledge to this day.

"You can't miss what you never had," he says. "I think I should take to my marriage bed what I would want my bride to bring."

Carmyn Bledsoe, who manages a high-end hair salon in Atlanta's trendy Buckhead neighborhood, keeps daily contact with her only son, encouraging him in his football pursuits as well as life in general.

"Brady is such a blessing," Carmyn Bledsoe says. "But I tell him that with success comes great responsibility. He's got a gift, and I'm proud that he's doing so well. I really think he's got a shot at the Heisman."

And Brady Bledsoe carries his mother's teachings with him whether he's at football practice, in the classroom, at church, or interacting with fans.

"I want to be a role model, especially to young black kids," says Bledsoe. "With so many thugs in the world, kids today need a positive example, and I embrace that role."

College football is defined by the quest for perfection. In the Bowl Championship Series era, undefeated teams with superb players are rare, and with the perfect tailback,

Central Georgia has a head start on what could be a magical season. But Brady Jamal Bledsoe isn't just a perfect football player — he seems to be an all-around perfect young man.

BRADY'S FAVORITES

Football Players — Tom Brady and Eddie George

Basketball Players — Dwayne Wade

Favorite Meal — Medium-Well Steak and French Fries

Favorite Actor — Don Cheadle

Favorite Actress — Beyoncé Knowles

Favorite Comedian — Dave Chappelle

Favorite Male Singer — Yung Joc/Jay-Z

Favorite Female Singer — Ciara

Favorite Movies — *Remember the Titans* and *We Are Marshall*

Words To Live By — "You only get to make one first impression. Make it a good one."

■ ■ ■ ■

BOOK ONE
THE SETUP

■ ■ ■ ■

CHAPTER 1
BRADY DROPS THE BALL

Yeah, I guess I *am* almost too good to be true, I thought as I read the *SPORTS: The Magazine* cover story for the third time. That is, if you believe the hype. But the truth is I almost ruined my life one night, but I somehow managed to right a wrong and come out basically unscathed.

It was a cool October night and my football team, the Central Georgia University Jaguars, had just recorded our biggest victory in CGU school history over the Louisiana State University (LSU) Tigers.

It was a beautiful night for football, with a crowd of over 80,000 fans. I remember the smell of the grass and how great my teammates and I looked in our green and gold uniforms under the lights in a nighttime atmosphere that only college football can provide. It was an incredible feeling when the team raced from the tunnel to the field surrounded by a thunderous roar from the

CGU fans.

I was a redshirt freshman, and in this my first start I gained over 150 yards against a tough LSU defense.

After the game, I decided to join my childhood best friend, Delmar, and some of my teammates for some postgame festivities. In the past, for me that would have meant reviewing film of that night's game. But I was getting tired of all my teammates ribbing me and saying, "Brady can't hang" and "Brady ain't down with that," so I surprised them and myself by going to drink my first beer with them at senior Teddy Miles's apartment.

After a couple of beers, I decided to call it a night and trek back to campus on foot. When I got to the parking lot of Teddy's apartment building, I saw a girl getting out of a car in a white dress and white stockings. When the headlights hit her face, I realized I knew her. Naomi Brasswell. A girl from the church I attend in Scarlet Springs.

Naomi was one of several people who said they were interested in being a part of Saving Ourselves when I tried to start the group at the church, but she was the only one who showed up for the first meeting. So I gave up the idea of starting the celibacy club, but still talked with Naomi several times about how tough it was playing football and trying to stay celibate.

Naomi was a local girl, was majoring in nursing at CGU, and lived with her mother and little sister near campus. Sometimes we attended Bible study on Wednesday nights and went to the movies on Sunday after church. A couple of times she invited me to her house for Sunday dinner. I always accepted that invitation, because her mother could throw down with the pots and pans.

I liked Naomi a lot, but I was trying to follow my mother's advice and stay focused on football and my studies. Still, I thought my mother might like Naomi because she was a virgin and went to church three times a week.

I approached Naomi, and she appeared nervous until she realized it was me. She flashed a beautiful smile and said, "Oh, it's you, Brady. What are you doing over here?"

"Hanging with some teammates, celebrating the big win," I said. "What are you doing?"

"Apartment-sitting for one of my friends who went home this weekend," she said.

"What apartment does she live in?" I asked.

"Up there," Naomi said as she pointed toward an apartment on the third floor, almost directly over my teammate's place.

"Why don't I walk you up? Make sure nobody messes with you," I said, realizing that several of my teammates were now most likely drunk and ready to hit the prowl.

"That would be nice," Naomi said as she locked her car door. As we walked toward the apartment, I took notice of her beautiful bright eyes and black hair tumbling over her shoulders. The evening light accentuated her white uniform and outlined her body, making her look like a sexy, naughty nurse and not the church girl I was used to.

When we got to the apartment, I realized I was a little tipsy, so I asked Naomi if I could come in for a while, get some water and rest. She said yes, and minutes later I crashed on the sofa and fell asleep.

A couple hours later, I woke up and Naomi was standing in front of me holding a bottle of water and wearing an oversized white T-shirt with no bra. I could see the shadow of her nipples pushing into the cotton, the soft, heavy curves of her breasts standing out perkily in front of her. An image flashed through my head of me raising up her shirt, getting on my knees, and sucking those breasts. I felt a twinge in my jeans, but I tried to ignore it.

"I thought you might need this," she said

44

as she handed me the water, leaning toward me as her overpowering but welcoming feminine scent washed over me. I found myself breathing deeply, wondering what her skin would taste like.

I took a sip of water, then put the bottle on the floor, stood up, and just looked at her. She stared back. I was nervous, and the bulge in my jeans grew tighter.

"Would it be all right if I kissed you?" I asked.

"Yes," she whispered.

I leaned in, put my arms around her waist, and pressed my lips softly against hers. They were sweet, like I always thought they would be.

Her body was tense at first, but then I parted her lips, slid my tongue into her mouth. She closed her lips around my tongue, and a shiver ran through my body.

I leaned out of the kiss. "Where's the bedroom?"

"Back there," Naomi said, pointing behind her. "What about your celibacy vow?" she asked.

I thought about the question for a moment, then said, "We don't have to go all the way."

"Are you sure?"

"We can just . . . you know . . . dry grind."

"Okay. I think that'll be okay."

I followed Naomi into the dark room. It took my eyes a minute to adjust before I saw that there wasn't a bed, just a mattress on the floor, a flower-print bedspread over it.

"What should we do first?" Naomi said.

"Take off your clothes," I said.

"No. You go first."

"Let's do it together."

We slowly took off our clothes. I pulled off my sweater and she pulled her T-shirt over her head. I pushed down my jeans. I took off my boxer briefs, and she slid off her ivory panties.

Naomi lay across the mattress on her back.

I stood over her, my erection sticking out and slightly curving up.

"It's so big," Naomi said.

"It's not that big," I said.

"It looks so big and hard," Naomi said, gently touching the tip.

I moaned, "You got me so brick, girl."

I lowered my body onto hers. Her skin was soft, her hips wide; her nipples, pointing up, were thick and hard like ripe cherries. Her body seemed to cradle mine as I lay fully on top of her.

"I'm nervous, Brady."

"I know. Me, too," I said.

"I'm so wet, Brady. Do you want to feel me?"

"Yeah."

She took my penis in her hand, rubbed it softly over her vagina.

I moaned.

"Do you feel it?" She moaned, too.

"Yeah."

"Does it feel good?"

"Yeah," I said as I started to push myself into her opening.

"We can't do anything. We don't have protection."

"I know. We aren't going all the way," I said sincerely. But it was feeling so good, better than I ever thought it would. The tip of me was throbbing, pulsating. I started to glide in and out in short strokes. Then I went a little deeper with each one, and I felt like I was losing control.

"Brady, maybe we should stop," Naomi said.

"I'm sorry!" I said, pulling out. "I'm sorry. We can stop."

Naomi looked up at me, her thighs still open, her eyelids low. She looked so beautiful right then.

"I . . . I . . . don't want you to stop. I like the way it feels," Naomi stammered.

"Are you sure?"

Naomi didn't say anything, just nodded and grabbed me between the legs. She started stroking me, making my head spin. Then she put my tip back inside of her and said, "Don't push too hard and don't come inside me."

"Okay," I said, already starting slowly to grind on top of her. I moaned, and I heard her, too. She wrapped her arms around me, clawing my back.

"Oh, Brady," she whispered.

And then I started to feel what I never felt before. Like an impending explosion, racing through my body toward my groin. My muscles tightened, my head spinning. "I . . . I . . ."

It was too much. I couldn't handle it. And before I knew it, I was gripped so tightly by a pleasure so overwhelming that I couldn't move. My back arched, I cried out and pushed farther into Naomi and then started to explode while I tried to pull out. But I couldn't. I rolled off her onto my side, feeling exhausted. My first time, and I didn't even last two minutes.

All I could think about was how much better this was than my palms and Palmer's cocoa butter lotion.

A cloud of guilt followed both of us during

the weeks that followed. I thought how disappointed my mother would be, but I couldn't forget how off the chain the sex had felt, and I now knew why sex was all my teammates thought or talked about. I called Naomi a couple of times, but our conversations were weird, like we knew that we both wanted to do it again but we couldn't live with the remorse.

At the end of the season, Naomi called me and said she needed to see me. It sounded like she was crying, and when I asked her what was wrong she asked me to meet her in the reading room at the school's library.

When I got there, I saw Naomi dressed in a green sweater and blue jeans, looking beautiful but nervous.

We exchanged polite hugs, and Naomi whispered, "I'm pregnant."

For minutes I maintained a stony silence before finally muttering to myself, "Damn, son."

In the days that followed, I spent long hours in my apartment thinking about God and how pissed off at me He must be. Still, that would be nothing compared to my mother's disappointment and sadness.

I spent a lot of time praying. I spent a lot of time telling myself that I wasn't ready to be a father. The one thing my mother had warned me about, I'd gone out and done. Even though she didn't talk a lot about my father, she'd admitted that they were both too young when I was conceived.

I chastised myself for ever thinking I was better than my friends and some of my teammates because I wore a celibacy ring.

I thought about how this was going to affect something that I truly loved — playing football, which had always been a part of my life since the first time I put on my #2 jersey. Even though my mom wasn't in favor of my playing at first, I convinced her at age six that it was a part of my DNA. Something I had to do to feel whole. I remember putting on a helmet for the first time when I was playing Pee Wee football and how it made me feel important. I remember the first time I touched a football on a kickoff return and how I outraced all of the other guys for a touchdown.

Maybe God answers prayers after He gets your attention. A day before finals started, Naomi came to my apartment and told me she decided to get an abortion and transfer to Savannah State, but that she would need my help.

I didn't know how I felt about abortion, but I definitely did not want to become another statistic, a young African American man who'd become a father before he escaped his teens. I made a promise that if I could come out of this situation free and clear I would reclaim my vow of celibacy and maybe only God, Naomi, and I would know what I'd done.

CHAPTER 2
RAQUEL, NOW AND LATER

Raquel Murphy smoothed the gloss over her lips and took a glance at her makeup in the lighted mirror. She smiled at herself and thought, *You're still the most beautiful girl in the room — any room you enter.* She yanked her hair into a high ponytail and walked back into her bedroom one final time.

The large master suite was dark with the exception of the quivering glow of the candles on the dresser. The Louis Vuitton suitcase on the bed was still open, and she stuffed the cosmetics bag inside before she zipped it up. She sighed as she looked around. She didn't want to leave but knew it was no longer safe to stay.

Raquel picked the large envelope off the dresser and spilled the contents onto the bed. There was a driver's license and credit card, both with her new name, *Barrett Elizabeth Manning,* a cell phone, a BlackBerry, and pictures and newspaper articles about her next job.

Maybe the fifth time would be the charm and this would be her last assignment, she thought as she picked up her purse. It wasn't like she really enjoyed her work. But how could she turn away from the lifestyle that the money she earned afforded her? She would have never been able to live in a lavish condo near the University of Washington near downtown Seattle. Neither would she be able to drive the expensive Mercedes sports car she rolled around town in. She'd come a long way from how she grew up, but that had been no way to live.

With that thought, Raquel took a deep breath, swung her purse over her shoulder, and took one last look around. There would be another condo like this waiting for her — maybe a better one. That's what had been promised.

Just before she got ready to leave the condo, the phone rang. She assumed it was someone making sure that she'd gotten the information for her flight and was on time.

"Hello," Raquel said.

"Bitch, where is my shit?" The loud male voice boomed over the telephone line. "I'm gonna get your ass, Bethany, when I get back to Seattle. Watch your back, bitch!"

Raquel didn't respond to the voice and

53

with characteristic calmness hung up the phone, mouthed *Stupid asshole,* then laughed and thought, *Bethany Lewis doesn't live here anymore.*

She pulled the suitcase into the carpeted hallway. As she pressed the button for the elevator, she thought about all that awaited her. This next gig would be easy but would have a big payoff — if the notes she'd just received were any indication.

The elevator door opened.

"Hey, Bethany."

She stepped back, startled by the voice, stepped into the elevator, and then smiled at her neighbor, Jenna.

"Hey."

Jenna eyed Raquel's suitcase and asked if she was going on a trip.

"Yes."

"Vacation?" Jenna quizzed.

"Business."

"Gone for long?"

"Back in a couple of weeks," Raquel lied as she thought that she wasn't going to miss this nosy bitch one bit.

"Is your handsome boyfriend going with you?"

"Is that any of your business?" Raquel asked as she shot Jenna an evil look.

"I'm sorry. Are you flying or driving?"

"What part of mind your own damn business don't you understand?"

"Just trying to start my day with a little conversation. Wow, what a beautiful watch that is," Jenna said, changing the subject, as she eyed Raquel's wrist. "I wish I was dating a professional athlete or somebody rich enough to buy me gifts like that. You're one lucky girl."

"Well, this is your lucky day, Jenna. I'm your fairy godmother," Raquel said as she slipped off the expensive watch layered in diamonds and put it in her surprised neighbor's hand.

"You're giving this to me?"

"Yes."

"But why?"

"Because I know if anybody around here is looking for me you're going to tell them nothing," Raquel said. "Do I make myself clear?"

"Oh, yeah. Loud and clear. But who would be looking for you?"

"There you go with those pesky questions. You want to keep that watch, don't you?"

"Yeah, but are you in some kind of trouble? Maybe I can help."

"All my trouble is behind me," Raquel said as the elevator stopped.

"Thanks and good luck, Bethany," Jenna

said. Raquel didn't respond and dismissed Jenna with a simple wave of her hand.

She wouldn't see Jenna again.

As she walked through the lobby, the doorman smiled, nodded, and then held the large glass doors open for her. A fine mist had settled over the city, and Raquel told herself she wouldn't miss Seattle's rainy days.

A limousine driver took Raquel's bag and opened the door for her. She looked up at the high-rise building, smiled slightly, and stepped gently into the car. Moments later, the driver took his place behind the steering wheel and Raquel slid on large, dark sunglasses, even though the sun was nowhere to be found.

It was time to go to work.

CHAPTER 3
CARMYN'S TRICK PLAY

My son looked over and noticed the tears streaming down my face, momentarily taking his eyes off the road. I had warned him not to do that ever since I first taught him to drive in the Kroger parking lot close to our home.

"Watch the road," I said.

"What's with the waterworks, Mom?" Brady asked as he came to a stop sign. He looked in the rearview mirror and noticed another car pulling up. He drove slowly for a couple of blocks, then pulled to the side of the road and turned the engine off.

"Brady, what are you doing? You know I've got to get back to Atlanta tonight. Why are you stopping?" I asked. I had surprised Brady by driving the 150 miles from Atlanta to take him to lunch after his morning football practice. When school started, there wouldn't be time for such midday adventures.

"Ms. Carmyn Bledsoe, we got plenty of time. I need to know what's up with my main lady," Brady said as he looked into my swollen eyes. He took my left hand and stroked it gently. "Tell me what's wrong, Ma."

"I know it's silly, but it just hit me that this is your last season of college football. It seems like yesterday we were driving up for the first time. I can't believe four years have passed." I gazed at my son and realized how much his face had filled out and matured. The cute little junior high school boy with skin that looked like butter and brown sugar combined, who had once had knock-knees and braces, was now a very handsome twenty-year-old. Wide shouldered, Brady had bright copper eyes with chestnut-orange interiors set deep beneath heavy brows. His gentle smile revealed perfectly aligned teeth and deep dimples that I knew would one day bring some young lady total happiness. The braces he'd hated had been worth every penny. My baby is a great-looking young man, and that's not just a proud mom talking.

"Is that what you're crying 'bout? Look on the bright side. This time next year, you'll be flying first class to who-knows-where to see me start my first professional football game.

I'll finally be able to take care of you."

"Stop that," I said. "How many times have I told you I don't need you to take care of me? I have my own money. I'll get to wherever you're playing on my own, and I'm not wasting money on first class."

"Whatever you say." Brady sighed and flashed that easy grin I couldn't resist. He started the car and we headed toward his off-campus apartment.

Moments later, we reached the parking lot and I directed Brady to pull up next to a sparkling silver Navigator. The car salesman had kept his word. It had the new-car sticker on the back window, and I had to keep myself from laughing out loud.

"Nice-looking truck," I said.

"Yep, it is," Brady said.

"Do you like the color?" I asked, and dug inside my large brown leather purse.

"Yeah, I do. When I go to the league, I'm gonna buy you *and* me one of those."

"Why wait?" I said as I tossed a ring of car keys to Brady. His mouth flew open and his eyes bulged. Tears stained my cheeks, but my face was now covered with a huge boy-did-I-pull-one-over-on-you smile.

"Damn, Mom," Brady said, catching himself. "I mean dang. These keys are mine? That truck is mine?" Brady said in disbelief.

"It's all yours, baby. You've earned it."

"Can you afford this? I mean, I thought you wanted to open another shop. I can wait for a truck until the season is over. I've made it all this time without wheels."

"You don't have to wait, Brady. Your football scholarship got you through college. Do you know how much money that's saved me? You're the best son in the world, and this is the very least I can do. Let's call it an early birthday present. Now you don't have to depend on your teammates to get you around."

"Wait until my boys see this. This is tight," Brady said. He turned and looked at his new SUV and then suddenly bolted from my car.

As I stepped out from the passenger side, he was gazing at the beautiful and awesome piece of machinery, at the headlights that glared from the front of the large hood. This was by far the most expensive gift I'd ever given my now speechless and sometimes spoiled son. He gave me a bear hug that made up for his loss for words. Before he inserted the key in the lock, he touched the door as if making sure it was real.

"Go ahead, get in. Let's test it out," I said.

"Okay, but how did you pull this off without me knowing?" Brady asked.

"That's my secret," I teased. "But you ought to know by now your mom's got skills." I walked toward the SUV's passenger side. Brady walked around the SUV and opened the door for me, and I eased into the car, relishing the firm leather seats and the new-car smell. He climbed into the driver's seat and caressed the steering wheel as though it was the sweetest thing he had ever laid hands on.

About two hours later, I drove away from Brady's apartment and pulled my cell phone from my purse. I speed-dialed Lowell Washington Jr., my best male friend and Brady's godfather. Lowell was a tenured professor in the Andrew Young College of Arts and Science at Central Georgia University. I first met him when he was young and handsome and poised to become the first African American United States senator from the South since Reconstruction. That is, until a jilted male lover set him up with steamy man-on-man sex tapes that were played over and over on BET and CNN. The revelation of the affair ended the political aspirations of Lowell, the son of one of Atlanta's first black multimillionaires. I had worked diligently on Lowell's campaign when Brady was a toddler. I knew Lowell to be a wonderful human being, whatever his sexual orientation, and I wanted him to always be a part of Brady's life. I was ecstatic when he agreed to be Brady's godfather and male role model.

It was tough being a single mom, so it was great to have Lowell around for those father-son Cub Scout meetings. And even though I had never missed one of Brady's sporting events, sometimes he wanted me in the background and Lowell front and center when he registered for Little League and Pee Wee football because all of the other boys had their fathers with them.

When Brady's little friends would ask if Lowell was his father, Brady would tell them no, but that he was his godfather, which was more special than a real father because God had chosen Lowell to look over him since his real father was in heaven with God.

Lowell's answering machine picked up, and when I heard the beep I began speaking. "Hey, Professor, I just dropped off the big surprise I was telling you about. He loved it. So thanks for your help in deciding what to get. Why don't you check on him later this evening or first thing tomorrow? Oh yeah, don't forget to keep those little hoochies away from our baby. Love ya. Mean it."

I savored the last sip of my warm spiced-tea as I glanced around the empty beauty salon.

It was Monday morning; the shop was closed but life still traveled forward as people returned to their weekly routines. Sometimes I would come in and do a little business, like balancing the books, ordering supplies, or taking care of that special customer who didn't like the hustle and bustle of a crowded beauty shop.

Back to My Roots had been in business for more than fifteen years in the Cascade area of Atlanta, the middle-class bedroom community where Brady and I lived until he reached the seventh grade. When I opened the salon, it had two stations, but it now had five regular stations and two for manicures. It was a cozy community business that had all kinds of customers, including welfare mothers, high school girls, as well as judges and local television anchors. I treasured them all, and they were one of the main reasons I had turned down offers to move the salon to the newly renovated historic downtown College Park. Every business day around noon, I would head across town and walk through the doors of the very exclusive Buckhead Day Spa and Salon, where the clientele was a little different from that of Back to My Roots. The customer base included Atlanta's socialites, mostly white, but a few blacks, as well as the wives of any celebrities who decided to visit the city. I had formed close relationships with several of the concierges at the nearby Ritz-Carlton, and they sent new clients almost daily. The menu of services was drastically different at the day spa. Patrons could receive everything from turning mousy brown hair to brilliant shades of blond, to the popular oxygen facials and Brazilian bikini waxes. At the day spa, I would put on a lilac smock with my name embroidered in white and *Spa Manager* directly under it. Even though that was not an accurate description of my current position, I saw no reason to let the world know that I was highly favored when a golden opportunity to become the owner landed in the pocket of my smock.

My start in Atlanta wasn't a good one. I didn't want to be here but had little choice in the matter. No one wanted to take a chance on me, a single mother, still a teenager. I finally got a few jobs: One was at a day care center, which gave me a discount so Brady could attend. I also had a job in the gift-wrap department at Rich's department store downtown.

One day, when I walked into the upscale day spa in affluent Buckhead by mistake, my life took a positive turn. There wasn't a black face to be found in the sleek white and chrome interior. When I decided to ask for an application, I figured I'd get turned down yet again. But then I met Jean-Claude, the owner, and he hired me on the spot.

"I see something in you," Jean-Claude said after twenty minutes of interviewing me. "I know you'll work hard."

I was offered the position of appointment clerk, which seemed easy enough, but after I had been on the job for only two hours, I realized there was nothing simple about what I had been hired to do. I was taking calls and arranging appointments for southern beauties who were convinced that being pampered was a fact of life, like housekeepers and rich husbands. But it didn't take me long to become a natural with the women, finding a way to make each person feel as if I were doing them a special favor. I quickly became everyone's favorite.

Months later when Jean-Claude's longtime prep girl left, he immediately promoted me. Within two years, I was managing the Buckhead Day Spa.

"I love you, Carmyn," Jean-Claude would always say to me. "I couldn't run this shop without you."

I still get misty when I think about Jean-Claude, a boss who became my friend, and whom I miss dearly. He was the first man who loved me unconditionally. I had no clue he had AIDS until the final stages, which he spent in a hospice in midtown Atlanta. When I found out, I invited him to move in with me and Brady, but he declined, saying children didn't need to be in a house with death hovering.

"I've got to stop thinking these old thoughts," I said to the walls of the empty shop.

A few moments later, my ringing cell phone broke the silence of the salon. *Unknown* flashed across the tiny screen, but I answered anyway.

"Hello," I said.

"Is this Ms. Bledsoe?" a somewhat familiar male voice asked.

"Yes. With whom am I speaking?"

"I see you forgot my voice, but that's cool. This is Nico Benson, CEO of The Great Ones Sports Agency. We talked last spring," he said.

"What can I do for you?" I asked, wondering what it was going to take for this man to get the message that Brady and I were not interested in him or his agency. I thought I'd made it perfectly clear last spring when he tried to convince Brady to forgo his senior year and enter the NFL Draft early.

"I was hoping, now that your son is entering his senior year, that I could sit down with the two of you and go over my firm's services. It still looks like Brady will be a first-round draft pick, and we can make sure he gets what he deserves."

"Mr. Benson," I said sternly, "Brady is busy getting ready for his final season and isn't talking with agents. I'm already familiar with what your firm offers, and we're not interested."

"Ms. Bledsoe, I apologized last year for contacting Brady without your permission. This year I hoped we could start with a clean slate. I thought all was forgiven," he said.

"Yes, but I'm still not interested. You need to stay away from my son, or else I will have to report you to the NCAA *again*. Have a good day, Mr. Benson," I said, and then I clicked off the phone before giving him a chance to respond.

I made sure that everything was in its proper place, and then I turned off the lights and locked the salon. I walked out to my car, and I was about to get into my beige E-class Mercedes when a hand grabbed my shoulder from behind.

I immediately dropped my purse, afraid that someone was trying to jack my car.

When I turned around, standing in front of

me was a brown-skinned man, 6'4" tall, broad shouldered, and well built. He wore khaki pants, casual shoes, and a knit shirt.

"I'm sorry I scared you," he said, looking disappointed.

"What are you doing here, Sylvester?" I asked as I bent down to pick up my purse.

Sylvester Monroe was handsome, with a strong jaw, beautiful straight white teeth (I have a weakness for men with nice teeth), and wavy black hair with a little gray at the temples. His only flaw was that he worked in a sandwich shop. Actually, a croissant bar called the Croissant Corner. It was a chain that had started in Macon, Georgia, and had expanded across the country.

When the shop first opened two years ago, I'd gone in for a croissant and a cup of soup, and there he was, smiling brightly, being helpful, telling me to have a wonderful day and he hoped to see me soon.

Every week or so I would go back, not knowing if it was the freshness of the croissants or Sylvester that had me continually walking through those doors.

He asked me out a dozen times, and a dozen times I told him I was just too busy. But he was persistent, and Brady was away at school, which left me lonely. So I took Sylvester up on his offer and let him take me out.

Sylvester took me to P. Diddy's restaurant Justin's on Peachtree. I made the mistake of offering to pay half of the check, because I wasn't sure if he could afford it on what he made at the croissant shop.

He looked hurt by the gesture, and I knew that he wanted to pay. I just wouldn't let him get too close to me. It sounded selfish even to me, but considering all that I had struggled to achieve, I didn't need to be settling for a man who made sandwiches for a living, or who might be embarrassed that I made more than he did.

I would see Sylvester once a week or so when Brady was away at school. But when my son was home during the summer, Sylvester became the Invisible Man. I told him not to call, and if Brady and I happened to go into the Croissant Corner and see him, I'd give him my order just like he was any one of the crew of employees working there. To keep him interested, every now and again I would text him a question such as *Miss me?* like I was a silly teenage girl.

"Why haven't you called me, or come to see me?" Sylvester asked me now, standing beside my car.

"Why are you sneaking up on me outside my salon?"

"Would I have seen you any other way?"

"I told you, I can't see you when my son is in town," I reminded him.

"But he's been back at school. He's at practice. I saw a story on him on television last night. And you still never told me the real reason for not allowing me to meet your son," Sylvester said as he stepped closer to me. "What's really going on?"

"There is nothing *really* going on," I said, turning to him. "I'm extremely busy right now, and I haven't had a chance to call you or come by." I put my arms around his waist. I didn't need him putting me through an inquisition right now. Besides, my relationship with my son was mine and mine alone. I hoped Sylvester wasn't going to make this complicated, because I did enjoy his company. He was the first man I'd dated more than once since Brady was born twenty years ago. If I expected my son to remain celibate, I needed to be a great example not only for him but also for the other girls and boys at our church. But when I met Sylvester, my morals betrayed me. I had to be sure no one, especially Brady, found out.

Brady was special, and I wanted him to live his life like he knew that. When he first got interested in sports, I knew I would do everything within my power to keep him from turning into a spoiled jock who thought the world revolved around him and owed him something.

"Are you too busy for me, Carmyn? Because if you are, just tell me, and I'll leave you alone so you can do what you need to do," he said in that mellow, masculine voice I loved.

"No, Sylvester," I said as I leaned closer and allowed my lips to linger near his. "I will make time for you. I just can't promise how soon that'll be. Do you understand?"

"Yeah," he said, and squeezed my hands. "And I'm sorry for walking up on you like that. I didn't mean to scare you."

"It's okay. I'll call you when we can get together. Okay?"

"Okay," Sylvester said. "But I want you to tell me then why you don't want your son to know about me."

"Okay," I said, not knowing if I was really going to tell him or not.

Chapter 4
Brady's Got a Secret

Just as I was getting ready for bed, the phone in my apartment rang. I looked at the caller ID and recognized the number. I felt a nervous energy in my stomach and I decided not to answer the phone, but it seemed my hand had a mind of its own and picked up the phone.

"Hello," I said.

"Welcome back, Brady. How was your summer?"

"Fine."

"What are you doing now?"

"Just chillin'," I said.

"Did you work out this summer?"

"Every day."

"I bet your body looks even more amazing than it did the last time I saw it."

"It's alright."

"Are you up for a session?"

"When?"

"Tonight?"

I thought about it for a minute and a part of me started to feel excited, but I told myself that what I was about to do was wrong.

"How about an hour. Do you need me to pick you up?"

"Sure," I said.

"Good. See you soon. Oh, and Brady."

"Yeah?"

"Don't wear any underwear."

"That's whassup."

I drove my Navigator out of the wash stall, jumped out, lifted the tailgate, and grabbed two towels. We had just finished our first week of brutal two-a-day practices, where we worked out in humidity that felt like steam rising from a hot iron.

"Hey, nigga, how much money did you get for that movie they made about you?" Delmar asked.

"What movie?" I asked as I wondered why Delmar always had to use the *N*-word.

"*The 40 Year-Old Virgin,* or in your case, *The 20 Year-Old Virgin,*" Delmar said, laughing. There was nothing Delmar loved more than teasing me about my alleged celibacy vow.

"Oh, snaps, fam. I see you got jokes from the summer. Let me see what you can do with this," I said as I tossed a towel to Delmar.

"What's a nigga 'posed to do with this?" Delmar asked.

"Help me dry my truck. Hurry up. Then I'm gonna give you some paper towels so you can clean the windows," I said.

"I'll help you dry, but I ain't cleaning no windows. Delmar don't do nobody's windows," he said as he started to wipe away some of the excess water on the truck's body.

"Whatever. Just keep moving those guns and be thankful I let you ride in the front seat," I said.

"Son, ain't that the new shawty who was serving that cold-ass attitude at the spirit squad mixer?" Delmar asked.

"Where?" I asked as I looked around the parking lot of the Super-Suds car wash. Washing my new car had become an almost daily event for me and Delmar — or Three-D, as the team sometimes called him.

His full name was Delmar Dewitt Dawkins. At 6'1" and 236 pounds, Delmar was among the elite on the team when it came to physical qualities. His toasted-almond skin was as smooth as marble and he looked more like an action hero than a college football player. Coaches and sportswriters called him the perfect fullback. I couldn't count the number of times he had been approached by photographers wanting to shoot him for posters and books. Sorority girls wanted him to strip at their private parties. His cornrows were always designed into patterns that only a man with his confidence could get away with.

"Over there," Delmar pointed.

That's when I saw her. She was wearing flannel gray short-shorts and a gold T-shirt with *Jaguars Cheerleading* stretched across her chest. Her long, auburn hair was pulled into a perfect ponytail, and she was putting coins into the vacuum machine.

"Yeah, that's her," I said. I checked her out while she bent over to vacuum the mats of her expensive, sleek, silver-toned sports car. Both Delmar and I had noticed the new coed when the football team and spirit groups got together for a barbecue after the first week of practice. It was an annual event before the season started where the two groups would be formally introduced. We noticed her because she was so beautiful and it had been a couple of years since the cheerleading squad had had a sistah as a member.

"How you doin', shawty?" Delmar yelled out.

"D, leave that young lady alone," I said as I slugged Delmar in the shoulder.

"I need to hit that. I bet that ass is tighter than a parrot's pussy. You can stay over here and act all shy if you want, but I'm not wait-ing for the rest of the knuckleheads on the team to try and hit that," he said.

"You see she ain't even trying to hear you," I said as the girl continued to vacuum her car mats.

"That's 'cause she don't know what she's missing." Delmar smiled with that crooked grin that caused me to shake my head. I knew the young beauty could get into deep trouble if she didn't watch herself.

Delmar went after the opposite sex like he was competing on the field, and that meant with a vengeance. Three-D and I had been best friends since the ninth grade at West Lake High in Atlanta, even though we were competing for the same position. I won out and Delmar moved to fullback, where he spent most of his time blocking for me. When it came time for me to pick a college, I chose CGU because they offered both Del-mar and me scholarships. Some of the other schools I considered were worried about Delmar's grades and hood-boy mentality. We were very different, but we never allowed those differences to get in the way of our friendship. I was the serious student of both my studies and football, while Delmar, who had been blessed with natural athletic abil-ity, was a jokester who was always in the coach's doghouse. He was also popular among our teammates for his wicked sense of humor.

We both came from single-parent homes, but Delmar was raised by his father, Jesse, a bus driver for the city of Atlanta. As long as I'd known him he'd never talked about his mother, and I wasn't sure if she was even alive. Being raised by a man, Delmar had a confidence when it came to females that I lacked. He was so experienced that by his junior year in high school he wound up with a Delmar Jr. to prove it. But the birth of his son did not slow down his chase of any female who would look at him, and even some who ignored him.

"Hey, lil' mama, don't you know who we are?" Delmar shouted toward her.

Again, there was no response as she placed the hose in its proper place and reached inside a brown and pink purse and pulled out some keys.

"Damn, son, who does that bitch think she dissin' like that? I'm going over there," Delmar said.

"D, leave her alone. Get in the truck and let's ride," I said, pulling out my keys.

"Naw, Dawg," Delmar said, walking toward the beautiful girl. "I'm going to introduce shawty to Three-D up close and personal."

I walked around my truck, then leaned against the hood, knowing I was in for a show.

Delmar stopped in front of the girl just as she was about to lower herself into her convertible silver Mercedes.

"Can I help you?" I heard her ask Delmar in a very snooty tone.

"Yeah, shawty. Ain't you that new cheerleader?"

"Yes, that would be me."

"Don't you know who I am?" Delmar asked, sucking his teeth, which he thought was sexy.

"No, I don't know who you are, and why don't we leave it that way?"

"I thought I would do you a favor, introduce myself, and save you the trouble of having to fight with all the other women once the school year starts. I can make room for you on my roster now, but slots are filling fast, so what you wanna do?" Delmar said, casually leaning against her car and crossing his arms over his double-barreled chest.

"I'm sorry, I didn't get your name," she said.

"Delmar Dewitt Dawkins. But you can call me Three-D," he said coolly.

"Well, Delmar, since slots are filling fast,

what I'm going to do first is tell you to re-move your sweaty, dirty, baggy, jean-wearin' ass off of my car. And next, I'll save *you* the trouble of saving me trouble by telling you if you ever see me coming your way, you can just turn around and save yourself the em-barrassment of knowing that your little bub-blegum game don't work on a grown-ass woman like me. Later," she said, putting a palm to his face.

"What!" Delmar said, rising up off the car. "Bitch, do you know who you talking to? I'm Three-D!" he said, waving his arms and looking like he was about to do something crazy.

That's when I ran over, threw my arms around Delmar, and pulled him away from the car.

"Fuck that bitch!" Delmar yelled, fighting me, trying to get away.

I held on to him tight, dragged him back toward my truck, and pushed him up against it. "Chill," I yelled. "Remember what Coach said about staying away from trouble."

Delmar calmed down a little, but he was still looking back at the young lady with total disdain.

"Get in the truck, D!" I shouted at him as I walked toward her car.

"Where you goin'?" Delmar said.

"I'm going to make sure she's all right. Just get in the car."

When I reached the car, she was rubbing a smudge from the driver's door. When she turned to me, she looked like she hadn't been the slightest bit affected by Delmar's antics.

"What do you want?" she asked. I was startled by how beautiful she was. She looked like Ciara, my favorite female singer. A part of me couldn't look away and my mouth suddenly didn't want to work. There was an awkward silence, and then I heard Delmar yelling, "Come on, B. Let's ride." I noticed her beautiful hazel-green eyes and her perfume that smelled like fresh flowers.

"Can you talk?" she asked.

"I wanted . . . I mean to apologize for my friend," I finally stuttered. "Sometimes he's just a little less than a gentleman. Please accept his and my sincerest apologies."

"Yeah, whatever," she said. She got in her car, slammed the door, and drove off.

I stood in the parking lot dumbfounded, not knowing if I had just met the meanest or the most beautiful girl I'd ever seen.

Maybe she was a little bit of both.

CHAPTER 5
BARRETT IS A BAD MUTHER
. . . SHUT YOUR MOUTH

"Hey, beauty, I'm going to need to see some ID," the overweight bartender with an unruly beard said as she walked into the dimly lit bar.

"Will this do?" she asked as she handed him a piece of identification.

"Barrett Elizabeth Manning, twenty-two years old," he said as he studied the ID, then looked her up and down to make sure they matched.

"Are you finished staring at my tits so I can get to my business?" Barrett quizzed.

"You sure got a smart mouth on you."

"Fuck you and give me back my ID," Barrett said as she snatched the driver's license from the stunned bartender.

She turned, quickly spotted someone in a corner booth, and walked over. Nico Benson was well dressed and wearing dark shades. He was a peanut butter brown man with a smooth face, who measured over 6'6" and looked like he could still fit into his Duke University basketball uniform. He smiled at Barrett and nodded toward the empty seat next to him. Barrett smiled back as she slid onto the cool wooden bench and placed her hands on top of the table. He placed his large hands over hers, and Barrett's eyes met his penetrating gaze.

"How you doing, Barrett?"

"I'm okay, but I miss you," Barrett said.

"That's why I'm here."

"I'm glad." Barrett smiled.

"So you met him? That was quick."

"Yes, and it was easier than I thought," Barrett said.

"How did you meet him?"

"I overheard him telling some of his teammates how he washed his new car every day after practice. So I had to spend a couple of hours at that filthy car wash pretending to do something my man should be doing for me," Barrett said.

"Do you think he's interested in you?"

"Are you kidding? This is going to be easier than getting a Bengal tiger to eat raw meat," Barrett said, and laughed.

"You're so confident, Barrett. That's what I like about you. But I got a white girl and a dude on reserve, just in case that's what he's into."

"I know there are a lot of things you like about me, and you know very well that you won't need anyone but *me* to close this deal and get what we want." Barrett smiled as she increased her grip on his hands. They held hands for a few minutes in silence, smiling at each other like they were teenagers on a first date.

"Not only are you beautiful, but you're clever as well."

"And that's why you'll never be able to do without me," Barrett said confidently.

"You think so, huh?"

"I know so. So tell me, have you decided how we're going to get him to sign with your agency? What about the technique we used on the guy from USC when we drugged him, put him in bed with the gay dude, and took pictures. Black guys always do what you want after that. They don't mind being called thugs, but no one wants to be called a fag."

"That's not going to work this time. You read the information on this kid. He doesn't drink and probably has never been naked in front of a camera. The dude is so lame he probably takes a shower in his underwear," said Nico in his deep voice.

"Then why do you want him so bad?"

"Because if Brady Bledsoe has a season

like he had last year, he'll get a Reggie Bush–type signing bonus and we'll get paid. Besides, that bitch of a mother of his turned me in to the NCAA last year."

"But nothing happened," Barrett said.

"I got a slap on the hand, but she doesn't know who she's fucking with. I guess she's so uppity that she doesn't realize that the governing board for college sports doesn't give a damn about some black woman and her superstar son."

"Then I think we need to come up with a more elaborate plan."

"All you need to do is get him in your bed and he will be all ours," he said.

"Then consider him your first new client of the season," Barrett said with a smile.

CHAPTER 6
CARMYN'S PAST MAKES A COMEBACK

I walked from the laundry room back into the salon, when a woman sitting in Zander's chair looked up at me and measured me with her eyes. Her lap was filled with pink plastic rollers that she was handing to Zander as he rolled her hair.

Zander was my most popular stylist. His customers affectionately called him the "Hair Nazi," because he was known for turning down customers for a myriad of reasons if he didn't like them or thought they didn't take care of their hair. If they said things he didn't like, he would tell them, "Don't ever try to get on my book again in this lifetime." I put up with him because he was so good and a percentage of his clientele helped pay off the salon. Besides, he never said anything nasty to me or my clients.

"Here are some clean towels," I said to Zander. I could feel the woman's eyes on me like a high-beam spotlight. I gave her a polite but distant smile. She looked familiar, and I couldn't remember if I had seen her in the shop before or if she was one of Zander's out-of-town clients. It was nothing for women to come from Augusta and Columbus to get him to do their hair.

As I was going back to my office, I heard her say, "Excuse me."

"Yes," I said, turning to face her again. As I tried to study her face without staring, memories from my youth suddenly started to flash before me. I was unable to get the picture of my daddy's church out of my head. I saw my mother sitting proudly on the front row in one of her fabulous hats and waving a cardboard fan.

"Aren't you from Houston?" she asked. I looked at her again. She was a small, brown-skinned woman with bright white teeth and too much hair for her head. She was dressed in an expensive pantsuit.

"No," I said firmly.

"Are you sure?"

"Positive."

"I guess you got a twin that lives in Houston, or used to. You sure your name isn't Niecey Johnson? Weren't you in Jack and Jill?"

"No to both questions," I said.

"What about Daphne Mitchell? Do you

know her? She was in Jack and Jill and she went to the University of Texas. I think she dated a football player."

"I can't say that I do."

"You sure do look like Niecey," she said as she gave me a wry little smile and looked away.

"Sorry," I said as I shot Zander a puzzled glance and walked back into my office. I turned to close the office door, but I left it slightly ajar so I could hear their conversation.

"What was that about, Ms. Rena?" Zander asked.

"Who is that woman?"

"Carmyn Bledsoe. She owns this place."

"How long have you known her?"

"Five years. Why?"

"She looks like this girl I went to church and high school with. It wasn't like we were hanging buddies or anything, but Niecey Johnson was Miss Everything at Yates High School, and I think her first name was Carmyn. Her family was big-time in Houston. She was closer to my sister's age, but I knew her more from church. We've all aged a little, but that woman looks just like Niecey."

"They say everybody has a twin, but I've never heard Carmyn talk about being from

Houston. Come to think of it, she never talks about her family at all except for her son," Zander said.

"Don't you find that odd?" Rena asked.

"Find what odd?"

"That she doesn't talk about her family."

"Mind your own business, Ms. Rena, or else you gonna have to find somebody in Auburn, Alabama, to do your hair, you hear what I'm saying?"

I closed the door and pressed my back against it as I took another deep breath. Being one of the most popular girls in your high school wasn't all that it was cracked up to be.

Especially for a woman of thirty-eight who thought she'd outrun her past and the secrets it held.

CHAPTER 7
BRADY'S GOT IT BAD . . .

I was walking back to the athletic complex after morning practice and watching film when I saw the girl from the car wash. I could have sworn that I saw her looking in my direction, even though she was on top of a male cheerleader's shoulders.

As I entered the complex, I noticed Shante Willis, one of the squad's two black pom-pom girls. Shante smiled at me and then started running in my direction. I liked her and we had hung out a couple times during my sophomore year, but I'd put my guard up after Delmar told me she'd asked if I might be gay since I didn't make a pass at her. The fact was I viewed her more as a little sister than a romantic possibility.

"Brady Bledsoe! How have you been? Did you miss me over the summer? Of course you missed me," Shante said as she gave me a big hug.

"Hey, Shante. I see you are in two-a-day

practice as well," I said as I looked over at the cheerleaders. The girl from the car wash was talking to one of the male cheerleaders.

"Two-a-days? Honey, we practice three times a day. Got to get ready for the football season. Are you excited? It's finally our senior year," Shante said gleefully.

I didn't answer. I was too busy watching the girl from the car wash. She was wearing tight pink shorts and a black sports bra. Her hair was pulled into another ponytail and her golden-brown legs looked perfect.

"Brady. Did you hear me?" Shante asked. When she noticed me looking toward the cheerleaders, she rolled her eyes.

"I'm sorry. What did you say?"

"I said aren't you excited about the season? I just read that you're one of the leading candidates for the Heisman. I sure hope you win," Shante said.

"Shante, who is she?" I said, nodding my head toward the group of cheerleaders, both male and female.

"Her?" Shante asked as she motioned toward the new beauty.

"Yeah . . . She's new. Boy, is she beautiful," I said without looking at Shante.

"She's a transfer. I don't know from where. You know how women can be sometimes, so we haven't exactly bonded," Shante said.

"Do you know her name?" I asked.

"I heard someone call her Barrett. We haven't done a lot of mixing with the cheerleaders yet. We don't do that until we start getting ready for pregame stuff," Shante said.

"Barrett," I repeated. She had a name as beautiful as she was.

"So you wanna hang out sometime before everybody gets back to campus?" Shante asked. The last session of summer school had ended and the only people on campus were football players, students on the spirit squads, and band members.

"Yeah, we can do that, but right now I got to run and grab a bite to eat," I said as I continued to gaze at Barrett. I knew my mother would tell me talking to one person and looking at another was rude, but there was something about this new girl, this Barrett, that made it hard to look anywhere else.

Chapter 8
Barrett Doesn't Play Well with Others

August 27, 2006

Dear Diary,

I found out today that Brady is definitely interested. I assumed he liked me, since no man can resist me once I turn on the charm, but getting confirmation did make me feel good. I caught him staring at me again today.

I was at cheerleading practice drinking a cup of water when one of the only black pom-pom girls, Shante, came sashaying up to me. This is the part of my job I hate: having to make friends with other females, be it ex-girlfriends, wannabe girlfriends, or mothers.

Bitches have a way of getting on my nerves. Always have.

I guess Shante could be all right. But she just tries too hard. Just because we're both black doesn't mean we have to be friends. I'm not here to make friends anyway. I'm here to get paid. In full.

Anyway, Shante tried to get all up in my business, asking if I was dating anyone and telling me she would approve if I decided to date Brady since at least he would be dating a sistah. Like I really need her approval. Or anyone else's, for that matter.

As she kept talking she really started getting on my nerves, so I finally had to let her know that Barrett Elizabeth Manning gets whatever or whomever, whenever she wants. She looked at me like I was crazy. So I finally said, "Bitch, I'm not listening to anything you got to say. Go tell that shit to someone else." And you know I had to cap that line off by sticking my nose toward the sky and giving her my best beauty contestant spin before I walked away.

I love doing that to females.

Chapter 9
Carmyn's BF or Best Girl

Me and my best friend, Kellis Glover, walked out of a gourmet coffee shop drinking skinny lattes under a summer pink and blue sky blended together like cotton candy at a county fair. It was almost nine o'clock in the morning.

We had just finished a Pilates class and Kellis was once again trying to get me to go out on a blind date with a friend of hers. Kellis didn't know anything about Sylvester, because the first thing she would ask was what he did for a living. Like the Kanye West song said, Kellis wasn't necessarily a gold digger, but she wasn't looking for a broke man either. Kellis was working hard searching for husband number two and was not going to lower her standards.

"Kellis, how many times have I told you? I'm not interested in dating. My life is quite full. You know I stay busy," I said. We located my car, and I clicked the remote so we could get in. I was taking her back to my shop, where she had left her car. "Yeah, that's what you say. I need to meet your vibrator, because it's got you on lockdown for real, honey," Kellis said, and laughed. "Stop talking like that, Kellis. I told you that in confidence. Somebody from my shop or church might hear us talking," I whispered.

"Come on, Carmyn, loosen up. We all got a little freak in us," Kellis said as she tried to tickle me.

"Stop it," I said as I moved in front of her.

"Are you telling me you lead a nun's life so your son will remain a virgin?"

"It's important I set a good example for Brady," I said.

"How many men have you been with in your life?" Kellis asked.

"I'm not answering that," I said swiftly.

"More than three? Five? Twenty?"

"Let's change the subject."

"Have you ever been in a threesome?"

"Kellis! Stop it!"

"Whatever, girl. You don't know what you're missing." Kellis laughed again.

A sturdy woman with skin as smooth as chocolate milk and a well-maintained weave, Kellis looked older than me although she was actually two years younger. She was only thirty-six but looked at least forty because of the chain-smoking habit she had picked up during her very public divorce. Kellis was the former wife of Rashard Smith, an all-star NBA player she married during her freshman year at Florida A & M. Kellis and I met when she became my customer at Back to My Roots, and she was one of the few customers I still provided personal services for. Even though she'd been divorced for several years and her financial situation had changed drastically, she loved expensive clothes and handbags. She told me when we met that it was her goal in life to marry another professional athlete. And since she had succeeded once, she could do it again.

Kellis and I shared the plight of being single moms of boys, and for years Brady and Ramon, Kellis's son, were close. But when Brady got interested in sports, Ramon became obsessed with girls, fathering two kids before he was eighteen. I made sure Brady knew he was on a different mission and that it didn't include becoming a parent so soon.

"What did Brady think of the gift you got him?" Kellis asked.

"Oh, honey, he was so excited. It took everything I had not to cry a river of tears when I saw my baby driving his new truck," I said as we approached the parking lot of the spa.

"You know you spoil that boy."

"Well, he's my life. And you do the same for Ramon and his babies," I said.

"I guess that's what being a mother is all about. I just wish Ramon would make better choices. The mother of Ramon Jr. showed up at my house a couple days ago talking about how she needed some money for Pampers and formula. I told her, first of all, she needed to use them big titties that lured my son into her bed to feed her baby, and second I wasn't giving her any money because it wasn't my problem. She said she was going to talk to Rashard and I told her good luck, she'd have to find him first," Kellis said.

"When is the last time you talked to Rashard?" I asked.

"About three years ago when I got my last child-support payment. Now I'm running low on cash, so I need to find me a new husband soon. Why do you think I have season tickets for the Atlanta Hawks and Falcons? I really wished Ramon had been interested in tennis or something he could make a living at. This time next year, you'll be rolling in paper when Brady goes pro."

"Now, you know I'm not interested in Brady's money. If he makes it into the league I will be happy for him, but I'd be just as happy if he came home and helped me run my business or got a real job."

"Has he found a girlfriend yet?" Kellis asked.

"Kellis, you know he's not looking for one," I snapped. I know I shouldn't have, but I got sick of people always asking when Brady was going to get a girlfriend. I had raised Brady right and he was going to wait until he met his wife before having sex. I mean, with all the diseases out there and the way young girls are today, I was happy Brady wasn't preoccupied with girls. Besides, I know there are a lot of young women out there, like Kellis, looking for soon-to-be professional athletes on college campuses. Once Kellis had implied that maybe Brady wasn't interested in girls, that he might be gay. I told her that wouldn't bother me, but I called Lowell anyway and he assured me Brady didn't have a gay vibe.

"Touchy, touchy," Kellis said.

"Honey, you're not getting my dandruff up, but I don't think I'll be a grandmother before I'm forty," I said. "Where is your car?"

"It's over there," Kellis said as she pointed toward the end of the strip mall where the Croissant Corner was located. I hoped we wouldn't run into Sylvester, although I didn't really know what his hours were.

When I asked him why I didn't see him in the store if I came by in the afternoons, he told me the owner sent him to work at some of the other locations in Atlanta.

I pulled behind Kellis's car and gave her a kiss on the cheek.

"Thanks, sweetie. You sure you don't want to meet my friend? You might like him."

"I'm sure. Now get out of my car so I can get back to the shop," I said.

CHAPTER 10
BRADY'S TRAINING TABLE

"Let me have a T-bone done well done, some of that shrimp scampi bullshit, the salad bar, and bring me two sweetened iced teas," Delmar said to the thin white waitress with slumping shoulders.

"Dang, D, didn't you have two burgers for lunch?" I asked.

"I'm still a growing boy, and didn't I tell you this was my treat? You ain't got to pay for shit," Delmar said as he positioned his body more securely against the wall in our booth, facing the other Logan Steakhouse patrons.

"And what can I get for you, sir?" the waitress asked as she looked at me, but before I could answer, Delmar had something else to add.

"Oh snaps, let me have a baked potato, loaded. Nah, I don't want none of that sour cream crap. That shit don't look or taste right. And I think you should bring us some more bread with extra butter."

"Are you finished?" I asked.

"For now," Delmar said. He reached into his shirt pocket and pulled out a red Tootsie Pop and started sucking, like it was providing him with some sort of lifesaving serum.

I looked up at the waitress and said, "Just let me have a New York strip medium rare, with fries and the salad bar, please."

"What would you like to drink?" she asked.

"Root beer," I said.

"Thanks. I'll be right back with some plates for the salad bar," she said as she picked up the plastic menus.

As she walked away, Delmar looked at me and said, "Damn, that bitch is skinny. She needs to take her ass to the dessert bar and sit a spell. The bitch's chest is as flat as yesterday's Coke."

"D, leave that girl alone," I said, looking around to make sure no fans had heard Delmar. The coaches were always telling us that people looked to us as role models. Some of the players, like myself, took that seriously; Delmar, on the other hand, did not.

"I ain't messin' with her, just stating a fact."

"So how many hours are you taking?"

"As few as possible, and I'm gonna drop them as soon as I can," Delmar said.

"Then what are you going to do if we go to

a bowl game? You have to pass six hours to play in a bowl game."

"I'll work it out," Delmar said confidently.

"What if we go to a major bowl?"

"Don't mean shit to me since they ain't given me none of the money," Delmar said.

"What about next spring?" Brady asked.

"Dude, if we play our cards right, the two of us will be at a gym like The Thoroughbreds getting ready for the combine."

"Man, that would be cool, but I heard they only take a few players every year," I said.

"Then we'll be their few players next spring."

"I hope you're right."

"Haven't you learned I'm always right?"

"So whatcha wanna do when we leave here?" I asked. "I know you're not looking for love."

"I ain't doing shit with you. I'm tired of hanging round you hardheads. I need to smell some females. That's what I hate about the beginning of the season: All you see is bulging chests and swinging dicks. Not that I miss going to class, but I'm glad school is starting back. I need some love from the opposite sex," Delmar declared.

"You mean sex, don'tcha?" I asked.

"Aw, here we go. Mr. Ain't Never Had No Female Joy trying to hate on me 'cause I tap sumthin' new anytime I want. I wonder what the freshman class of 2006 will bring me."

"Poor girls," I said. There were times when I wished that Delmar knew about Naomi and me so he would stop kidding me about the virgin stuff. But I knew how he liked to talk when he got drunk — there was no telling what he'd say under the influence. So I kept my secret to myself.

"You mean lucky young bitches. I'm just making it do what it do, boi. Did you get the digits from Miss Oreo Cookie?"

"Her name is Barrett, and why do you call her an Oreo?"

"You see how she be up in those white boy cheerleaders' faces. What the fuck is that about? Those dudes probably more interested in fucking each other."

"Who else is she going to talk to? It ain't like there's brothas or sistahs on the squad she could talk to," I said.

"Whatever. Where is that skinny bitch with my salad plate? I'm hungry like a mofo," Delmar said. I looked around the restaurant and saw the waitress coming with the salad plates.

After two trips to the salad bar, Delmar started back up again.

"Nigga, sumthin' up with you and this chick. Now, don't go get whipped and tricked before the season starts. Somebody like you might explode like a terrorist's suitcase if you get a little taste," Delmar joked.

"Besides, a girl like her probably got three or four dudes. She ain't trying to holla at me."

"Yeah, that's what you say."

"So, how you think we're going to do this season?" I asked in yet another attempt to change the subject.

"If you run the rock like I know you can, ain't no way we shouldn't go undefeated," Delmar said as he finished up the last of his salad.

"That would be awesome," I said.

"Awesome? Where in the hell did that come from, son? You sound like one of them corn-fed white boys. What's dude name the center, Gilbert Hillbilly?"

I ignored Delmar's comment, knowing full well I should have said "crunk." My mother didn't really like me using slang all the time. "You know, for some strange reason, I do feel a special connection to Barrett, even though I haven't really met her. I mean, I've seen hundreds of beautiful girls on campus, but none of them have got me curious like this girl," I said.

"It wouldn't take much for a female to open your nose, since you haven't had any."

"See, that's why I can't talk to you about nothing serious," I said as the waitress placed two sizzling steaks on the table in front of us.

"Come on, pimpin'. I'll quit playing, but you got to give me all the details."

"I hear you, but right now there ain't no details to talk about. What do you think of blue-chip Koi? You think I should be worried?"

Koi Minter, the son of an African American father and Italian mother, was a freshman running back from Oakland, California, who was the heir apparent to me. In his senior year of high school, he rushed for over 5,000 yards and broke all the prep rushing records in the state of California. A lot of schools shied away because of his grades and a few brushes with the law. Dude looked like a movie star and had an amazing body for an eighteen-year-old, but had not made a lot of friends on the team because of that. He made the equipment manager mad when he insisted on wearing his own special jock and shoes, which were Adidas while everybody else wore Nike.

"Worried about what? That Pretty Ricky motherfucker ain't got shit on you. Nigga too busy looking at himself in the mirror to run the ball. When I see niggas like him, it makes me wish I was on the other side of the field just so I can lay a hit on his ass," Delmar said.

"He'll be good for the team next year," I said.

"That's cool, but I heard that nigga say he planned to be in the running for the Heisman during his freshman year."

"On what team — not this one. This is my year."

"Damn straight. He should have left that shit in Cali with Reggie Bush," Delmar said, and laughed.

"I'm going to make sure that young dude don't ever see the field," I said as I wolfed down the last piece of my steak.

"Whatever. To me it sounds like the nigga is just plain simple. Have you seen that Kate Moss–looking chick with our check? I need to get out of here and get on the prowl. I also got to wire my baby's mom some support money before she have Johnny Law on my ass," Delmar said as he pulled out a wad of what looked like hundred-dollar bills.

"Where'd you get all that money from?" I asked.

"Mind yo business, son. I busted my ass this summer for these dollars."

"Whatever, son," I mumbled as I climbed

out of the booth.

"Oh yeah, dude, I was down in Savannah this summer and I bumped into that little church girl you used to chop it up with and thought nobody knew," Delmar said.

"Who?" I asked, knowing full well who Delmar was talking about.

"I don't know the bitch's name. She had a nice little body, but I knew if she was hanging with you she wasn't giving out no goodies."

"Naomi. She transferred," I said.

"And I know why," Delmar said.

"Why?" I asked, wondering where this was leading.

"Oh, girl got knocked up. She had a kid," Delmar said.

"How do you know that?" I asked. I felt my eyebrows move up my forehead. An expression of deep angst covered my face, and Delmar noticed it.

"B . . . you look like you just saw a ghost. What's up with that?"

"Nothing. You sure it was her and she had a baby? How old was the baby?" I asked as the memory of that night in the library returned like it was imprinted in my head.

"Saw it with my own eyes. I don't know how old. It was a baby, but he was walking," Delmar said.

As we walked out into the stiflingly hot night, I told myself that there was no way I was a father.

It was the start of classes and most students were still wearing shorts and T-shirts. I walked into the Walker Business School wearing white linen slacks, a short-sleeved pink linen shirt, and sandals.

I stopped by the dean's office to see if I could add an advanced business law class before it was too late. I had actually completed my marketing degree requirements at the end of my junior year by attending classes the previous two summers. I wanted to work during the summers, but my mother told me to stay focused. She always emphasized that getting my degree was more important than playing football. This semester, I was going to finish a second degree in transportation and logistics.

As I walked through the hallway I could feel the stares on me, but it was something I had grown used to. It probably happened to all the football players, even though more students knew me now since I had been the cover boy on several preseason football magazines. When someone caught my eye, be they male or female, I would flash a smile and hope my classmates would feel as though they had made a connection with me. It was cool being one of the most popular guys on campus. I got so many e-mail messages and people asking me to sign up as one of their friends on my Facebook account that it sometimes interfered with my studies.

I thought about finding Naomi's e-mail address or seeing if she still had an account on Facebook and making sure she was doing okay. I hadn't decided if I was going to ask her about the baby Delmar said he saw her with. I figured if she had something to tell me she knew how to get in contact with me.

While I was waiting in line, the dean's assistant told the student in front of me that they weren't doing any more overrides for the b-law class. But she quickly changed her answer when I passed her my form with a smile. After processing the form, the young lady asked me if I would do her a favor.

"Sure," I said.

"My father is a huge fan of yours. Will you sign an autograph for him?"

"Not a problem."

"Could you take a picture with me also?"

"Yeah, but don't make me late for class," I teased as I folded my schedule and pushed it into my back pocket.

She quickly pulled a pad from the top of her desk and a camera from her lower desk drawer and scurried to where I was standing. She placed her arms around my waist and said, "April, will you take this picture for me?"

I stood patiently as several other workers from the dean's office asked for the same photo opportunity. It took the dean walking out of his office to stop the impromptu photo session.

Just as I was walking toward my class, the bell sounded and I noticed Barrett walking toward me. She was in a short jean skirt and a green sleeveless top, carrying the same designer bag my mom and Kellis had.

This was my chance to finally speak to her again. My body and hands began to perspire. I knew that I had the courage to introduce myself if only I could make my mouth work. Taking a deep breath, I smiled at her and said, "Hello, Barrett."

She looked startled and then said, "Do I know you?"

I stuck my hand out like I was in a business meeting and said, "I'm Brady Bledsoe. I met you at the car wash a couple of days ago, and of course I've seen you around campus and practicing your cheerleading."

"How do you know my name?"

"I asked a friend of mine," I said.

"A lot of people here don't know me," she

said. She looked like she was looking for someone, or annoyed that I was trying to invade her space.

"Hopefully, that will change," I said.

"I have to find my class," Barrett said as she moved a few inches from me. I needed to do something quick.

"Barrett," I called out. She turned around but didn't say anything.

"Is there any way I could get your number? Maybe we can go and get a cup of coffee sometime?"

"I don't drink coffee."

"A milk shake or, you know, it's whatever, just come chill wit me," I pleaded.

"Why? Because you're a big football star?"

"So you do know who I am," I said. A smile covered my face and I could see the hint of a smile from Barrett. I told myself I didn't have to beg, this girl wanted me. She was just playing hard to get.

"I didn't say that," Barrett said.

"So what do you say? Can I get your number?"

"No," she said quickly as she started to walk away. But before my smile could turn into a frown, she walked back toward me and pulled her cell phone from her purse. She handed me the cell phone. "Put your number in here and maybe I'll call you."

"Maybe?" I mumbled as I pressed my cell number into her phone.

"That's what I said, Brady Jamal Bledsoe."

"Look at you. Who told you my name?" I asked.

Barrett gave me a cute sneaky smile and said, "A friend of mine."

CHAPTER 11
BARRETT PUTS ON HER
GAME FACE

Dear Diary,

Today, I was formally introduced to Mr. Brady Jamal Bledsoe. I'll call him in a day or two. I can't seem too eager. Besides, he wants me. I can tell — and who wouldn't?

At 5'6" and 112 pounds, it was me and not Beyoncé who put the licious in bootylicious. My skin is the color of cinnamon toast and I have long hair that falls like silk to my shoulders — and the hair is all mine and not some scratchy horse-tail weave. Although I'm almost thirty, I can still pass for twenty — or nineteen on a good day even *sans* makeup — (that's a little French word I just learned that means without).

Anyway, when I ran into Brady I was wearing an ultra-short jean skirt that would make most mamas roll their eyes and a too-tight top, and guess what? I caught Brady staring at the twins. Unlike those phony Hollywood bitches, I admit to paying for a little enhancement. Well, I didn't pay for them, my little upgrade was another gift from Nico. I can't wait until Brady sees them live and in person.

Nico was a little nervous that Brady hadn't already called me. I don't know why, since he knows how quickly I get these young bucks under my spell. I've done enough of these jobs for Nico, successfully, I might add, so he should know I will deliver.

Nico's concerned that Brady might be gay, but I know that's not the case, not with the way Brady's been sniffing behind my scent. The boy might be a little square, but he ain't gay. Brady's nose is already wide open, and gay boys don't stare at the twins the way he did.

Nico said the sooner I finish, the sooner I can get out of this hick town and back to a real city, and that really bothered me, especially when he asked where I wanted to live. Has he forgotten that we're supposed to get married in a few months? When I asked him what was going on with his wife, Nico said everything was under control. And then he had the nerve to hurry me off the phone.

Nico better be telling the truth, because nobody, and I mean *nobody's*, gonna make a fool out of me.

It had been less than a month and Barrett was already tired of Scarlet Springs, so she called a limo company in Atlanta for a shopping spree at Phipps Plaza. She told Ms. Jean, the spirit coordinator, that she had a doctor's appointment. Ms. Jean wasn't happy and told Barrett if she missed another practice, or was even late, she wouldn't cheer the first two games.

Barrett knew it wasn't wise to cross Jean Nail. Miss Jean, as all the cheerleaders and pom girls called her, was a soft and deliciously southern woman in her mid-forties. The raven-haired beauty with a school-girl figure and sparkling eyes told Barrett she'd soon figure out how she'd gotten on the squad without a traditional tryout.

She also let Barrett know she'd be watching her and added, "This is a top program, and everyone must abide by the same rules."

A good-looking black man named Julius, dressed in a black suit, white shirt, and black tie, opened the door to the limo and pointed to a bottle of champagne and cold water for the two-hour trip to Atlanta.

"Just let me know if I can get you anything, Ms. Manning. I'm here for whatever you need," Julius said.

"Thank you, Julius, but I think I'm going to have a little champagne and take a nap," Barrett said.

About five hours later, Barrett took a seat at an outdoor café at Phipps Plaza. Over $10,000 worth of new Louis Vuitton luggage and about $15,000 worth of jewelry from Tiffany's were in the car with Julius. She felt good about her purchases and couldn't wait to taste the vodka gimlet and Maytag blue cheese chips.

Barrett smoked a cigarette lazily and was enjoying the bright blue and silver-edged skies when she noticed two women, one black and one white, at the table next to her, laughing. Barrett looked over her shoulder to see if she was missing something funny happening near her, but didn't see anything.

She looked at the two bony-shouldered Buckhead Bettys with silicone-enhanced breasts. Each woman was beautifully dressed; one wore an apricot silk dress, while the other had on a peach-colored shell and a short white pleated skirt.

The two women looked like new money, but when they continued gazing at Barrett while whispering and laughing, their actions suddenly made her a bit paranoid.

Who did they think they were? Barrett thought. And why were they laughing at her?

Barrett tried to look at them more closely to see if maybe she knew them.

Barrett became frustrated when she couldn't make out what their syrupy southern voices were saying and she was convinced they were talking about her. With a feline quickness, she got up from her table to confront the two southern belles.

"What are you two bitches saying about me?" Barrett demanded.

"Excuse me?" the blond woman asked as the black one responded with a blank gaze.

"You heard me! What the fuck are you saying about me?" Barrett asked as she moved closer to the women.

"Looks like somebody's having a nervous breakdown," the African American woman said as she smiled a superior smile.

"Bitch, I will slap you back to the Section Eight housing you came from," Barrett said.

"Do we have a problem here?" a tall white guy in a police uniform asked as he approached the table.

"You'll have to ask this woman on the verge of a nervous breakdown. We were just enjoying our lunch and some private jokes about our recent trip to the South of France," the blond said.

"Miss, are you all right?" the officer asked as he extended his hand to Barrett.

"Don't touch me," Barrett screamed as she raced toward the limo and Julius, who was patiently waiting about a hundred yards away.

CHAPTER 12
CARMYN'S KINDNESS

"Look at you," I said as I patted my client Shelby's hair one final time. I took a can of hair spray and sprayed her dark brown hair until it glistened.

"I want to see," Shelby said anxiously.

I picked up a mirror from my station and handed it to the young lady.

"See," I said, smiling.

"Oh, Ms. Carmyn, it's wonderful. I don't think I've ever looked this good," Shelby said as she admired her new hairstyle.

Shelby Beale was a sixteen-year-old I'd met at church when she joined the celibacy circle Saving Ourselves. I was hopeful that Shelby, in a sea of Lil' Kim wannabes, would find a way out of her surroundings and aspire to do something big with her life. The only daughter of a single mom, I somehow connected with Shelby and had promised her free services as long as she kept at least a 3.5 average and honored her vow of celibacy.

Her mother, who also had two small boys, was still trying to find her Mr. Right and didn't pay enough attention to Shelby. Although she was only sixteen, Shelby had a body that most boys found dangerously tempting. Even Brady had once commented that Shelby wasn't a little girl anymore. But that conversation ended when I gave him my *Mama don't wanna go there* look.

Today, I'd also treated Shelby to a manicure and pedicure and had thought of surprising her with a little shopping spree at Lennox Mall before school started.

"Shelby, don't you look cute," I said.

"I do. I do. Wait until Torrian sees me," Shelby said.

"How is Torrian?" I asked through a tight, fake smile. I knew Shelby was dating him, but he seemed a little older than his actual age of seventeen. He had been a part of Saving Ourselves, too, but had dropped out last summer, and I thought that was a bad sign.

"He's doing well. You know he's going to UGA this fall. He got a full football scholarship," Shelby said proudly as she continued to look at herself in the mirror.

"That's good. I guess I'll see him when they play Brady's team," I said.

"How is Brady?" Shelby asked.

"He's doing well. They already started

practice," I said.

"So has Torrian. I really miss him. Ms. Carmyn, can I ask you something?"

"Sure, darling."

"Do you think I will lose Torrian to a college girl?"

"Listen to me, Shelby darling. If Torrian is the right one for you, then you won't lose him. He'll do things the right way."

"It's going to be hard," Shelby said softly.

"Why?"

"Because he'd been pressuring me for sex, but since he's been up in Athens he's stopped," Shelby said.

"Maybe he's busy with football, and that's a good thing that he's not pressuring you anymore. Remember our agreement and your Saving Ourselves pledge. You will graduate with honors and save yourself for your wedding day no matter what these boys say to you," I said.

"I know, but I'm the only one in my group at school who's a virgin. Sometimes the other girls hound me about it. Other times they tell me how wonderful sex is. I want to make sure I'm Torrian's first, and I don't think he's going to wait," Shelby said.

I walked over to Shelby and took her hands and said, "Sweetheart, I know it's tough, but you see this ring you're wearing?"

Shelby looked down at the silver celibacy band and nodded her head.

"Well, don't take that off until your husband replaces it with a wedding band," I said.

"I know what you're saying is right, but if I lose Torrian I don't know what I'll do," Shelby said.

Just as I was about to tell Shelby that maybe Torrian wasn't the right young man for her, my phone rang. I decided to answer it, because I felt it would give me a little time to think of what else I should tell Shelby about why she should wait.

"Back to My Roots. This is Carmyn," I said.

"Are you the owner?" a female voice asked.

"Yes, who's calling?"

"This is Rena. I was in the shop a couple of days ago to see Zander," she said.

"I see," I said. "How may I help you?"

"Why are you lying about who you are?" she asked point blank.

"What?"

"You're Niecey Johnson, aren't you? I know you from Houston and also from the University of Texas. You were dating a football star. You thought you were all that," she said in an accusatory tone.

I suddenly found myself wordless. I looked

at Shelby, who was standing by my chair waiting patiently. My mind traveled back to a time when I was seventeen and in love for the first time.

"I told you, you have the wrong person," I finally said.

"I don't think so, and I don't know what you're hiding from, but I plan to find out," she threatened.

"You have the wrong person, and if you call my shop threatening me again, you will be looking for another shop to get that hair of yours done," I said. I was suddenly restless with anger, and I felt a cloud of guilt hover over me.

"Oh, I can't lose Zander," she said quickly.

"Then stop asking questions about something that doesn't concern you," I said, and hung up. I took a long, troubled breath and told Shelby

I needed to get home quickly.

"But, Ms. Carmyn, I had a few more questions," Shelby said.

"Sweetheart, I'm sorry, but your questions will have to wait. E-mail me," I said as I showed her to the door.

Having finished a hasty dinner of grilled salmon, I was rinsing my plate to put it in the dishwasher when my cell phone buzzed with a text message: *I'm five minutes away from your house. Can't wait. SR*

After the disturbing phone call I'd received at the salon, I'd nearly forgotten Sylvester was going to drop by. So much for enjoying a night of my latest guilty pleasure, *Project Runway.* One night when I couldn't sleep, I came upon the show and just couldn't stop watching. I had fallen in love with the fashions made by Michael Knight, a young African American who reminded me of Zander, and the white lady, Laura, who made stuff I would wear.

As I was refreshing my makeup, the doorbell rang. *That was quick,* I thought. *No time to put on something special.* But I did have time to slip in my Jill Scott CD.

I looked through the tiny hole on my door and there stood Sylvester, a bit distorted but smiling like a clown at a fair. I took a deep breath and opened the door.

"Hey, pretty lady," Sylvester said as he handed me a bouquet of daisies. He moved his lips toward mine, and I immediately pulled him inside my house.

"What are you doing?" I asked as I slammed the door.

"What's the matter? I was just trying to give you a little kiss," Sylvester said.

"My neighbors could have seen you," I said.

"I'm sure it wouldn't be the first time they've seen lovers kiss," Sylvester said.

"Lovers? We're not lovers," I said. I thought our relationship was more like friends, with benefits.

Sylvester moved close to me and placed his hands very gently on each of my shoulders. "Did you have a tough day, baby?"

"Not really," I said. *Stop being a b,* I told myself. *It wasn't his fault you had a crazy woman digging around in your past.*

"Then why are you talking to me like this? I wasn't being disrespectful. Is everything all right with your son?" Sylvester asked.

"Brady? Oh, Brady's fine — you know his focus is football and school. Not girls," I said. I was feeling very guilty, because I'd been preaching the virtues of a chaste life to Brady ever since he first asked about sex, and here I was entertaining a man who wasn't my husband. And then there was that sweet little Shelby.

"I understand. I like hearing when a young man is serious about school. You're way too young and good-looking to be a grandma anyway," Sylvester said.

I gave Sylvester a hint of a smile. The man did know how to get on my good side.

"Why don't you let me use these to take some of that stress out," Sylvester said as he wiggled his large hands in the air like they were magic mittens.

"I don't know. Maybe we should do this later," I said.

"Come on now, Carmyn, I've been waiting to see you all day."

"Look, Sylvester, I'm sorry. I'm dealing with some stress. The football season is about to start, and you know how I worry about my son. Please, let's not make a big deal out of this. I promise to call you tomorrow. I'll make it up to you," I said as I moved closer and took his hands in mine. His eyes looked so forlorn.

"You promise?" Sylvester said slowly.

"I promise," I said.

Sylvester took me in his arms and gave me a deep, reassuring kiss. Then he pointed at me like a kindergarten teacher instructing a toddler and said, "You got to start living your life for you, Carmyn, because very soon your son won't need you as much. Make sure you don't kick a good thing like me to the curb."

And then he walked out the door into the muggy Atlanta night.

CHAPTER 13
BRADY MAKES A MOVE

After a quick meal of a double cheeseburger, onion rings, and strawberry limeade, I pulled out of the Sonic drive-in. With one hand on the steering wheel, I picked up my cell phone from the empty passenger seat and hit the automatic dialing feature. After a few rings, I heard my mom's very cheerful voice. "How's my baby doing?" my mother asked.

"I just got my eat on. Whatcha got going?" I asked.

"Getting ready to head home and get me something for dinner this evening. I feel like maybe some baked chicken and spinach."

"You need to watch out for that spinach. Haven't you been watching the news? Something about *E. coli* in the bags they put the spinach in. You can't be getting sick before my first game."

"Okay, baby. I won't eat spinach tonight. What did you eat for dinner?"

"Sonic."

"What did I tell you about that stuff? Look at you warning me about what I shouldn't be eating. That stuff isn't any good for a top athlete. You and Delmar need to learn how to cook and leave that fast food alone."

"You know I can't cook. Like mother, like son," I said, and laughed.

"You better be glad I'm not there. I would have to pop that smart mouth of yours," my mother teased.

"Oh, before I forget, I got some good news today from the sports information director," I said.

"What?"

"ESPN's *College Football Today* is coming to do a profile on me. It's going to be about the leading candidates for the Heisman, and I'm also on the Doak Walker watch list."

"What is the Doak Walker watch list?" Mom asked.

"What did you do with my mother, lady?" I teased. Usually, my mother knew everything about college football.

"I haven't even heard of him," Mom said.

"It's the award for the best running back in the country, named after this player from SMU who played halfback in the old days. Reggie Bush won it last year. At the beginning of the year, they put out a watch list of the candidates. It just means they gonna be watching your boy's every move," I said.

"Aw, baby, that's wonderful," my mother said proudly.

"And that's not all."

"No?"

"Nope, they mentioned wanting to talk with you and maybe coming to your salon. Are you ready for your close-up?"

"Baby, I don't know about that. What would I wear? You know I haven't ever been on television."

"You'll be the most beautiful mom ever on television," I said.

"I hear you talking, baby. Please give me as much notice as you can. I'll need to stop by Lennox and get something new to wear," my mother said.

"I'll let you know as soon as I find out. Oh yeah, one of the girls in football marketing set up a photo shoot for a poster they're doing to promote me. Can you believe it — me doing a photo shoot?"

"Sure I can. My baby is very handsome. But don't let all these outside distractions take away from school and football. Remember: Stay focused," she said.

"Don't worry, Mom, I will. I'm almost back to my apartment. I'll call you before I get ready to crash." I paused for a few moments and then I asked, "What do girls like?"

"What?" my mother asked. Her tone seemed startled.

"What do girls like?" I repeated.

"What do you mean?"

"I mean, do they really like flowers — and if so, what kind?"

My mother had to know this day was coming, I thought, but she probably hoped it wouldn't be this soon. She told me that flowers were nice but I had to make sure flowers didn't send the wrong message. She explained that if I sent red roses, that meant I was in love. Red is for passion. Yellow roses are for friendship.

"What should I do if it's a strong like?" I asked.

"Maybe you could send something like daisies," my mother suggested.

"Okay, that sounds cool. Maybe I'll send a box of chocolates or something," I said.

"Well, make sure she's not on a diet," my mother teased.

"No, I doubt she's on a diet. She's already perfect," I said.

"So does she have a name?"

"Yes, she does. Her name is Barrett, and Mom, I can't wait for you to meet her."

"Then I can't wait either."

"I love you, Mom."

"I love you more, Brady. Please be careful, and don't forget that you need to be careful. When it comes to girls, we can be trouble. The Heisman voters pay a lot of attention to character."

"I know, Mom, I know."

I smiled to myself as I hung up the phone. I wondered if my mom was going to like Barrett when she met her. Now all I had to do was convince Barrett to go on a date with me.

I was a few blocks from my apartment when a blocked call came in. I figured it might be a reporter or the sports information guy, so I answered it.

"Hello," I said.

"Is this Brady?" a sweet-sounding female voice asked. My heart started pumping fast and my foot pressed down on the gas pedal of my truck. I needed to stop before I had a wreck.

"Yeah, this is Brady. Who is this?"

"Do you give your number to that many girls? This is Barrett Manning," she said.

"Barrett, I was hoping you'd call," I said as I pulled over to the curb and parked my truck. I needed to devote all my attention to this call.

"You were?"

"Yes. How're you doing? I mean, how's school and cheerleading? Are you guys ready for the first game?" I asked nervously.

"Which question do you want to me to answer first?"

"Whichever one you want," I said. "Why don't you have a Facebook account? I looked up your name to see if I could send you a message."

"I closed my Facebook account," Barrett said confidently.

"Why, too many dudes jockin' you?" I asked.

"Yeah, something like that," Barrett said.

"That's whatsup," I said. Now what could I ask? I was out of questions.

"So I have a question for you."

"Holla at me," I said.

"Would you like to meet me in the Union coffee shop tomorrow?"

"Bet. That's whatsup. What time? You just tell me where and when. I'll be there."

"What time is your first class?" Barrett asked.

"Let's see — tomorrow is Wednesday, so that would be ten," I said.

"Then meet me at the Union at nine," Barrett instructed.

"I'll be there."

"See you then."

"Barrett."

"Yes."

"Thanks for hollering at your boi."

"Just don't make me regret it," Barrett said.

"Bet," I said. "You never will."

A few minutes after I hung up from Barrett, I got a text from C asking me to meet at ten that night at the studio. There was no way I could go there and still be fresh for my meeting with Barrett, but I needed the money, so I sent back a text that I would be there in about thirty minutes.

How long can I continue to do this, I thought as I started my car and headed for the highway.

I arrived at the house just as a bright orange sun set behind the clouds. I usually didn't arrive until after it got dark, but I was glad the text had come early. I parked my car behind the garage and went around to the side door as always.

Before I could knock, C greeted me with an anxious smile.

"Brady, how are you?"

"I'm straight."

"You're early."

"Yeah. That's whatsup. I got some studying to do later on."

"How was your day? How was practice?" C asked as we went through the kitchen into the studio. There wasn't much in the way of furnishings: two white leather love seats that faced each other, wood shutters on tall windows, and several camera lamps. There were several nature paintings on the wall.

"Fine. How're your classes?" I asked.

"Class. I'm only teaching one this semester. An advanced sculpting class," C said.

"You want me to change in there?" I asked as I pointed to the bathroom door, which was slightly ajar.

"Sure. I'm going to put on some music and get my equipment. Would you like something to drink?"

"A bottle of water would be cool," I said.

"Okay."

I went into the bathroom and removed my T-shirt, jeans, and underwear and placed my celibacy ring on the bathroom sink. I felt a slight breeze over my body as I walked back into the studio butt naked and with a slight erection. I had thought of Barrett as I removed my clothes and wondered what she might think of my part-time job that only C and I knew about. I felt as I did most times, an uncomfortable mix of lust and guilt.

The job had started innocently enough. When Naomi got pregnant and I needed money for an abortion, I answered an ad from the school newspaper looking for art models. I figured it was a quick way to make some money. I didn't know what to expect, but when I found I had to pose nude I needed the money so I did it. Chloe assured that no one would see my face. It turned into something else.

Chloe Perez was an art instructor at CGU and I had known her for almost three years. She was a regal lady in her early forties, with amazing bone structure. She had long dark hair and a deliciously round and feminine body. Even though she was Hispanic, there was a hint of something African American about her mouth.

During our sessions, Chloe began talking to me about her personal life. She told me she was in a sexless marriage with a man she no longer loved. She told me he taught at a university in Vermont and that they had a "commuter marriage."

Chloe walked back in with a bottle of water, and I noticed her dark brown eyes slowly travel up and down my body.

"How is it that your body looks more awesome every time I see you?"

I didn't answer. I just opened the water and took a long swig. I heard the Cuban music she normally played and asked her if she was ready to get started.

"Yeah, I got my trusty camera right here.

Why don't you stand over in that corner by the window," Chloe instructed as she pointed.

I put the water bottle on the stool and walked casually to the corner. I thought how nervous I'd been the first time I'd posed almost three years ago, and how now it was as simple as brushing my teeth.

Chloe took several shots of me, advising me to use my hands to shield my manhood at times, then telling me to turn around and raise my arms toward the sky like I was getting ready to fly away.

"So are you excited about your senior year?" Chloe asked.

"I just want to get it over with and move on to the NFL," I said, not looking toward her. I wasn't very good at small talk, especially when I was naked.

"You should cherish this time. You only get it once."

"Yeah, I know."

When she pulled the stool to the center of the studio, I got excited knowing the photo session was about to end and the finale was only moments away.

"Are you ready?" Chloe asked, her voice gentle.

I didn't answer.

"Of course you're ready," Chloe said as she

removed her white linen dress and stepped close to me, separating my thighs with her soft but cold hands. She took my manhood in her soft palms and, a few seconds later, with her warm mouth made my body feel like it was knocking at the door of pleasure.

CHAPTER 14
BARRETT MAKES HER GAME PLAN

"I'm going to move in for the kill tomorrow," Barrett said.

"That's great. What are you going to do?"

"I'm meeting Brady at the Union for coffee first thing."

"Cool. Keep me posted. How's everything else?"

"Where's my new American Express black card?"

"Oh, shit, I forgot. It's on my list of things to do. I've got to run, Babe."

"Forgot? You better make sure you're handling your business. You know I don't like to wait."

"Look, Barrett, don't forget who you're talking to. I said I'd do it and I will. 'Bye."

When Barrett hung up the phone, she took a deep breath and told herself she might as well make the phone call she was dreading. She went into the kitchen and got a bottle of water from the well-stocked refrigerator.

When she got back to her bedroom, she got on her knees and pulled from under the bed a small red lacquer box that held her stash of weed. Barrett knew that before the night's end she would need a toke or two.

Then she picked up the phone and dialed the numbers she didn't want to dial.

After a few rings, her mother picked up.

"Hello," she said, clearly annoyed.

"Hey, it's me. I just called to see if you got the check," Barrett said.

"Why do you always call when my stories are on? Your timing is always off, girl."

"They're called soap operas."

"Bitch, I know what they're called. You think your ass is so damn smart."

"I was just making sure you got the check."

"Yeah, I got the check. If I hadn't, you know I would have called you. Is that cell phone number of yours still the same?"

"I told you I would always keep one cell number the same in case something happened to Wade."

"Whatever. That boy Chris hasn't been back looking for you. I guess he gave up."

"Good," Barrett said. "Make sure you don't give him this number or any of the others, either."

"Did you give him back his money?"

"I don't want to talk about that.

How's Wade?"

"Wade is Wade."

"What does that mean?"

"I got to get back to my stories."

Barrett didn't say good-bye as she held the phone close to her chest and muttered to herself, "Yeah, get back to your stories, woman."

CHAPTER 15
CARMYN GETS DEFENSIVE

It was one of those days when the air was so stifling in Atlanta that I daydreamed of living in San Francisco or Seattle. Kellis and I were sitting in her warmly golden-lit, cathedral-size kitchen, drinking herbal tea and eating salty Spanish peanuts.

The 4,300-square-foot Buckhead split-level house was something that Kellis was proud of, even though she was constantly complaining about the costs of keeping it up. At times I wondered how she was able to do it, since Kellis had never shown any interest in maintaining a full-time job. She earned some money doing interior decorating, even though she had no formal training. Her home, which she had decorated herself, became her calling card and professional résumé.

Kellis had called me right before I left the spa and invited me to dinner at Houston's, one of our favorite restaurants. I hated eating alone in restaurants, so I welcomed the invite. Many evenings I would stop at the restaurant on Lennox Road and order my dinner from the bar, then take it home. Sometimes when I got home I would place my entrée on fine china and imagine I was having dinner at a fancy restaurant with Brady across the table, enjoying the superb meal with me.

"I need to stop eating these things," I said as I placed the peanuts I had just picked up into a napkin in my lap. When I was a young girl and had gone to my first tea at church, I loved the taste of salty peanuts and candy mints mixed together. It's been a favorite ever since.

"Me, too," Kellis said as she picked up the bowl from the table and moved it to the granite island in the middle of the room. "Oh, did I show you this?"

Kellis picked up a beige leather bag and displayed it proudly.

"When did you get that?" I asked.

"Today. It's the latest Marc Jacobs bag. I had to have it."

"It's beautiful. So, you ready to go, girl?" I said as I dusted salt off the palms of my hands and into the napkin.

"Yeah, but before we go, I need you to do something for me," Kellis said.

"What?" I asked as I got up from the table.

"Wait a minute. I'll be right back," Kellis said as she left the kitchen and entered the hallway that led to her master suite.

I walked over to the sink and rinsed my hands and thought about calling Brady to see if I could find out more about the girl he had mentioned. His first game was a week away and he needed to be focused. I looked around for a paper towel, but all I was able to find was a stack of pressed white linen napkins. I smiled to myself at how Kellis always kept her house like it was a four-star hotel. I picked up my purse so I could get my cell phone and refresh my lipstick.

As I opened the purse, Kellis walked in carrying a cloth-covered jewelry box.

"What's that?" I asked.

"Something I need you to keep for me," Kellis said as she placed the box on the bar.

"Keep what?"

"Just a few things I need to keep out of the house for a bit," Kellis said.

"Sure, but why?"

"Do you want the truth, or will you just do it?" Kellis asked.

"Kellis, what's in the box and what's going on?"

"Take a look," Kellis instructed.

I looked in the box and saw a woman's gold Rolex watch, some diamond studs with a matching necklace, and Kellis's five-carat wedding ring.

"Why do you need me to keep this?" I asked.

"Carmyn, you're my friend, so I don't want to lie to you. I am in a little financial bind. I've been helping Ramon out with his child support, and I'm running low on money. I'm going to call the police when we get back home tonight and tell them these things were stolen. They're insured, and I think that will hold me over until I can get another decorating job," Kellis said in a voice steeped with sadness.

I was shocked, and I resisted an overwhelming urge to grab Kellis and shake some sense into her. Why did she let her son take advantage of her like this?

"Kellis, you can't do that. How much money do you need?" I asked. I didn't like to loan money to friends, but I didn't want to see Kellis get herself in even more trouble by committing fraud.

"I don't want to borrow money from you, because I don't know when I'll be able to give it back," Kellis said.

"I don't know if I even have the money to loan you, but you've got to come up with something else, Kellis. Have you thought of putting your house on the market? This is a beautiful place; it would sell in no time," I said.

"I can't sell my house. This is all I have," Kellis said.

"Kellis, you could take the money you make from selling this house and buy something over near me in Cascade. Some real nice town houses are going up just a couple blocks from me."

"I can't get a town house. Carmyn, you know the type of man I'm trying to snag. I need to have a place like this to get that kind of man."

As much as I loved my friend, I knew that she measured her life by her house, clothes, car, and material things she wasn't willing to give up. Like expensive pocketbooks she couldn't afford.

"Why don't we go look at those homes Martha Stewart and KB Homes are building. I bet they're really nice," I said.

"KB Homes? Child, please! Nothing against your girl Martha, but I saw a billboard for those homes and they start at around two hundred thousand, so they can't be that fabulous. So will you do it?"

Without taking a second to think about it, I said, "I can't, and I'm disappointed you'd even involve me in such a scheme."

"Are you mad at me? What is that shit about? You ain't got to worry about paying your bills. When Brady finishes school and signs his big contract, you might not have to work another day in your life," Kellis said, her face sculpted in anger.

"That will be Brady's money. Have you tried putting yourself on a budget?" I asked.

"You can't make a budget if you don't have any money, Carmyn. I've maxed out my credit cards as well as the line of equity credit I have on this house. I don't know how long I can go on like this. It's like trying to stay dry when you're standing naked in a rainstorm," Kellis said.

"Kellis, you're my friend and I want to help you any way I can, but please don't do this. It would be so sad if my best friend went to jail."

"I won't get caught. There've been a few robberies in the neighborhood lately. This real handsome policeman stopped by my house a couple of weeks ago to warn me. Come on, Carmyn, this is a white folks' neighborhood. My insurance company will write that check fast, because that's what they do when Miss White Lady's jewels are stolen."

"That's fine, but that happens when something's *really* stolen," I said.

"They won't know that," Kellis snapped.

I picked up a magazine with Martha Stewart on the cover and handed it to Kellis, then said, "I bet Martha didn't think she'd get caught either."

Kellis slammed the magazine on the table and said, "Martha made jail work for her, and if I get caught, I'll do the same."

"Are you ready to go to dinner?" I asked as I picked up my purse from the counter. "Maybe we can think of something else you can do."

"I've lost my appetite," Kellis said.

"Do you want me to go and pick something up?"

"No, thanks. The way I feel, I might just drink my dinner tonight," Kellis said.

"Please don't do that."

"Don't worry, I will be fine, Carmyn. I have some leftovers from P.F. Chang's from lunch. I promise, when I get on my feet I'll take you out for a real nice dinner," Kellis said, embarrassment replacing the anger on her face.

I walked over and hugged her tight and whispered, "I'm going home and getting on my knees and praying for you. Prayers are powerful and God hears them, Kellis. Things will work out just fine."

Kellis fought back tears and said, "Keep your prayers for yourself. If I want to talk to God, I know where He is."

CHAPTER 16
BRADY'S FIRST DOWN

It had been very hard to sleep the night before as I tossed my body from one end of my bed to the other thinking about Barrett and our morning coffee date. I wished that I'd dated more so that I wouldn't come off looking lame in front of this young lady who I knew was much more sophisticated than most of the girls at CGU. I didn't consider my situation with Chloe a relationship, but I knew it would have to stop if things got serious between Barrett and me. Chloe knew we didn't have a relationship beyond the occasional posing and pleasure we provided each other. I mean, I was never at her house for more than a couple of hours.

I got up around 5:30 a.m. and went to the weight room and lifted for over an hour. I loved early-morning workouts, so as team captain I set some up for my teammates. They were pissed as hell at me, but I told them if we wanted to be champions we had to start our day like winners and quit complaining.

I stopped at Wal-Mart and picked up some flowers, then rushed back to the apartment, showered, and pressed my jeans for the second time.

When I walked into the Student Union's coffee shop, the first person I saw was Barrett standing at the counter. She looked like she was posing for a picture for a high-fashion magazine. She was the only person I could see.

"These are for you," I said as I nervously handed her a bouquet of daisies.

"I love daisies. Thank you, Brady," Barrett said as she admired the flowers. "How did you know I loved these?"

"I just took a guess," I said. Moms was right again.

"Should we order something and find a table?" Barrett suggested.

"Sure, what would you like?" I asked.

"A latte," Barrett said quickly.

When I walked back with our order, she was seated at a table and absorbed in her notebook, so I cleared my throat to get her attention.

Barrett was wearing a short-sleeved pink sweater and a short khaki skirt. She was the picture of confidence and composure. Her hair was neatly pulled back into a slick pony-tail and she was wearing a thin strand of pearls. I couldn't help but notice how beautiful her skin was — it was the color of café au lait, a delicious blend of heavy cream swirling through a cup of black coffee.

"So they don't have an athletic dorm or somewhere where all you guys live?" she asked.

"Can't do that. The NCAA won't allow it. You know us athletes can't be treated special. Might get us put on probation or something," I said.

"So you live off campus?"

"Yeah, in some apartments about ten minutes by bike, which used to be my mode of transportation. Now that I have a truck, it takes me just a couple of minutes to get to campus, and then maybe a half hour just to find a parking space," I said.

"So your truck's pretty new?"

"Yeah, it was a surprise from my mom," I said as I gushed with pride.

"What does your mother do?"

"She owns a couple of beauty shops in Atlanta," I said proudly. "One of her spots is the most popular day spa in Buckhead."

"And your father?"

"I never knew my father. He was killed in a motorcycle accident on his way to the hospital when I was born," I said. Maybe I was telling her too much about myself for a first date.

"Oh, Brady, I'm really sorry."

"Thanks, but I always say you can't miss what you never had. Besides, my mother makes up for it. She's better than having two parents," I said, staring at Barrett. I was unable to take my eyes off her beautiful face.

"I don't know what I would do without my parents. Do you have any siblings?"

"No, it's just me and my moms," Brady said.

"Your story is so sad, but in a way kind of romantic. The thought of your father on a motorcycle rushing to see you being born," Barrett said as a smile crossed her lips.

"I never thought of it that way," I said as my shoulders rolled in a shrug. "What about you?"

"I'm an only child. My father is a businessman, my mother does volunteer work in Atlanta. I guess you'd call her a socialite or a black Buckhead Betty," Barrett said.

"Where does your family live in Atlanta? Buckhead?"

"Yes, we live in Buckhead."

"Where do you attend church?" I asked.

"What?"

"Where do you attend church?"

"We're Catholic. We go downtown," Barrett said.

"What's the name of it?"

"Is this a quiz on Atlanta?" Barrett asked, slightly annoyed.

"I'm sorry," I said.

"That's okay."

"So where did you transfer from?" I asked.

"Spelman."

"Why?"

"I needed to get out from under my parents. I stayed in the dorm one year, but I was going home almost every day. I didn't want a big school like UGA or Auburn, so this place seemed perfect."

"Yeah, I like it down here and will miss it next year," I said.

"Why did you come to school down here? I mean, you must be a city boy."

"I knew they were building a good football program and I could play as a freshman. Also, they promised to give my homeboy, Delmar, a scholarship as well," I said.

"So why don't you have a girlfriend?" Barrett asked.

"I could be a playa," I teased. I suddenly felt comfortable with Barrett and wondered what she would think if I told her about Naomi.

"Tell me why a beautiful young lady like

you doesn't have a boyfriend," I said.

"It's a long story," Barrett said quickly.

I looked at my watch and said, "I got about a half hour until my first class. Why don't you start in the middle?"

"You might have the time, Brady, but I have to stop in the bookstore and pick up a few things. I need to know you better before I'm ready to tell you more," Barrett said as she unzipped a small leather purse and pulled out a set of keys.

"Would you like for me to go with you?" I wasn't ready for this date to end.

Barrett stood up, pushed the chair back with her legs, and said, "Thanks, but I'm a big girl."

"That I can see, but big is not a word I would use to describe you," I said as I eyed Barrett from the top of her head down to the shoes she was wearing. It was not the vulgar, *what a nice piece of ass* look I had seen Delmar give girls, but more the look of someone admiring a nice piece of art — the way my mother had taught me to look at women. Chloe had taught me the body could be viewed as a piece of art as well.

"So would you like to see me again?" Barrett asked softly.

"No doubt. Would it be okay if I had your number?" I asked, looking down sheepishly.

"I'll call your cell and leave my number when I'm ready, or maybe I'll just text you," she said.

"I hope it'll be soon."

"Don't worry, it will," she said as she walked toward the door.

I watched her until she was out of sight and a tiny voice in the back of my mind said, *Dude, you're about to be in trouble. Big-time.*

After lifting weights and running a few skeleton drills, my teammates and I headed toward the athletic complex for a much-needed shower. I marched into the locker room to the sounds of laughter and sighs of relief. You could always tell who'd had a great workout: They led the lineup of muscular young men, carrying helmets and dressed in shorts and cut-off T-shirts.

The first day of class had signaled the end of our two-a-day practices. Now practice started around three and ended at six. Almost every day, I was the last player to reach the locker room because of the number of reporters, both print and broadcast, who wanted to interview me about every practice, what I thought of our offensive line and passing game. Rushing for over 1,500 yards during my junior year had made me not only a fan favorite but a media favorite as well.

Reporters were always commenting on how polite I was when I answered questions with "Yes, sir" or "Yes, ma'am." My mother always told me to represent the young black male athlete the best I could.

I couldn't wait for the opening game against Big 12 foe Texas Tech. I would put on my new green jersey with the gold #2 outlined in black on the front and back and *Bledsoe* emblazoned across my shoulders. I was excited but also a bit sad when I thought ahead to the season's final game against Georgia Tech. The last home game of the season was Senior Day. The last time I would play on Jaguar Field. On that special Saturday, I would run out of the tunnel, greet my mother with a hug and a kiss at midfield, present to her a signed football, and then have our picture taken with the coach. If I knew my mother like I thought I did, she had already purchased the outfit she would wear that day. Earlier in the summer, Mom and I had talked about how we were both looking forward to Senior Day. It would be a milestone of sorts for us, the end of the first part of my football career and the start of something new — and even more exciting, a chance at the Heisman and the NFL.

As I walked to my locker, I removed my underarmor and shorts and stood wearing only a jock as I searched for my brush, toothpaste, and body wash. I listened to the chatter of the locker room lawyers, so to speak, who always had something to say about the girls on campus or the upcoming opponent. The football locker room was in many ways like a beauty shop for men. In fact, sometimes conversations I heard weren't that different from the ones I heard growing up in my mom's shop Back to My Roots. Only, in the locker room the conversations about the opposite sex were held in the midst of cheap aftershave, hot steam, and naked bodies.

I removed my jock, grabbed a towel, and walked to the shower with my body wash and shower shoes.

"Nigga, what's that?" Omar Whitmore, one of the starting linebackers, asked.

"What's what?" I replied. Now everyone in the shower area was focused on the bottle in my hand.

"That," Omar said as he pointed to my hand.

"It's soap, playa," I said with a *what's the big deal?* look.

"This is soap," Omar replied, holding a white bar of soap in his left hand. "That's some of that female Victoria's Secret bullshit. Did your mommy buy that for you?"

Omar asked as he and several other team-mates exploded in laughter.

"Hey, don't say nuthin' about Brady's mom. Have you seen how fine she is? Damn, she looks like his sister instead of his mom," said Pierre James, a linebacker from Alabama who, like me, had already completed his degree requirements but still had a year of eligibility remaining on the field. I'd even been to his house a couple of times, and his parents were two of the coolest grown folks I'd ever met. I loved the relationship he had with his father. When I saw Pierre with his dad, it made me happy and sad at the same time and I felt sorry for myself. It was like they were boyz, not father and son. They talked about football and girls and played Madden NFL like their lives depended upon it.

"You ashy-ass niggas ain't got no class," Delmar said as he walked in to defend me. He knew I didn't really mind the teasing about how meticulous I was with my grooming. It didn't bother him that I used body washes, scrubs, baby oil, and cocoa butter to keep my skin baby soft.

"Why can't Brady just use some good old Ivory soap like the rest of us?" Omar asked as they all moved into the community showers.

" 'Cause he ain't no ordinary nigga. This man's gonna win the Heisman and be playing for more paper in his first NFL game than most of you motherfuckers are gonna make your entire life," Delmar said.

I just smiled at Delmar as I squeezed my body wash into the loofah and began to massage my chest and shoulders. I knew the attention on me would soon shift and the conversation would change to sex and how much everyone was getting. They would put certain young ladies in categories like "wifey material" and "flat-out freaks." They might talk about how much ass I could be getting since I was considered a football star. But that was cool — what they didn't know wouldn't hurt them. How many of these knuckleheads had an older woman paying to see them naked and bust a little slob on their knob every now and then?

CHAPTER 17
BARRETT TAKES A BOUNCE

Barrett was about thirty minutes into her afternoon cheerleading practice when it happened again. Her partner Dan almost dropped her while doing a pop-up chair, which is a very basic cheerleading stunt. She didn't know if Dan was just a weakling or doing it on purpose. She'd told him how she and her former cheer partner had come in first nationally in stunting and she expected him to live up to her expectations. But of course that wasn't true, since Barrett had never been a college cheerleader. Still, T-Mack, a former college male cheerleader and Barrett's private instructor, told her all the time how she could win partner stunt competitions.

Nico had hired T-Mack and a lovely blond girl named Barrett Rawlins to teach Barrett how to pass as a college cheerleader. They had told the male and female cheerleader who were from the University of Arkansas,

160

that "Bethany" was an actress preparing to play a college cheerleader in a movie. The real Barrett was so nice to Bethany, even on days when she was a complete bitch, that she had decided to take her name along with the skills she taught her.

"I'm sorry," Dan said. "I guess I need to dry my hands," he added as he looked around for his towel.

"You need to learn how to stunt," Barrett said as she walked off to get something to drink. She spotted Brooke, one of the cheerleaders who had questioned her on how she was able to get a spot on the squad without trying out.

"Looks like you guys are having some problems stunting. Are you two going to be ready for the first game?" Brooke asked with a cool, self-possessed smirk.

"Bitch, mind your own damn business before I have to make you disappear," Barrett said, restraining herself from slapping or pouring her cup of water on the captain of the cheer squad.

When she spotted Kraig, the head cheer coach, she told him she needed to talk with him in private.

"Sure, Barrett. Let's take a walk," Kraig said as he put his arm around her and guided her toward a private area next to the gym where the cheerleaders practiced.

"You have to give me another partner," Barrett said firmly.

"What?"

"It's just not working out with Dan and me. He can't even do a popup chair and he drops me all the time. If it wasn't for Tim always spotting us, my body would be black and blue, and that's not what I signed up for." Barrett hoped she could accomplish her mission before the football season ended, leaving the squad short one female member. It would serve Dan and the rest of them right. Besides, college cheerleading took up more time than Barrett wanted to spend.

"Just try and work with him. I can't change partners a week before the first game. Maybe he's just nervous because this is his first year on the gold squad."

"I don't give a shit if it's his tenth year. I am not used to working with amateurs. I was told that I would get to pick my partner, and I want Tim," Barrett said. Tim was a handsome ex–football player with black hair and green eyes. Not only was he one of the best-looking guys on the squad, he was also one of the strongest. His current partner was a tiny blue-eyed blonde who was attractive but unexceptional as a cheerleader. Like most of the others, she had practically ignored Barrett since Barrett had joined the squad without a tryout. She was obviously not impressed with Barrett's skills.

"Barrett, I can't do that. Tim and Julie have been partners since last year," Kraig said.

"All the more reason to make a change," Barrett said with a stony look on her face. "I don't think it's good to have your best cheerleader being dropped in front of the fans. That'll make you look bad, since you're the coach."

"I'm sorry, I just can't make a change," Kraig said with a rising edge to his voice.

"Look, Julie is the size of an American Girl doll. Dan won't drop her. You need to make a change and do it before the next practice, or else you have to find yourself another black girl, because this one don't play that being dropped crap," Barrett said, then walked off in a huff.

Barrett found a private spot outside the athletic complex, pulled out her cell phone, and dialed Nico's number.

"Hello?" he said.

"Hey, we got a problem. This cheerleading bullshit has *got* to go. The way that boy is throwing me around and dropping me, I might break my neck, and you're not paying me enough for that."

"Listen, baby, I paid a lot of money to get you onto that squad, and you know what's at stake. You have a job to do, so do it and I'll make it up to you later."

"You will?"

"You know I know how to make your pussy sing."

"In that case, I'll make it work, even if I have to pull a Tonya Harding on one of those bitches," Barrett said.

"I knew you would, baby girl. Thanks. Oh, I need you to get homeboy's social security number or his checking account number."

"Consider it done," Barrett said.

"Thanks, love."

CHAPTER 18
CARMYN GETS A SCOUTING REPORT

I was in my bedroom, matching a couple of my blouses with the new white linen pantsuit I'd bought for Brady's first game. Even without working out like I should I was a perfect size 6, the same as when I entered college. When the phone rang, I looked at the caller ID and recognized Lowell's number, so I picked it up after a couple of rings. "How're you doing, Professor?"

"All's well in academia," Lowell said. "How's the beauty business?"

"You know it's good. Women will still miss a meal or not pay a bill to get their hair done," I said as I took a seat at the desk in my bedroom. On top of the desk were my Bible, a compact, and about four pictures of Brady at different ages. Above the desk was a picture of Brady at the ring ceremony at church when he joined Saving Ourselves. It was one of the happiest days of my life when, without much encouragement from me,

Brady told me he would join the group and was willing to be celibate.

"I just called to see if you were coming in on Friday or Saturday?" Lowell asked.

"I checked the Web site today and kickoff is at two, so most likely I'll come on Friday night," I said.

"Do you need a place to stay?"

"I might. I made hotel reservations for most of the games, but not for this one. You got room?"

"Always got room for you, love. I had that handsome son of yours over for dinner the other night and we had a good time," Lowell said.

"Did he mention somebody named Barrett?"

"Yep. I think your son is smitten with a new coed."

"Have you met her?"

"No, but I'll see her soon enough. She's a cheerleader," Lowell said.

"Is she black?" I asked. I felt my heart beating — no, make that thudding — as I thought about the lineup of CGU blond-haired cheerleaders from previous years. I know it was wrong of me, but if Brady was going to have a girlfriend I at least wanted her to be a sister. I remember how the little white girls who were Pee Wee league cheerleaders used to make a fuss over him after the first time he made a touchdown. I hoped Lowell was wrong and that Brady was keeping his attention on football. I'd spent most of my life keeping him focused on academics and sports. I wasn't ready to be a mother-in-law or, even worse, a grandmother.

"I think she might be black. He didn't say. But maybe if Brady does fall in love, it'll put you back on the market. You still got a lot of good years left, Carmyn," Lowell said, chuckling.

"Why does everybody think I don't date because of my son?" I asked.

"Because it's true," Lowell said quickly.

"You're one to be talking. How many times have I told you that you need to be teaching at Morehouse or Tech, or at least in a major city where you could meet someone your own age?" I said.

"I might do that in a year or two. But I got tenure down here and they let me do what I want. Besides, things might be looking up for my love life," Lowell said.

"Have you met somebody?"

"I don't want to say. I might jinx it."

"Is there somebody new on the faculty or staff?" I asked. Lowell had a strict policy against dating his students, even though I know he was flattered when some of his male students made subtle passes at him for grades. Every time I met somebody gay in the shop, I tried to introduce him to Lowell, so I guess I was just as bad as Kellis. When I hired Zander, I thought he would be perfect for Lowell. I was disappointed when I found out Zander was straight and acted gay only because it helped him bed more women. He would slowly gain their confidence in a gay-boy way and then go in for the kill. I was surprised by how that strategy worked for him. I hadn't told Lowell about Sylvester because I didn't hold much hope for it lasting much longer, and I knew Lowell would definitely have something to say about my dating an hourly worker.

"My lips are sealed, Carmyn. But if something happens, you'll be the first to know."

"Okay. Can I let you know tomorrow if I need to stay with you?"

"Sure."

"Hey, Lowell, see what you can find out about this girl Brady's interested in," I said.

"Okay."

"And one more thing I need you to do for me," I said.

"What's that?"

"Make sure Brady is still wearing his celibacy ring," I said.

"What if he's not, Carmyn? Will you be able to handle it?"

"Why worry about that until I have to?" I said.

CHAPTER 19
BRADY: THE BODY
BEAUTIFUL

When Delmar and I opened the door, there was a guest on our doorstep. She was an African American woman in, I would say, her mid-forties with short reddish-blond hair with black streaks. She was wearing skintight white jeans and a glittery top that seemed to bring attention to the gold strips outlining her two front teeth. She looked like an over-the-hill cleat chaser, a term players used to describe groupies.

I glanced quizzically at Delmar and then asked, "Can we help you?"

"Yes, you can! Which one of you is my baby?" she said.

"What?" Delmar asked.

"You heard me. You got problems with your hearing, chile? Which one of you fine young specimens is my baby?" she asked as she stepped into our apartment like her name was on the lease.

"Are you sure you have the right place?" I asked.

"Let me see," the lady said. She pulled a little piece of paper from her purse and adjusted the tiny glasses that she rested on her nose.

"Man, shut that door. This woman is crazy," Delmar said.

"Well, now I know for sho it's you, 'cause you act and look just like your daddy," she said, pointing toward Delmar.

"What do you know about my daddy?" Delmar demanded.

"Oh, I know plenty because I'm your mama. I'm Maybelline Jean LaRue. May-Jean for short," she said as she moved over and tried to hug Delmar.

He pushed her back and said, "What are you talking about, lady? You must be smoking crack. I don't know you and don't want to know you."

"Of course you do, baby. Don't you remember when the two of us used to go to Chuck E. Cheese? As a baby, you loved pepperoni pizza," Maybelline said. "Honey, I was living in New Orleans until that bitch Katrina came through. My place is a mess now. Them motherfuckers are crazy if they think May-Jean is staying in some damn FEMA trailer."

"Delmar, are you all right?" I asked as I placed my hand on his shoulder. I was trying to prevent him from falling over.

"I'm straight, B."

"You want some private time?"

"Yeah, baby, we got a lot of catching up to do," Maybelline said.

"I ain't got no time to talk. And I have a class to go to," Delmar said. I looked at Delmar strangely, because he *never* wanted to go to class. He always told me that he only went to class so that he could stay eligible for the bowl games, and then it was "so long, school!"

"I'm glad to hear my baby is tending to his books. That's fine; we got plenty of time to talk. Here, let me give you the number to my celly. Call me when you get some time. By the way, I need a ticket for the game this Saturday."

"I ain't got no extra tickets," Delmar mumbled.

"What about you, handsome? You got a ticket I can use?" Maybelline asked as she looked at me.

"Uh, let me check," I stuttered as I looked at Delmar for some clue as to what to do. Mom usually gave one of my tickets to Lowell, but he could always get a ticket because he was tenured faculty.

Maybelline wrote down some information on a piece of paper and handed it to a still-shocked Delmar.

"And what's your name, baby?" she asked as she turned to me.

"I'm Brady Bledsoe," I said, extending my hand to her.

"Nice meeting you, Brady. You sure are a handsome young thang. I bet you treat your mama real nice."

"Come on, dude, let's bounce. I don't want to be late for class," Delmar said as he moved out the front door.

"I bet my baby is smart. Ain't he? Look at him going to class and shit," Maybelline said as she walked out the door.

I laughed to myself and moved swiftly to catch a fast-moving Delmar. I looked back and saw Maybelline take out her compact, touch up her lipstick, and then pull out her cell phone.

Delmar and I rode in silence for a few blocks before I finally spoke.

"So, how are you feeling, man?"

"What you talking about, how am I feeling? That was some fucked-up shit that just happened," Delmar said.

"Are you mad at your dad for lying to you?"

"My dad didn't lie to me. I mean, I knew she wasn't dead, but to my dad and me, she was. She didn't want to be a part of our lives, so to us she was dead."

"You knew she was alive? Why didn't you tell me?" I asked.

"Tell you what?"

"That your mother really wasn't dead."

"Look, dude, I don't want to talk about this shit no more. Didn't you hear me say she didn't want to be a part of my life? The only reason her ass is showing up now is to try and make some money. Crazy bitch didn't even know which one of us she gave birth to. That shit is whack. So don't ask me another fuckin' thing bout it. All I want to do is get to campus and hang at the Union till practice. Let's not talk about this anymore. Understood?"

As we pulled into the parking garage, I said, "Understood."

"You don't shave down there, do you?" asked the wiry photographer with untidy blond-streaked hair and small round glasses.

"Excuse me?"

"I want you to take your hands and act like you're about to pull your pants down. We will tease them with a little pubic hair peeking from that jockstrap," he said.

I gave the photographer a *you've got to be kidding* look, then, as I started to feel nervous sweat spill down my back, I asked if Kevin Trainor, the sports information director, told him to take a shot like that.

"Nobody tells me how to take a picture," the photographer barked.

I was in the middle of a photo session for the "Run" poster, another special promotion the university marketing department had come up with in support of my campaign for the Heisman Trophy and I hoped, making an All-American team. The plan was to come up with a poster that included my career rushing stats with glossy color photos of me wearing my football uniform and practice clothes in ways that highlighted my body. They had also given students who bought season tickets a T-shirt that said ♥ *BB.*

At first, I didn't want to do the poster because I thought awards like the Heisman Trophy and All-American honors should be based on what I did on the field. But Kevin reminded me that even though I was big at school, I was an underdog for a lot of the postseason awards and we had to be aggressive with our marketing efforts. CGU didn't have the advantage that players from long-standing football powers like Arkansas and Michigan had.

Kevin pointed out that the leading candidates, Brady Quinn from Notre Dame and Troy Smith from Ohio State University, were on television almost every Saturday and that even South Bend and Columbus were much more glamorous locales than Scarlet Springs, Georgia. We were lucky to have a few games on ESPN2 every season. Still Kevin had managed to secure interviews for me with two of college football's best writers, Clay Henry and Dudley Dawson. Everybody who followed college football read these guys.

"I don't feel comfortable doing that," I said. I didn't object to the photographer when he took photos of me wearing only my shoulder pads and tight football pants, with a jock clearly visible under the sugar-white pants. He'd also taken several of what could only be called ass shots of me in my tight white uniform, which made me feel a bit uncomfortable, because he was one weird dude. Chloe had made me comfortable in front of the camera and had often said my ass was one of my best assets. I hadn't objected when the photographer's assistant sprayed my face and hair with water and then spread something that felt like Vaseline across my lips. But showing my pubic hair was going too far. I grimaced at the thought of my mother seeing a photo like that or any of the ones Chloe took.

"What are you talking about? If I had a body like yours, I would do everything buttnaked," the photographer said. "You're a natural, Brady. Besides, sex sells."

"Maybe that's the problem. I'm not for sale," I said as I grabbed my jersey and headed for the dressing room.

CHAPTER 20
BARRETT'S CHANGE OF
HEART

"Are you going back to the locker room?" Barrett asked as she left the pep rally at Founder's Square. A shocked Shante turned around to face Barrett and quizzed, "Are you talking to me?"

"Yes. Are you going back to the locker room? Why don't we walk down there together?" Barrett said. Shante raised her eyebrows, rolled her head, and said, "Whatsup with being nice to me? You trying to pledge my sorority or something?"

"I'm sorry. I know I wasn't so friendly when we first met but I think we should try and be friends. I mean we are the only two black girls on the squad," Barrett said.

"So now it's *let's be friends because we sistahs.* I get along with my white girls just fine, thank you."

Shante picked up her green and gold pompoms and started toward the center of campus. Barrett didn't like to beg, but she needed information on Brady.

"Shante, wait. Please, I'm sorry," Barrett called out. Shante turned around and said, "Come on, girl. You right. We sistahs and we should get along. Give me a hug."

A hug wasn't at all what Barrett had in mind. She wasn't used to females touching her in any way unless they were trying to bring her physical harm. Still, when she pulled away from the awkward embrace, Shante was smiling at her.

"So, how are things going with Brady?" Shante asked.

"I'm taking it slow," Barrett said.

"Well, I think you've gotten farther with him than the rest of us. And let me tell you, honey, we've all tried. Black, white, Hispanic, you name it," Shante said.

"Why do you think that is? Is he really that much of a Boy Scout?" Barrett asked.

"I know he's really focused on football and school. I mean how many jocks do know who've finished their college requirements in three years? He's just hanging around to play football and he's working on a second degree, too."

"Yeah, that's pretty amazing. Do you know his mother?"

"I've met her a couple of times. She's a beautiful woman. Looks more like his sister than his mother. She seems nice, but I know it might be a different story if I'd made that move on Brady like I'd wanted to. Notice, I said that in the *past tense*," Shante said.

"So you're no longer interested in Brady?"

"I wouldn't kick him out of my bed, but that's where the problem starts."

"What do you mean?"

"Girl, you know that Brady Bledsoe is a virgin and he even wears a little silver celibacy ring that looks like a wedding band."

Barrett had noticed the ring and knew it wasn't a wedding band but she hadn't asked him what it stood for. So, the information Nico had given her about Brady was true.

"Brady Bledsoe is the Chris Leake of CGU," Shante said laughing.

"Who is Chris Leake?" Barrett asked.

"That phine ass quarterback at the University of Florida who said he wouldn't have a girlfriend until he won a national championship. I know Brady looks up to him. Let's hope whatever they feeling ain't spreading," Shante said.

CHAPTER 21
CARMYN DEFLECTS A PASS

I kicked off my heels by the door, browsed through the mail I held in my hand, then dropped it onto the table without opening anything and slowly climbed the stairs. It had been a long, grueling Wednesday — first at Back to My Roots and then with the rich and the wannabe famous in Buckhead.

I crept by the exercise room. As tired as I felt, I wouldn't be doing anything in *that room* for days. But a smile filled every part of me once I stepped inside my bedroom. I took off my blouse and dropped my skirt to the floor. The soft azure walls embraced me with comfort, stealing the day's tension away. I reached for some of my Carol's Daughter hand cream and rubbed my hands as I inhaled the wonderful aroma of lavender. I slipped my Yolanda Adams CD into the Bose CD player. It took just a few steps for me to reach my bed and fall into the softness of my overstuffed comforter and my super-plush pillow-top mattress. I moaned with pleasure. *This is probably better than sex,* I thought. *At least it's more consistent.*

I rolled onto my stomach and stared at the telephone. I had been thinking about Kellis all day, but both salons were so busy I didn't have a chance to call her. I hoped she'd reconsidered her insurance scam. I thought I might have a plan to prevent Kellis from doing something she'd regret even if she didn't get caught. I picked up the phone and dialed her number. She answered on the first ring.

"Hey, Kellis," I said as lightly as I could. "What are you up to this evening?"

"Girl, you just caught me. I'm going to the Blue Point for dinner." Normally, a mention of that upscale Buckhead restaurant known for its atmosphere and outstanding food would have made me smile. But tonight I couldn't — because I knew it was probably more than a dinner for Kellis.

"That's pretty fancy for the middle of the week, isn't it?" I asked.

"Yeah. I won't have to pay for it, though." Kellis laughed.

I didn't laugh with her. I took a breath before asking, "Who are you going with?"

"Some guy I met at the gym. He used to play for the Atlanta Hawks. I could ask him if he has a friend. But I must warn you, he's young," Kellis said.

"Don't do that. I'm waiting for Brady to call," I said.

"You sound worried. What's going on? Is Brady all right?"

I hesitated for a moment and then said, "Nothing. Brady's fine."

"Come on, Carmyn. I know you didn't call just to check out my dinner plans."

"I guess you know me too well, huh?"

"We're friends. I'm supposed to know you."

Friends. I wanted it to stay that way. But more important than Kellis's feelings was her well-being. I had to say something. "Well, what I'm about to say may not be good for a friendship, but I've been worried about you." Before Kellis could respond, I continued before I lost my nerve. "I've looked over some of my accounts and . . . I think I can spare five thousand dollars if that will help."

When there was only silence on the line, I called out Kellis's name to see if she was still there.

"I'm here, Carmyn," Kellis said softly.

Oh, no, I thought. *I've offended my friend.* I couldn't help but think about when we first met and Kellis was always spending money

183

and had paid for what seemed like hundreds of dinners for Brady and me. Back in the day when she was an NBA wife, she used to drop five thousand dollars just walking through the door of the Louis Vuitton store at Lennox Square.

Kellis said, "I'm just trying to fight back the tears."

It took a moment for her words to make sense, and I sighed with relief. "I don't want you to cry. I just need to know if this will help you out."

"More than you know."

"Good. I'll drop the check by tomorrow."

"I'll never be able to thank you enough."

"Don't mention it. I know things are tough right now, but I want you to know they will get better."

"Carmyn, you know I didn't really want to file that false police report. But there was no other way."

"There's always another way," I said. "You're going to be fine."

"Because of you."

"Well, thank God for hair grease and pressing combs," I said. We laughed together. I said, "Go out and have some fun tonight."

"I will." Kellis paused. "And Carmyn, thanks for being a real friend." "You would do it for me," I said.

"Yeah, I would. I'm here if you ever need me," Kellis said. "I wish you'd let me find you a boyfriend after I find husband number two."

"Good night, Kellis." I hung up, suddenly filled with an energy I didn't have when I first came home. Maybe, instead of a night of fattening snacks, I'd venture into my exercise room instead.

It was a little after 6 a.m. and I was on my second cup of coffee when the phone rang. Nobody but Brady called me this early. "Good morning, sunshine. Have you finished your workout?" I asked.

"Yeah, Mom, I have. My teammates have been stepping up with the workouts. I'm really proud of them. What about you? I hope you're not letting your exercise room collect dust when I'm not there to push you," Brady said.

"That's because you're a good captain and you would be proud of me. I actually did the treadmill for thirty minutes last night. I want to look my best when I greet you on the football field on senior day. How's practice going?"

"We're ready. I think we can run the table this season. Are you coming on Friday or

Saturday morning?"

"I'm coming Friday. I'll hang out with Lowell. I think he's met someone. So I need to either pry it out of him or do some spying," I said.

"That's good. Hey, do you know if he's going to use your other ticket?"

"I don't know. Why?"

"I might need it for someone," Brady said.

"Who?" I asked. I sent up a silent prayer that it wasn't this girl he was interested in. Lord knows I didn't want to spend the first game of the season with a total stranger. Someone who would try to get pointers on how to snag my one and only son. But then I remembered Lowell telling me she was a cheerleader, so I knew the ticket couldn't be for her.

"You're not going to believe this, but I want to give it to Delmar's mother," Brady said.

"What? I thought she was dead," I said.

"Me too. But it turns out she's not. Just showed up out of the blue the other day. She said she had been living in New Orleans."

"Was Delmar shocked?"

"You know Delmar, he's not talking," Brady said.

"Is she going back to New Orleans?"

"I don't know, Mom, but I'll tell you she's

a character," Brady said, and laughed.

"I'm sure Lowell can get a ticket. He might be able to sit in the president's or dean's box. When do you need to know?"

"Whenever," Brady said. I detected a note of sadness in his response.

"Brady, are you all right?" I asked.

"Yeah, but I'll tell you that meeting Delmar's mother got me to thinking about my dad and how I wish he was alive to see me play," Brady said in a serious tone I rarely heard from him.

I didn't respond right away. No matter how many times Brady brought up his father, I always got nervous and didn't have anything to say. It was easier when he was younger and accepted my response that his father was up in heaven helping God. Brady took great pride in that, and when his classmates in first grade asked him where his father was, Brady boasted what I'd told him, word for word.

"Mom, I got to ask you a favor," Brady said after a few moments of silence.

"Sure, baby. Whatever you want," I said.

"Do you have a picture of my father? I want to tape it to my helmet this season. It'll be like he's with me during every run I make."

A heavy silence followed Brady's question.

How was I going to handle this? All of a sudden, horrible images of my youth flashed before me like a bad movie. I'd become an expert at blocking painful events from my memory. Now my son was tampering with the movie of my life he knew nothing about.

"Mom, are you still there?"

"Yeah, Brady, I'm still here," I said softly.

"I didn't upset you, did I?"

"No, Brady, you didn't. I just wish I could help you, but I don't have any pictures of him," I said.

"Okay, I just thought I'd ask. I've made it since Pee Wee football without him, and I guess I can make it this year, too," he said mournfully.

It was breaking my heart not to be totally honest with my son. But how could I tell Brady I didn't know who his father was?

■ ■ ■ ■

BOOK TWO
THE SEASON

■ ■ ■ ■

CHAPTER 1
BRADY'S LITTLE PRAYER

It was Friday night, hours before the first Saturday in September. It was time to play some football, and even though I'd played in hundreds of games before, I felt an indescribable blend of excitement and calm.

The team had just returned to a hotel right outside of Scarlet Springs where we were going to spend the night. Just before we went into our rooms, I spotted Koi Minter dancing in the hallway while a couple of our teammates cheered him on as he showed off his "Cali moves." I had a bone to pick with Koi and thought now was the time, so I went over and tapped him on the shoulder. He took out his earplugs and said, "Whatsup, Brady boi?"

"Can I speak with you for a moment?"

"That's what's up, Mr. Team Captain. What can I do for you?"

"Why don't we step over here," I suggested, nodding my head toward the corner near the vending machines.

Koi followed me, and when we were out of earshot of the other guys, I turned around and stood so close I could see my reflection in his eyes.

"Why haven't you been making the morning workout sessions?"

"Man, that shit is whack. Do you know when it's five A.M. here in the dirty South that it's two A.M. in Cali? A brother just be getting in from study sessions or whatever."

"Yeah, I know, but that's not the question. The workouts are MANdatory and you need to man up and be there. Do I make myself clear?" I barked in my best captain voice.

Koi looked me up and down real slow in one of those *Is he smoking crack?* looks and then said, "Yeah, I hear you, dawg."

"Good, I'll expect to see you first thing Monday," I said, and headed for my hotel room.

Delmar walked through the door wearing an oversized, team-issued warm-up suit and a black do-rag. He was talking on his phone, but I could tell from the look on his face that he wasn't happy.

"Trifina, why you got to always be a bitch? I sent you five hundred dollars last week, which means I'm only a hundred dollars behind in my child support. Why in the hell is that not enough money for you to bring your punk ass down here for the game? I want my son to see me play," he shouted.

I hoped Delmar fighting with Trifina, his baby's mom, wasn't going to affect his game tomorrow. Not that their arguing was something out of the ordinary. I thought about Naomi, whom I had found an e-mail address for but hadn't heard from. I wondered what my life would be like if I had the responsibility of a child and a wife.

I picked up my cell phone and debated whether or not to call Barrett again. I had called her twice but figured she was busy with the pep rally. I listened to my messages, including one from my mother telling me she had arrived safely at Lowell's.

When I clicked off my phone, Delmar was ready to talk.

"Son, can you believe that trick Trifina? Talking 'bout she ain't got enough money to drive down here for the game because gas is so high. I pay her over five hundred a month, and that's more than enough for gas. She's just being a bitch. I bet when I make it to the league she'll find a way to get to my games," Delmar said.

"Where are you getting that much money from?" I asked.

"Mind your own business, son. I know how to handle my shit," Delmar said.

"Don't do anything that will make you ineligible, D."

"Stop trippin', Brady."

"I wish you would have said something earlier, because D Jr. could have ridden down with my mom," I said.

"This shit just pisses me off. My dad could have brought him," Delmar said as he lay back in frustration on the double bed on the left side of the hotel room. I didn't think now was the time for me to tell him that I'd gotten a ticket for Maybelline. He hadn't mentioned her since she showed up at our apartment.

"There will be other games," I said.

"I wanted him at this fuckin' game. It's going to be a sellout, and I got about three agents who will be there. I wanted them to see D Jr. so they know I got mouths to feed. They need to know I'm hungry."

"D, I hope you're being careful and not taking money from agents. They'll feel like they own you."

"That's bullshit, dude. Do I look like Kunta Kinte to you, dude?"

Just then my cell phone rang, and when I looked, I saw Barrett's beautiful face and name flash up. My heart quickened. I looked at Delmar and told him to hold up.

"Hello," I said.

"Brady. How're you doing?"

"I'm straight, Barrett. How are you? How was the pep rally?"

"I'm good and the rally was awesome. So much better than the freshman pep rally. I would say there were over four thousand people there. The campus is so geeked about the game tomorrow. Are you ready to play?"

"Yeah, I'm ready. But I want it to be over so I can see you. I can't wait for you to meet my mother," I said.

"Do you think she'll like me?" Barrett asked.

"How can she not like you?"

"So what are you doing? I bet ya'll got some boppers waiting for you at the hotel," Barrett teased.

"Come on, girl, you know that ain't my style. Besides, the coaches look out for that kind of stuff," I said.

"So have you been thinking about me?" Barrett asked. Her voice sounded so sweet and irresistible.

"Would you believe me if I said every minute of the day?" My statement was pretty close to the truth.

"Should I?"

"Barrett, I told you my mom raised me

right, so every word that comes out of my mouth is true. Especially when it comes to you," I said.

Delmar got up and went into the bathroom and closed the door, making the room dark.

"Do you have any pregame rituals?" Barrett asked.

"Nothing but prayer with my mom," I said.

"What do you sleep in?"

"What?"

"I asked, what do you sleep in?" Barrett repeated.

"My drawers," I said.

"What kind?"

"Boxer briefs."

"I want you to do something for me."

"Sure, Barrett, whatever you want."

"You promise?"

"Yeah, what do you want me to do?"

"I want you to take those boxers off when you get through praying and sleep totally naked tonight. Make sure you continue to spend every minute thinking of me. Will you do that for me?"

I waited a few moments and then said, "Sure, I can do that." We said good night, and I was thankful that Delmar couldn't see my hard-on in the dark as I got under the covers full commando — naked as the day I was born.

I had been in bed for about an hour, Delmar snoring like a grizzly bear, when my phone rang. I saw that the call was from my mom, so I answered it.

"Mom, is everything all right?"

"Sure, Brady, everything is fine. Lowell wants to take me to breakfast first thing in the morning, so I thought we could do our prayer tonight," she said.

"Sure, Mom. Let's do this," I said.

"Lord, we come before You as your humble servants. We ask that You look after Brady tomorrow. Please keep him and his teammates safe from harm. Allow him to do his best as he glorifies Your name. We thank You for all that You give us: the many blessings; the love. In Jesus' name we pray. Amen," Mom said.

"Amen," I said. Then I started my prayer. "Dear Lord, we come to You on bended knee. I ask that You look after my mother tonight and tomorrow. Make sure that she arrives home safely. I also ask that You look after both teams tomorrow. Allow us to play our best and keep every player, coach, fan, and cheerleader from harm's way. Make sure that we all understand that this is only a game and nothing is important unless we put You first. Thank You for the blessings and the talent You have given me. And thank You for the best mother in the world. Amen."

"That was lovely, Brady. It all starts again tomorrow. Good luck, baby."

"Thank you, Mom. I love you."

"I love you and I'm so proud of you."

"You think my dad would be proud of me?" I asked.

My mother didn't answer. There was silence sandwiched between Delmar's snoring.

"Mom? Are you still there?"

"Yes, your father would be very proud of you," she said in a hushed voice.

CHAPTER 2
BARRETT'S BACKFIELD IN MOTION

Dear Diary,

Nico came by last night real late and put it down on me. My call to Brady had me all amped up and I sure did need some loving, so seeing Nico was perfect timing. When that man gives it to me, it feels like he's sending shocks of pleasure through my body. He had me straddle him, and in his booming voice he whispered, "Make that pussy talk, baby. Make it talk." I don't care how fine these college boys are, none of them can compare to my Nico and his experience.

In honor of the first football game of the season, we played a little game ourselves — the football player and cheerleader. I put on my uniform, and I arranged my hair in two long ponytails with gold and green ribbons tied around them.

The girls on the squad wear these little green A-line skirts that are really short, with gold tights under them. I wore my skirt but said fuck the tights. Nico went crazy. The top is a midriff halter, gold and green with *Jags* across it. Most of these girls are so flat-chested they can get away with a little nude bra, but me and the twins need a full-fledged sports bra.

Nico told me I looked like a teenage girl, and I told him he looked like the older brother of my high school friend who I was secretly having an affair with. We drank champagne and just laughed together until the wee hours of the morning.

The sun woke me up and I rolled over and realized that Nico was gone, leaving behind his T-shirt for me to caress and inhale his masculine scent.

It's game day, and at age twenty-nine I'm making my debut as a college cheerleader, and for some strange reason it excites me. I remember wanting to be a cheerleader when I was in junior high and my mother telling me she wasn't wasting her hard-earned money for some pleated polyester skirt for me to shake my ass in.

It's funny how things sometimes turn out.

CHAPTER 3
CARMYN VS. MAY-JEAN

Today was the day I'd been waiting for since the end of last season: game day at Central Georgia University. I got to the stadium about three hours before the game so I could greet Brady and his teammates as they unloaded from the buses and walked to the stadium in the pregame ritual known as Jaguar Walk. My heart was bathed in such a feeling of pride when I got a glimpse of my son leading his team through the crowd. Brady was dressed in a dazzling white shirt, gold tie, and blue pin-striped suit, and as team captain he was the first player to follow the coaches and state troopers as they strolled into the dressing room. Along the way, they gave handshakes and hugs to the fans who lined up on both sides of the route to welcome their football heroes. Since I was at the beginning of the line, I got to give hugs to both Brady and Delmar. A lot of fans had posters of Brady shirtless, which I wasn't sure I liked, and they were grabbing at him to sign them. Didn't they know he had a game to play?

At the start of the game, I stood up with over 80,000 cheering fans as the band played the national anthem and then the school song. When the band started playing the CGU fight song, I screamed even louder as I looked for Brady, and the cheerleaders led the team through the band and on to the field.

"CGU . . . CGU . . . CGU," the crowd cheered. "Go Jags Go! Go Jags Go!"

My heart burst as Brady and two of his teammates met the opposing team at the center of the field. Just as the coin was tossed, a woman wearing a faux mink jacket, carrying a tub of popcorn and a liter of Coke, moved in front of me, blocking my view. I figured the Jaguars had won the toss when I heard the roar of the crowd.

"You must be Brady's mom. I'm Maybelline, Delmar's mom. May-Jean for short. He told me I would be sitting next to you," Maybelline said. "It sho was nice of yo boy to give me a ticket, since that son of mine gave all his tickets away."

"Hello," I said with a smile and a glance at her tight-fitting getup, thinking, *The 1980s want that outfit back.* But I quickly told myself to stop being judgmental, folks are entitled to wear whatever they want.

"So sorry to hear about how Katrina forced you to move," I said.

"Girl, that bitch did me a favor. I needed to git my ass up and out of humid New Orleans anyway, and I'm making a little money off it," Maybelline said.

I fought hard not to raise my eyebrows and turned my attention back to the game. On the first play, the quarterback took the snap, faked a pass, and then handed the ball to Brady. At first he did a stutter step and it looked like he was going to be tackled in the backfield, but he sidestepped a defender, then ran behind Delmar, who plowed through several more defenders, giving Brady a clear line to the end zone.

The first play of the game — and Brady had scored with an eighty-yard run. This was going to be my baby's year for sure. The entire stadium was on their feet, cheering, waving flags as the band played. I was jumping up and down, clapping my hands while I watched Brady race to the sideline into the huge arms of his teammates.

"Yeah, Brady. You go, baby," I yelled.

"Eat 'em up. Tear 'em up. Give 'em hell, Jags," the crowd cheered after the band played the fight song.

"Yo boy is good, but I don't think he would have done that if my son wasn't blocking for him," Maybelline said.

I didn't respond, but something inside of me just wanted to haul off and give Maybelline a good slap, or at the very least tell her what I thought of any woman who would leave her son because she wasn't ready to be a mother. Who was ever really ready to be a mother? You just did it.

"Do you think she's mixed?" Maybelline asked.

I was trying to watch the game and ignore her, but I heard her voice again.

"I think she is mixed. Honey, after a while everybody gonna be mixed with something. Just a bunch of mutts. I bet she is mixed with sumthin' — don't you think so, Carmyn?"

"Who?" I finally said, hoping she would stop her yacking.

"That girl down there on the field. I guess they call them pep girls."

I glanced down on the field in front of the bench and saw a pretty, light-skinned black girl. I wondered if this was the Barrett Brady had mentioned.

"I don't know."

"I think she is. She remind me of one my girlfriend's daughters from New Orleans. But that bitch was too evil to go to college.

Just like her mama," Maybelline said to herself, because I wasn't listening. I was watching my baby play.

For most of the first half, I watched Brady as he raced for over 143 yards; still, I couldn't really enjoy the game because of Maybelline's constant jabbering. Whenever Delmar ran the ball, blocked for Brady, or made any kind of play, Maybelline would say, "You go 'head, Delmar. Run that ball. Do it, baby! My baby gonna be making plenty money real soon. . . ."

All of a sudden, Maybelline grabbed my hand. "Girl, is that ring real or is it cubic zucchini? Look like you're doing all right for yourself."

I quickly pulled my hand back and said, "Of course it's real."

When halftime arrived, I quickly grabbed my purse and started to move away from my seat.

"Where you going?" Maybelline asked.

"Uh, I'm going to the ladies' room," I said, wondering why I had even told her that.

"Good. I gotta go, too. That cold drank is running right through me like beer normally do," Maybelline said.

"What?" I asked a bit more abruptly than I had intended.

"You got wax in your ears, darling? I

got to pee."

During the trip to the restroom, Maybelline wobbled beside me on leopard-skin pumps that were way too high for her. I noticed that we had become the center of attention. I didn't know exactly what it was that was getting so much notice, because there were so many possibilities.

It could have been her fur, or maybe the green, skintight Capri pants clinging to a shape that was long past its prime. Or maybe it was the striped tan shell that was struggling to contain the heavy, sagging breasts that bounced as Maybelline moved through the stadium thoroughfare as though the fans had come to see her.

I was thankful when we came to the entrance of the restroom. I quickly ducked into one of the stalls. When I saw the spotted shoes beneath the wall of the stall next to me, I just shook my head, wondering how I could get rid of Maybelline.

Suddenly, I heard a knock on the metal stall and heard Maybelline say, "You handling yo' bizness over there, Carmie?"

I didn't respond, silently praying that the second half of the game would move faster than the first.

When the game was over, Maybelline hung

around outside the players' dressing room, clinging to me like a bad skin infection. I would have preferred to savor the Jaguars' 35–14 victory over Texas Tech and Brady's 234 yards rushing and two touchdown passes alone, rather than listen to Maybelline ramble on about nothing.

"That was a good game, wasn't it?" she said.

"Yes, it was."

"Our boys make the perfect team. If they keep playing like this, they'll win all the games, don'tcha think?"

"Yup," I said, trying my best not to encourage this woman into any additional conversation as we waited for our sons.

"We should get together before the next game. Maybe you can come by my place," Maybelline said.

"You live up here?" I asked incredulously.

"Yep, but let's keep that to ourselves. Delmar don't know I took a little six-month lease on an apartment."

"Why are you hiding that from him?"

"Because, honey, you know what they say. You got to spend money to make money," Maybelline said, laughing.

I didn't have a clue as to what this crazy woman was talking about, and I really didn't want to know.

"Are you and your son real close?"

"Very."

"Where's his daddy?"

"Dead."

"I know that ignorant-ass Jesse wishes I was dead. Look at him standing over there acting like he don't see me. Can you believe he told my son I was dead just because I was trying to follow my dreams and make something of myself," Maybelline said, smiling sorrowfully at me. "I was going to be a model slash dancer."

"How did that work out for you?" I asked, thinking I knew why Jesse wanted to protect his son from embarrassment. Fathers, like mothers, sometimes have to make decisions that will protect their children. I certainly understood that.

"It didn't. I wasted so much of my life, bouncing around here and there, letting men lie to me, tell me that I was going to be this and that, when all they wanted was one thing. A little taste of what's between my legs. I ain't got shit to show for all the joy I brought them men. But God has a plan. One day I was reading some magazines at the supermarket and I was thumbing through a sports magazine because there was a fine-ass man on the cover, and I see my baby's name, and how he's gonna be drafted and make a lot of money."

"So that's why you got in touch with him?"

"I was always planning on gettin' around to it, but when I read that, I told myself it wasn't no time like the present. I hear all the time 'bout young athletes buying houses and cars for they moms, and I'm Delmar's mom. Ain't no way around that."

I saw my son walking toward me, so I stepped away from Maybelline and met Brady halfway. Maybelline walked over toward Delmar and his dad, who had a big smile on his face as he hugged his son.

When Brady approached me, there was someone beside him, a young lady wearing a cheerleader's uniform with a very short skirt and sporting a bare midriff. She was the same girl I saw down on the field.

Brady gave me a huge hug and I kissed him on the cheek. I patted him on the back and whispered in his ear, "Great game, baby. This is going to be your year."

"Thanks, Mom. I love you," Brady whispered back as he gave me another big hug.

He tried to step out of our embrace, but I still held tight to him.

"So where are we going to dinner? I need to call Lowell and let him know where to meet us," I said.

"Ma," Brady said, seeming to avoid the

question. "This is Barrett. Barrett Manning," he said, urging her forward with his hand placed at the small of her back. The gesture was too familiar for my taste.

Barrett stepped in front of me. She was pretty enough, I thought, in a fake-boobs, too-much-makeup kind of way. She had long hair that was styled nicely, very keen features, and a nice little shape. She looked like a poor man's version of Ciara — that singer Brady had a photo of on his wall back home. Barrett looked like she could be a mixed-race child, but I wasn't sure. But immediately, there was something that I didn't like or trust about this girl. I couldn't put my finger on it, but I knew I would discover what it was if she stuck around.

"Hello, Ms. Bledsoe," Barrett said, extending a hand. "I've been looking forward to meeting you."

"And I, you," I said, shaking Barrett's hand and adding nothing else.

I directed my attention back to my son and asked the question again.

"So what do you feel like for dinner? I'm starving," I said. I was hoping that Brady hadn't invited Barrett to dinner.

Brady seemed hesitant. He dropped his head and looked down at his gym shoes.

"Brady, what's wrong?"

"Ma, why don't you and Lowell go on without me? I promised Barrett I would go to dinner with her at this private club I've been dying to go to. Didn't I tell you?"

"No, you didn't tell me," I replied. My feelings were hurt that Brady wanted to spend time with this girl rather than his godfather and me.

"Sorry, Mom, but tell me you understand?"

"No, Brady, I don't quite understand," I said softly. Ever since his freshman year, Brady and I had had a football-weekend ritual. I would drive up a couple of hours before the game, then join Brady and Lowell for dinner after the game. It was always that way, and now Brady wanted to change it. It was something I looked forward to, a way of spending quality time with my son while he was away at college.

"Ms. Bledsoe," Barrett said, stepping forward and opening her mouth when she shouldn't have. "I wanted to invite you to the private club, too, but they only had a reservation for two. I called to see if we could change it, but since it's a football weekend the club was booked solid."

"Thanks, but I wouldn't have intruded anyway. What's that expression? Oh yes, 'three's a crowd,' " I said as I eyed Brady, who looked away. Where was this little heifer getting money to take my son to a private club? I thought. It wasn't that I didn't want Brady to have a girlfriend. I did. But it had to be the right one. I could tell minutes after meeting Barrett that she wasn't the one.

"Thanks for being so understanding," Barrett said.

I ignored Barrett and looked at Brady and said, "So will your godfather and I get to see you before I leave?"

"Sure, Ma. I'll come by Lowell's as soon as we finish dinner."

"Okay, baby," I said as I gave him a half-hug.

"Brady, I don't know if you can do that," Barrett said as she tugged on Brady's shirt.

Brady released himself from me and turned toward her.

"What?"

"I have something else planned. I'll tell you about it later," Barrett said.

"Okay," Brady said. My son looked like a puppy eager to please.

"I hope to see you again real soon," Barrett said.

I gave her a fake smile as I thought, *Don't count on it, sister.*

"Ma, before we go, let me take a picture of you and Barrett," Brady said as he took his digital camera from his backpack.

I didn't want to take a picture with this girl, but it was hard to say no to my son. So I stood next to Barrett and forced a smile. Thankfully, she didn't put her arm around me, and I didn't put mine around her.

"Okay, say *'Go Jags!'* on three. One . . . two . . . three," Brady said.

"Go Jags," I said through clenched teeth and a tight smile.

"Is something wrong with your steak?" Lowell asked. After ordering my regular surf-and-turf dinner, I had spent most of the evening looking aimlessly at the other patrons as I picked at my steak with a fork.

The Smokey Bones restaurant was filled with the Jaguar faithful, celebrating the team's win, so the beer and on-the-rocks drinks were flowing. The space was large, with a ceiling that seemed to soar off into the sky. The smell of beef being grilled drifted throughout.

"Oh, it's fine. I guess I'm just not that hungry," I said after I realized that my picking was bothering Lowell.

"What's on your mind?"

"Brady's little friend. Barrett. What do you know about her?"

"Just what Brady told me. I think he's

smitten, to say the least. Talks about how beautiful she is and how she makes him feel special. I think she's good for him," Lowell said.

"Why?" I demanded.

"Come on now, Carmyn. Don't tell me you didn't think this wasn't bound to happen. Brady is a good-looking young man. He has been the catch of the campus since he got up here. It seems somebody has finally caught him," Lowell said as he took a swig of his beer. There was a trace of judgment in his voice.

"Do you think she's a virgin?"

"I don't know. That's not my concern. Listen, you've raised your son right and he's not going to do something against his will. I think it's amazing that he's been able to hold out for this long."

"What do you mean by that? Brady has been taught the difference between right and wrong. I started to pull him out of sports when I saw some of the boys who he was getting involved with. Mothers protect their daughters when it comes to sex, but they don't seem to care about their sons," I said.

"I don't know how you can make a blanket statement like that."

"Now, come on, Lowell, you know I'm speaking the truth."

"Just let Brady grow up. I think it's great that he has a girlfriend. It'll be better than his meeting some old gold digger once he reaches the pros. I heard those women created the 'take no prisoners' mantra."

"Who said she was his girlfriend?"

"Carmyn, don't be so naive! If she wasn't, you wouldn't be sitting here with me. Looks like your baby boy got another woman in his life," Lowell said with a sly smile.

"You're getting a big kick out of this, aren't you?"

"Now, Carmyn, you know I love you, but I hope this thing with Brady will allow you to get out and meet someone before it's too late."

"I'm not looking for anyone. This is a critical time in Brady's career. I need to make sure he gets the right agent who will look out for his future. Some fast-tailed girl could ruin it for him with babies. Or he could end up with some arrogant SOB agent, like that agent Nico Benson. I am not going to let that happen."

"I think you're overreacting," Lowell said.

"Let's talk about something else. Brady will soon grow tired of that girl. You wait and see," I said. "There's something about her that just ain't right."

Sometimes I felt Lowell didn't quite understand the depth of my relationship with my son or how hard it was to raise a black man in this day and age. Since Lowell had been outed, almost a decade ago, and given up his political dreams, it seemed that all he had to worry about were his lesson plans and where he was going to vacation for the summer. Ever since his father died and left him very comfortable, little else seemed to concern him.

"Good, let's talk about me. Ask me something," Lowell said.

"Do you miss Atlanta?"

"Sometimes, but there's something to be said about living in a city where you can leave your doors unlocked."

"How are classes?"

"Going great. Another group of smart students. There's one who's trying to get my attention out of the classroom, but I guess he doesn't know the rule."

"What rule?" I asked as I looked toward the door of the restaurant, hoping that I would see Brady walk in. Although I was enjoying my time with Lowell, I felt lonely. Brady had never chosen to dine after a game with someone other than me.

"Now, Carmyn. You know what I always say — never shit where you eat, which translated means, don't date students."

"What if he is *the one?*"

"The *one* has to have a job, and I don't mean work-study. Feel me?"

"I hear you," I said.

"Damn, these ribs seem to get better every time we come here," Lowell said as he picked the last rib off his plate.

"Lowell, do you think Brady has a chance of winning the Heisman?" I asked.

"If he keeps playing like he did today, we'll be planning a trip for our shopping spree in New York."

"What about that McFadden kid at Arkansas and the quarterback at the University of Florida, Chris Leake?" I thought about how Brady had strongly considered the Florida Gators when he came out of high school but I convinced him Gainesville was just too far for me to be able to make all his games.

"I don't think Brady has anything to worry about if he just keeps running the ball," Lowell added.

The waiter approached our table and said, "Can I interest you two in some dessert?"

"Oh, yes. I have to get some of that key lime pie," I said.

"None for me. Just some coffee with extra cream," Lowell responded.

After the waiter left, Lowell placed his

hand on top of mine and said, "Look, sweetheart, I know you're worried about your baby, but like I said, you raised him right and he'll be just fine. Don't you want him to be happy?"

"What kind of question is that? Of course I want him to be happy. But I know how women can be. Brady is not that experienced when it comes to these heifers," I said. My cell phone signaled a new text message. I looked at it and saw that it was from Sylvester, asking when he could see me. I tried to conceal my smile as I sent a message back — *Maybe 2nite.* It didn't make sense to hang around Scarlet Springs, since Brady was busy. I was taking my behind back to Atlanta.

"I could ask whose fault is that, but I won't," Lowell said.

"I could say thank you, but I won't." I smiled tightly, grabbed by pocketbook and got up from the table, and walked toward the exit.

CHAPTER 4
BRADY GETS A PENALTY FLAG

The week after my first game flew by quicker than one of Delmar's relationships with one of his stripper girlfriends. I won Southeastern Conference Offensive Player of the Week and several agents had somehow gotten my cell phone number, so now I had to deal not only with reporters but agents and runners as well. Runners were young dudes agents hired to befriend big-name players. So that means no new friends for me this year. Most of the agents backed off when I told them to contact my mother because I knew it was against NCAA rules for me to talk to agents about future business, although players could converse with them. Parents could talk, and I knew my mom would know how to handle them. Taking money from an agent at that point would get not only me in trouble but the entire team as well. The NCAA had made some teams, like Michigan's 1990s National Championship basketball squad, forfeit their championship because of a single player who broke the rules. That's why I was always on Delmar to follow the rules.

It was an exciting time. There were also a lot of scouts from professional teams showing up on campus, talking to players and coaches. We could talk to scouts, and it was a good thing when they showed up. One of my coaches told me the director of scouts from the Houston Texans had called about me, asking for game film. Houston most likely would have the first draft pick again.

Things were changing swiftly for me on many levels. I no longer spent my evenings doing my usual football routine of watching film over and over, downing fast food, and playing NCAA 2006 electronic football with Delmar. I still spent an hour after practice doing video conference interviews with sportswriters from all across the country inquiring about my chances for the Heisman, but all I could think about was Barrett.

Chloe sent me text messages a couple of times, but I didn't respond. I knew that was rude, but how could I tell her I couldn't pose for her anymore. Still no calls from Naomi, which was cool as long as she didn't show up on my doorstep with a baby that was mine.

Every moment that wasn't spent in class,

practice, or interviews was spent with Barrett. And that was all good.

We won our second game 31–24 against the South Carolina Gamecocks, and I rushed for over 211 yards and threw three passes out of the Wildhog formation. After the game, Lowell took my mother and me to dinner, and that made her very happy. She kept saying how this felt like old times. My mother didn't know it, but I had asked Barrett to join us, and Barrett had suggested that I spend the time with my mother and Lowell alone. I thought that was nice of her.

When I got home, I removed my jacket and placed my keys on the counter separating the small kitchen from the equally small dining room. Delmar walked out of his bedroom with nothing on but a towel. He was carrying a half-empty champagne bottle.

"Whatsup, son?" Delmar asked.

"Nothing much," I said. "What's up with you?"

"Just chillin'. Man, we played some ball today. All of these agents blowin' up my cell. Any calling you?"

"A few. I just tell them to talk to my mother. I'm going to let her narrow it down to the final two."

"Who's been calling?"

"The big ones, like XJI, the Poston Brothers, and Leigh Steinberg. I think it's going to be the Poston Brothers or XJI. My mother was really impressed with their marketing kits and wants me to sign with a black agent," I said.

"Are they willing to slip you some money under the table until you sign the big contract?"

"You know I ain't going for that. Remember that dude last year? If Coach and the school found out I was taking money, you know they'd kick me off the team," I said as I pulled a chair from the table and took a seat. I picked up the remote and pointed it toward the television and pressed the power button.

"Everybody does it," Delmar said.

"Does what?"

"Takes money from agents," Delmar said.

"I won't, and you better not do it either," I said.

"Would you turn me in?"

"I don't know, so don't put me in that position, D," I said.

"You want some of this?" Delmar asked as he held the bottle at eye level.

"You trying to send me straight to hell, ain't you, son? You know I don't drink."

"Yeah, I know you say you don't drink, but

I remember our freshman year when you drank some beer with us, so I was just checking." Delmar laughed. "You know this is the good shit. Dom goes for two fifty a bottle."

"Dude, where you getting that kind of money from?" I asked. Delmar was wearing a new pair of jeans almost every week and had bought dinner almost every time we had gone out since we had returned to campus this year. It was only last semester, after Delmar had spent all his Pell grant and housing money, that he was hitting me up for ten dollars here and five dollars there.

The monthly housing checks were more than enough for me, but Delmar was usually broke after a week. The main reason wasn't that he was being frivolous with his money, but that he had to send half of the check to his baby's mom for child support. Now, all of a sudden, he was spending money like a lottery winner.

"Who said I bought it? I got a little shawty in my shower right now whose only wish is to make me feel good. This makes me feel good. Bitch got peanut-butter legs."

"What? What in the hell are peanut-butter legs?" I asked.

"Legs spread easy as peanut butter." Delmar laughed.

"Anybody I know? Should I bounce?"

I asked.

"Suit yourself. But I can take her through the side door. I hope I remember the broad's name before she comes out of the shower." Delmar smiled.

"When did you meet this girl?"

"After the game. Some of us went to the strip club. That punk-ass Koi Minter was trying to push up on her, but I spit my game and cold-grilled Koi, who was left standing there holding his shit," Delmar said, laughing.

"Just like that?"

"You know how it goes for me. Just that easy . . . just that quick," Delmar said as he snapped his fingers.

Delmar walked back into his room and I called Barrett. She seemed really excited to hear my voice.

"What are you doing?" I asked.

"Getting ready to have dinner with my parents," Barrett said.

"Where are you?"

"In Atlanta," she said.

"I didn't know you were going to Atlanta," I said.

"I left after the game. Since I didn't have my man around, I decided to drive to Atlanta," Barrett said.

I had a huge smile on my face. She had called me "her man."

"When will you be back?"

"On Monday. Hey, babe, I got to go. My parents are calling me."

"Have fun," I said.

"Oh, trust me, I will," Barrett said.

A private call showed up on my phone after I finished talking with Barrett and I was not going to answer it. Then I remembered my mom's private line at the spa that she sometimes called me from, so I answered.

"Mom?"

"Brady?"

"Yeah," I said. The voice did not belong to my mother.

"Why haven't you returned my calls or texts? You said you would get back to me the other night and you didn't. What's going on, Brady?"

It was Chloe.

"I'm sorry I've been real busy with school and practice. I've had lots of interviews," I said. The truth was that I'd been avoiding Chloe.

"I figured as much. What are you doing now?"

I looked at my watch and lied, "I have to study."

"On a Saturday night? Come on, Brady, I'm not stupid. I need to see you," Chloe said.

"I don't think I can do that."

"Why not?"

"I just can't. Chloe, we're going to have to stop," I said, trying to make my voice firm.

"Why?" Chloe demanded.

I didn't answer right away.

"Brady, are you there?"

"Yes, I'm here."

"Tell me why."

"I have a girlfriend, and I don't think she'll like what we got going on," I said. It was the first time, I realized, that I was ashamed of what I'd been doing with Chloe no matter how much pleasure it brought the two of us.

"You think because you have some little girlfriend you can just drop me? I don't think so, Brady Bledsoe," Chloe said with bitterness.

"Sorry, but that's the way it's going to be."

"We'll see about that. Let's see what happens to your Heisman chances when I release some of these pictures to the press. Maybe ESPN or *Sports Illustrated* might like to see them as well."

"Are you threatening me?"

"Take it any way you want, but the Internet will be hot very soon. Let's see what the Heisman voters think of you then."

And then the line went dead.

CHAPTER 5
BARRETT RELEASES THE TWINS

Dear Diary

Celibate my ass.

Gay? Not hardly. If this boy is gay, I will send my gaydar in for a tune-up.

Brady is not going to be able to resist me much longer. I invited him over for a late-night swim. Of course, I needed his help with my top, so I walked out in just my bikini bottom. I had him in such a trance, he couldn't speak for a second. The twins did their job. As he helped me with my top, I made sure to lean against him, and it was pretty obvious he enjoyed my little show. I know he couldn't help but notice how flawless my skin was, how I smelled like lavender blended with an exotic musk scent. I know he wanted to kiss the back of my neck.

I have to buy that man some underwear. He had the nerve to show up wearing some military green baggy shorts and a gray crewneck T-shirt looking like a black Abercrombie and Fitch model. I asked him to take them off, and he said he only had a jock on underneath. When I told him I didn't have a problem with that and asked him for a full-body nude massage, he waved his little celibacy ring in my face and kindly refused my offer. I did get him to fool around with deep kissing and heavy petting, and although Brady seemed satisfied, I would be pissed if I was really his girlfriend.

The evening wasn't a total waste, though. I did manage to get his check card number and social security number off his driver's license when he left his pants and wallet in the bathroom. I called Nico to let him know, and he seemed pleased.

I told Nico he has to give me more money since I am going to have to buy some lingerie to help me to seduce Brady, and I'm sure I'll probably have to hire a cook. If I can't get to him with the joy between my legs, then maybe I can loosen him up with some food. I need to think of something else I might need so Nico will send me a lot of money. I'll use half for Brady stuff and keep the rest for myself.

I'd ordered a night shirt over the Internet made like Brady's football jersey, with his name and number on the back of it. Nico had once told me his college girlfriend (now his wife) had done that when he was in college and how much it turned him on when she wore it.

I also told Nico he's going to have to produce some parents for me real soon. Since I've met Mommy Dearest, I know Brady's going to start asking more questions about my parents. Nico says there are plenty of out-of-work actors in Atlanta and that I need to ask Brady about training for the combine. He told me to mention The Thoroughbreds, a training company he's co-owner of. Nico said Brady would know about this place because all the big-time athletes wanted to work out there. If Brady asks how I know so much about it, Nico told me to tell him that my dad works out there.

Nico wants to know when he's going to get some kind of return on his investment, and I assured him it's going to be as soon as Brady leaves my bed for the first time.

Speaking of soon, Nico says that I should still be moving into our house by Christmas. I reminded him of our conversation at the Ritz-Carlton in Atlanta where he said he was going to get a divorce attorney, and he assured me that things are under control.

I know that woman better be out of my house real soon. I have some Christmas decorating to plan.

Chapter 6
Carmyn's Telephone Games

If I hadn't seen it with my own eyes, I wouldn't have believed it. I was in the corner of Back to My Roots, counting supplies, when Maybelline walked into the shop like it was an every-Friday get-my-do-done evening. Wearing a too-tight blue jean miniskirt with white fringe, a black top, and white cowgirl boots, she took off her sunglasses and surveyed my establishment. It was a few minutes before the normal rush, and the place was quiet. A few of the stylists were preparing their stations for the day. The television was on *Ellen,* but muted.

"Where is Miss Carmyn?" she asked the receptionist. "Who may I tell her is asking to see her?" Laura asked. "Tell her it's her good, good girlfriend Maybelline. May-Jean for short."

I thought about what I was going to do for a few moments, then I stepped from behind the door and was face-to-face with

Maybelline.

"What can I do for you?" I asked.

"Come here, girl, and give me a hug," Maybelline said, not noticing that I wasn't smiling. She gave me the half-hug talk-show hosts sometimes give their guests.

"What brings you to Atlanta?" I asked as I pulled back.

"I came to Atlanta to do a little shopping and I heard about your lil' establishment and I want to give you a little business. Of course, with the family discount, since our boys are like brothas." Maybelline winked. "You know I got to look good at the game Saturday."

"You should have called for an appointment."

"An appointment? Girl, we family. What do you think you can do with my mop?" Maybelline asked as she ran her hand through her hair.

"I don't do walk-ins. Talk with Laura and she'll set you up with one of the stylists for the first opening," I said politely but with as much distance in my voice as possible. I knew from the first time I met Maybelline that she did not take hints quickly. I wished Zander was working here today, because he would fix her good. He would know exactly how to handle this woman.

"I ain't got all day — why can't you just do it? I bet if I was Whitney Houston or Halle Berry, you'd whip out that hot comb or whatever it is you use quicker than quick. Are we sitting together at the game this weekend?"

I wanted to respond with a firm "Hell, no," but instead I walked over to the receptionist's desk and looked at the appointment book. Then I turned in the direction opposite Maybelline and looked at a slim young lady who was putting on a pale pink smock.

"Kai, I see you don't have an appointment until eleven. Do you think you could take a walk-in?"

"Sure, Ms. B, what does she need done?"

"Excuse me, Ms. B and Kai, but I'm standing right here. Don't you bitches get all uppity with me. I will pull off my switchblade earrings in a New Orleans minute," Maybelline said.

"Excuse me, but I don't allow that type of language in my establishment," I said.

"What? Is this some kinda church or something? I don't see Jesus up in this camp. Excuse me, girlfriend, but ya'll ain't doing nothing but frying hair up in here. And I'm the kind of bitch that you ain't got to show me yo ass but once. I'm outta here," Maybelline said as she swept out of the salon, leaving the door wide open.

Right before closing, Kai came into my office and told me I had a phone call.

"Did you ask who it was?"

"No," she said.

"Okay, I'll take it. Close the door when you leave."

"Will do. See you tomorrow."

"Okay, have a good one."

I picked up the phone and said, "This is Carmyn. How can I help you?"

"Niecey Johnson. It is you," the somewhat familiar female voice said.

"Who is this?"

"This is Daphne Mitchell," she said. "Rena told me she thought she'd seen you. I've been looking for you. There is so much I need to tell you." Her voice was as friendly as a Wal-Mart greeter's. She was acting like we were best friends who talked every day.

"This is not Niecey, and I told that woman she has the wrong person. Please don't call me again."

"I need to talk to you about that night at college," she said.

The memory of that night twenty years ago was as fresh in my mind as a new layer of snow. When I could finally afford to go, I'd spent years in counseling trying to put that night behind me.

"I have to go. Don't call here anymore. Do you understand? Don't call me ever again," I said as my hands began trembling.

"But you —"

I hung up the phone, grabbed my purse, and rushed to my car after locking the door.

CHAPTER 7
BRADY FOR PRESIDENT

Fall was pushing its way onto CGU's campus amid all the excitement of the success of the Jaguars. We were ranked in the top ten in the country for the first time in the school's history and were a contender for a Bowl Championship Series game.

The oak trees were turning golden, and scattered acorns announced the official start of fall. Mix in the crisp autumn air that whipped across the open grounds under a glorious blue sky with gray empty clouds, and you had a postcard of what college life should be. I was going to miss all this next year.

I zipped my green and gold warm-up and rocked from one leg to the other as I stood in front of Founders Hall. "Would you come on?" I yelled at Delmar, who had stopped to talk to yet another female.

"Chill, B," Delmar shouted as he gave a wink, waved to the young lady, and raced to catch up with me. We were going to the Union for lunch.

The smell of grilled hot dogs wafted toward us and we saw a group of black students lined up at a table near the hot dog stand. The students were wearing "Vote Against the War" T-shirts, and I asked Delmar if he had registered to vote.

"Hell no," Delmar replied.

"Why not?"

" 'Cause my vote don't count," he said.

"I bet you won't say that if your behind is in Iraq next year this time eating sand sandwiches."

"Say, dude, what's up with the hot dogs?" Delmar asked one of the students passing out voter registration cards.

"Register to vote and get a hot dog and a free T-shirt," the young man said.

"Now you talking. Who said there was no more free lunch?" Delmar said as he took the card and pen from the young man.

"What are the fans talking about on the boards?" I asked.

"Same ole shit. But snaps, get this! I read on there that somebody was going to post some naked pictures of one of our teammates," Delmar said as he bit off almost half of his hot dog.

"What?" I asked, making sure that I'd

heard Delmar correctly. An unexpected shiver went through my body at the thought of my photos being on a message board. Maybe Chloe's threat wasn't empty after all.

"You heard me. Somebody said there were naked pictures of one of the players. You don't know who it is, do you?" Delmar asked with a sly smile on his lips.

"No, no, I don't know who it could be. I don't think anyone on our team would do that," I protested halfheartedly.

"I bet it's that dumb-ass Koi. Dude will do anything to get the press talking about him, but he could say good-bye to any hopes of winning the Heisman ever," Delmar said.

"You think it would hurt him?"

"Shit yeah," Delmar replied quickly. "I bet Troy Smith and Darren McFadden ain't got no naked pictures of them floating around on the Internet."

"Hey, Brady," another young man said. I recognized Wynn McDonald, the vice president of the Black Students Association. He was in my business law class.

"Whatsup, Wynn?"

"We're just out here trying to get everyone to register. You know we can make a change in this election. And somethin's gotta change."

"No doubt. I'm already registered," I said.

"That's great, Brady. I'm not surprised that a brotha like you is down for the battle," Wynn said as he smiled at me.

Delmar noticed this as he looked at Wynn and then at me. "B, let's get out of here."

I frowned as Delmar pulled me away. "Delmar, I thought you were going —"

"I changed my mind," Delmar said before I could finish my sentence. We'd only taken a few steps from the stand before Delmar continued. "Man, what you doin' letting that cake boy flirt with you like that?"

"What're you talking about?" I said.

"Don't tell me you didn't notice how that little queen was batting his eyes like a beauty contestant and sizing you up like you were a Thanksgiving turkey ready to be stuffed," Delmar said.

"Man, stop tripping. Wynn is a cool dude. Active in student government and on the Dean's List."

"That shit don't surprise me. All them gay dudes are smart and in shit. But it ain't good for your reputation," Delmar said.

"What are you talking about?" I asked again.

"Dude, everybody on campus know yo ass is a virgin, and if you go around letting them faggots smile and talk to you like y'all buddies, people will start to think you on they team," Delmar said.

"Their team? When did black men divide up into teams?" I asked.

"You know what I'm talking about," Delmar defended.

"D . . . you know me. I don't care what people think. I know who I am."

"Man, you need to worry about that shit. Come spring and after the NFL combine, they gonna be sending investigators to campus to check up on you, and I mean they check everything. You already got to deal with the fact that your godfather is light on his feet, then they find out you friends with the cake boys and that might cost you a few million dollars," Delmar said.

"Stop tripping and promise me you will at least go to the courthouse and register to vote," I said. I never understood why football players or athletes in general were so homophobic. We were the ones who were always naked in close confines with each other, or out on the field patting each other's butts.

I thought about something that had happened last winter that made me wonder about some of my teammates. It was snowing real hard and a bunch of us were in the Union coffee shop just shooting the breeze. In walked Darius, a guy who made no bones about being gay.

When he walked in from the snow, he suddenly slipped and his body flipped over, even though he did everything he could to prevent the fall. It was funny and everybody started laughing, including myself.

Darius got up and pulled himself together and walked over to the table where all the ballplayers were sitting and laughing. He put his hands on his hips and in his sweet-sounding but serious voice said, "I know you motherfuckers ain't laughing at me. I might need to start doing a little roll call of names of the ones who visit my dorm late at night. And we all know it ain't 'bout studying, don't we, boys?" Darius said. The entire table got silent, and Darius walked away snapping and popping his fingers over his head, saying, "Don't fuck with me, fellows!"

"Brady, just promise me you gonna watch yo step," Delmar pleaded, interrupting my thoughts of that funny scene.

"If that will get you to vote, then I promise," I said. I reached over and pulled Delmar's head toward mine and bumped it affectionately.

"Hey, man, cut that shit out. Somebody might see us," Delmar said.

CHAPTER 8
BARRETT'S BRIBES

When Barrett got home from another annoying cheerleading practice, she noticed a note taped to her door. She dropped the green duffel bag with her name embroidered in gold and opened the note.

Check under your bathroom sink and you'll find a little gift you need to give your boy. He will most likely reject it, but you must make him take it. I know you can do it.

Barrett walked into her kitchen and grabbed a bottle of water. She took a couple of swigs and went into her bathroom.

In the back of the cabinet, Barrett saw a silver bag with a royal-blue ribbon tied around it. Barrett took the bag and sat it on the counter as she caught a glance of her face. She noted that she needed to reapply her lipstick before Brady dropped by. She tore the ribbon from the bag and pulled out a leather blue box with the name Rolex embossed in gold. Barrett opened the box and saw a beautiful gold and silver watch with a blue face. It was very heavy and masculine-looking, and Barrett couldn't wait to see the look on Brady's face when he saw it.

"This is great, Barrett. Who taught you how to make food like this?" Brady said as he took a bite of a shrimp salad sandwich. He and Barrett were sitting on a blanket with a picnic basket in Barrett's living room.

"So you like it?" Barrett smiled.

"Yeah, it's hitting the spot. Did your mother teach you how to make this?"

Barrett started laughing, cupping her hand over her mouth.

"What's so funny?" Brady asked.

"Your question, that's what's funny. When you meet my mother, you'll realize right away that she is not the type who spends time in the kitchen."

"My mother doesn't cook much because she's by herself now, but she cooked for me all the time when I was growing up. So who taught you this? Your nanny?"

"What makes you think I had a nanny?"

"I don't know, you just seem like the type," Brady said, and smiled.

"I'm going to act like you didn't say that, and for the record I only had a nanny until I was six. Also, it was my father who taught me how to cook."

"You're kidding. Your father can cook?"

"Yes, he's an amazing man," Barrett lied.

"When am I going to meet your parents?" Brady asked.

"Hopefully real soon. They've been out of the country, but I'm going to get them to come to a game before the season's over," Barrett said.

Brady finished the rest of his sandwich and a cucumber and tomato salad, while Barrett told him about her father — that he was from New Orleans, an only boy with two sisters. Her grandmother was a single mom and a cook at one of New Orleans' most popular French Quarter restaurants.

"I thought your father was from Atlanta," Brady said.

"Naw, he moved there after he finished college."

"Where did he go to college?"

"Harvard," Barrett lied.

"Must be a smart guy," Brady said.

"Yeah, he's very smart. What team do you look forward to playing the most?" Barrett asked, changing the direction of the conversation.

"The dreaded University of Texas Longhorns," Brady said.

"Why the Texas Longhorns?"

Brady told Barrett that every major college in the United States had recruited him out of high school, but that the University of Texas hadn't even sent him a letter. He told her that he was ranked among the top twenty-five running backs in the country and that Texas had sent Delmar and even the third-string running back letters, but nothing to him. Brady said he dreamed of the day when he might line up against the evil Orange Empire and run for over a thousand yards as payback for their rejection.

"Are they any good this year?" Barrett asked.

"Well, they are the defending national champs, but I don't know. They don't have Vince Young. I guess we will see in October," Brady said.

"We'll beat them bad with you in the backfield," Barrett said, so happy she had taken the Women and Football course Nico had insisted on.

"I think you know as much football as my mom," Brady said. "So what else did your father teach you?"

"He taught me a lot about men, and how I shouldn't ever take shit from you people."

"I don't guess your father knew about men like me. My mother taught me a lot, too," Brady said proudly.

"Did you suffer from not knowing or having a father?"

"Yeah, at times," Brady said, his eyes beginning to glisten. Barrett saw this, and in a rare moment she felt sad for him. She recalled asking about her own father, and her mother telling her that she didn't know who her father was and if she did he probably wouldn't like her anyway.

"So do you ever visit his grave or anything?"

"No. I think he must have been cremated or something, because my mom never mentioned anything."

"Do you ever think what it would have been like to have him around?"

Brady told her he thought about his father often but kept it to himself because he didn't want to hurt his mother's feelings. He told her that once when he was in the sixth grade he wanted to take an item that belonged to his father to school. When he asked his mother for something, she became really upset.

"But it doesn't mean that I don't think about him and what he was like. Sometimes when I have a big game and I walk out of the locker room and I see my teammates greeting their fathers, I think how great that must feel, but I got my moms, and she's spent her life making sure I didn't miss anything."

"I know you're close to your mother, and I like that. Any man who loves his mother as much as you do — well, that bodes well for his future wife. I still think it's odd, though."

"What's odd?"

"That you haven't even seen a picture of your father," Barrett said. "Did he go to college? Where did he go to high school? I bet you could go to the school and look in the yearbooks and at least find out what he looks like. Who knows, you could look just like him."

"I never thought about that, but I don't think I could do something like that without my mother knowing," Brady said, moving closer to Barrett. He was tired of all this talk about a man he had never known, and he blinked back tears like he had done so many times before.

"Are you sure?"

"I'm positive. Let's talk about something else."

"Like what?"

"How about what else your father taught you to cook that you can make for me."

Barrett looked at Brady with a devilish grin on her face and rolled on top of him, whispering, "Let me show you something my father didn't teach me." And then she kissed him. Her lips were soft, and her scent stayed with Brady even after she had pulled away.

At the end of the night, Barrett said, "Oh, before you leave, I have something for you."

"I hope it's another one of those sweet, sweet kisses," Brady said, moving closer to Barrett as they sat on the sofa.

"You can get one of those anytime," Barrett said. She pulled back, got up, and went into her closet. Then she walked toward Brady seductively with her hands behind her back. She could tell from the look in his eyes that his curiosity was piqued.

"What are you hiding behind your back?"

"Guess."

"I'm not good at guessing."

"What if I give you three chances?"

"Come on, Barrett, just give it to me," Brady said.

"Now, you know I've been trying to do that since our second date," Barrett teased as she pulled a box from behind her and handed it to Brady.

When he saw *Rolex* on the box, his heart started beating at a very rapid pace. As he slowly opened it, he felt as excited as a kid meeting his sports hero for the first time.

"Man, this is tight," he said, giving a pleased Barrett a quick kiss on the lips.

"Try it on," Barrett insisted.

Brady studied it for a few more minutes and then said, "You shouldn't have done this. This is too expensive."

"I wanted to do something nice for my man," Barrett said.

"I don't know, but I want to make sure I can accept this," Brady said.

"Brady, I'm your girl. It's an early birthday present. You need to stop being such a straight arrow. Take the watch and wear it."

Brady gazed at the second hand of the handsome piece of jewelry for a full sixty seconds, then lifted the watch from the box, smiled, and said, "I guess I can't refuse a birthday present from my girl."

"Man, you're a genius," Barrett said.

"So the old boy liked the watch, huh?" Nico said.

"Loved it."

"Great! Now I can wire some money into his account. If choirboy doesn't go along with our little plan, then we can show he was taking money from a booster. Then I'll have him and that mother of his right where I want them."

Chapter 9
Carmyn's B-Boy Blues

I picked up a copy of *Baby Brother's Blues* by Pearl Cleage, one of my favorite authors, while Sylvester got dressed. We had just finished making love, and as usual we had both lapsed into silence. I knew why I did, but I couldn't really speak for him. I always felt shame and guilt, because here I was having sex without the benefit of marriage, something I had taught Brady was one of the worst things he could do. Not to mention all the young people who were members of Saving Ourselves and who thought of me as the perfect Christian mother.

I pulled a soft blue chenille blanket over me as if it was covering up my shame, then looked up from the book and gazed at Sylvester. He had on his boxers, and I couldn't help but notice how he looked like someone in their twenties, no paunch or sagging ass. He looked great for a man of forty-five. Sometimes after we made love, I would go weeks without calling him. But then I would remember his sweetness and his gentle touch and how he could flush my entire body with amazing sex. Why was it that underachievers were always so hot in bed? When Sylvester was in my bedroom, there was an aura of solid confidence about him that I didn't see when he was taking orders or wiping off tables at his place of employment.

"I saw your son on ESPN, Carmyn. Looks like he's off to a banner year," Sylvester said, breaking the silence between us.

"You did? I missed it. Brady usually calls me when he's going to be on television," I said.

"Maybe he didn't know. It was on Top Ten Plays of the Day. He looks like a helluva tail-back and he got a pretty good arm," Sylvester said.

"Yeah, my baby can do it all," I said proudly.

"I still would like to go to a game with you sometime. From what I've read and seen, your son seems like a fine young man. I'd really like to meet him."

"Maybe toward the end of the season, because right now I don't want to bring any further complications into Brady's life," I said.

Sylvester frowned. "You view me as a complication? What is that about, Carmyn?"

"I didn't mean it that way. It's just, like I've told you before, I don't know how Brady would react to me having someone in my life. It's always been just the two of us," I said.

"Sounds like Brady needs a girlfriend." Sylvester put on his tan pants, sat on the edge of my bed, and tied his shoes.

"That's the last thing he needs," I snapped. I wasn't upset with Sylvester, but when he said that my mind went back to the first game and how possessive that girl was, and it already seemed she had some sort of power over Brady.

"Has he signed with an agent yet?" Sylvester asked.

"Nope, too early. He can't do that yet," I said.

"Make sure you thoroughly check out whoever he signs with. There are a lot of snakes in that business."

"Yeah, we're well aware of that. I had to run one off last year," I said, wondering what Sylvester knew about agents — or anything, other than making sandwiches.

"You're a smart lady, Carmyn, and I'm sure you and Brady will make the right decision," Sylvester said as he nodded at me. He finished buttoning his shirt, then came to my side of the bed. He bent over and kissed me softly.

"See you next time, pretty lady," he said as he slid his finger playfully down my nose.

CHAPTER 10
BRADY'S SHAME GAME

A curtain of anger and shame covered me as I sat in my truck with my forehead on the steering wheel. When I finally looked up and saw most of the lights on in Lowell's house, I figured I might as well get this over with.

When I had called Lowell after Chloe threatened me, he told me he was out of town but would call me when he got back. He also asked me if it was important enough for him to come back right away, and I told him no even though I was really worried about Chloe. So I was relieved when Lowell left me a message and said that I could come right over. Right before I got out of my truck, I got a text. It was from Naomi. It was rather cold. It said, *Yes, I do have a child. No, it isn't yours, Brady.* Still, I breathed a sigh of relief and crossed that concern from my mind.

I rang the doorbell, and a few seconds later the stained-glass door flung open.

"Brady. Good to see you. Are you all right?" Lowell said.

"I'm doing okay," I said as I dragged myself into the house.

"You look tired. Is practice going well?"

"Same ole same ole. How was your trip?"

"It was cool. I needed a little adult conversation, so I went up to Atlanta for a few days."

"Did you see Mom?"

"No, so don't tell her I was there. It was a little romantic getaway," Lowell said.

"Cool. I didn't know you were seeing anyone."

"Well, it's kinda on the low."

"Gotcha."

"Do you want something to drink? Why don't we talk in the library," Lowell said.

"Can I just have a bottle of water?"

"Sure. Go into the library and I'll bring it to you."

I walked into the book-lined room and the first thing I noticed was a picture of my mother and me in a silver frame. I walked over and picked it up. What would my mother think if she found out about what I had been doing? Would she ever again be able to look at me as her perfect son? What would the public and my fans think?

"So what's going on?" Lowell said as he

walked into the library carrying a bottle of water and a glass of red wine.

"I did something stupid and it's come back to haunt me," I said.

"Come on, Brady. What could you have done?" Lowell asked. "Come on over here. Let's sit down."

I followed Lowell to a chocolate-brown leather love seat near the windows. There was a wooden trunk with a piece of glass on the top that served as a coffee table. Lowell took a sip of his wine, then sat it on the top of the glass. I unscrewed the cap off the cold water and took a swig. Then I started talking.

"Beginning of freshman year, I got myself in a bind and needed some extra money. I saw an ad for modeling in the school paper and called the number. I went to see the lady, and she liked me and told me I could make some good money."

"Why didn't you come to me or your mother?" Lowell said, interrupting me.

"I did something bad and I didn't want you guys to know," I said.

"What, Brady? You know we love you. Nothing you could have done would change those feelings."

"I know, but I needed to take care of this myself. I'd gotten myself in a mess and I needed to figure it out on my own. Anyway, the modeling job paid a hundred dollars an hour and sometimes she said I could work up to four hours."

"I don't see anything wrong with that. There is no denying you're a great-looking young man," Lowell said as he took another sip of wine.

"Yeah, if it had only stopped there, then there wouldn't be anything wrong with it. The first time she asked me to take off my shirt, it felt funny, but I did it anyway. Every time I went, she asked me to take off something else, until I was standing in front of her butt-ass naked," I said.

"In the nude?" Lowell asked in wide-eyed astonishment.

"Yes," I said, holding my head down.

"Brady. Brady. Who is this woman?" Lowell asked.

"Her name is Chloe Perez, she's on staff," I said. "Do you know her?"

"I don't know if I do."

"Right now she's on a leave of absence, working on an art book," I said.

"Okay, so you took a few pictures in the nude. Did you sign a release form?"

"No," I said.

"Then you don't have anything to worry about," Lowell said.

I didn't say anything right away. I was worrying about what Lowell would say when I told him the rest.

"Is that it, Brady? You didn't sign anything, did you? And is she threatening you?"

"Yeah, she is," I said.

"How?"

"By releasing the photos. It could hurt my Heisman chances if voters found out I posed nude. Also, taking the money from her might be an NCAA violation, since she works for the university. We can't hold jobs and that includes modeling without the school's approval."

"You said you did this when you were a freshman. Why is this coming up now?"

I told Lowell that I had continued to model for Chloe and that during the end of my sophomore year she wanted some pictures of me masturbating.

"Again, Brady, if you didn't sign anything, there is nothing she can do with those photos. What aren't you telling me?"

"Well, since I met Barrett, I thought I shouldn't pose for Chloe anymore."

"How old is this woman?"

"Mid-forties," I said.

"So how long have these sessions been going on?"

"At first once a month, then once a week

— since freshman year," I said.

"So she got mad when you told her you didn't want to pose anymore?"

"Yes."

"But why? There must be a hundred guys who would pose for this woman. What else happened?"

Again I went mute.

"Brady, what happened?"

I lowered my head and thought about what I would say, then suddenly blurted out, "She performed some sexual favors for me."

I glanced at Lowell, who looked like he was talking with a total stranger, and then he started laughing. He was laughing so hard that he held his stomach like he was in pain. He had always been so serious when I came to him with questions that I didn't think my mother could answer.

"What's so funny?" I asked.

Lowell took another sip of his wine and said, "This old broad is threatening you because you've pulled back the dick? Does she think it's hers?"

"Lowell, you've got to promise me that you won't say anything to my mother about this. It would kill her," I said in a pleading tone.

"You don't have to worry about that. But you know, in a way I think it's cool. A young man like you needs to sow his oats, so to speak."

"But I'm still saving myself. I mean, I haven't done anything else with her," I lied. "Plus, oral sex isn't really sex," I said defensively. I decided not to tell him about Naomi. I also didn't tell him that Chloe had taught me how to please her, and that she said I was a very good student. One confession for now would have to do.

"Hmm, well, that's a bit Clintonian of you, but I don't know if Carmyn would feel that oral sex isn't sex," Lowell said, getting up to walk around the room. "How can I help? Do you want me to go and talk to this woman?"

"I don't know if that would help. Maybe I should just keep doing it to save my career and any chances I have for the Heisman. I don't want Barrett to find out. This is my first serious relationship, and I want it to be an honest one," I said.

"So right now all she's threatening to do is to release the photographs," Lowell said.

"Word's out that there are photos on the Internet of a member of our football team. I don't think it's me, but I could be next. She said she would take them to the press and then the coaches. It would be a disaster for me. Everything I've worked for would just be thrown out the window. She paid me for the photos, and even though I doubt she has ever been to a game, I think the NCAA would consider her a Jaguar booster," I said.

"Don't you worry about this, Brady. Just concentrate on football and this new girlfriend. I'll talk to this Chloe woman. Two can play this game. I'm sure if the president of the university knew about this, Chloe would be out of a job," Lowell said. He patted me on the knee, then rose and said, "Stand up and give your godfather a hug."

So I did. While we hugged, I thought how lucky I was to have Lowell in my life. Then I thought of all the young men who were lucky enough to have not only a godfather but a real father, as well.

I did a double take when I looked at the balance in my checking account. I'd stopped at the bank on the edge of campus to withdraw twenty dollars so that I would have some cash in my pocket.

The receipt read *$25,359.43.* This couldn't be right. My mother hadn't won the lottery, so something was wrong.

I clicked open my phone, looked at the log of missed calls, and saw that Barrett and my mother had called. I pressed my mother's number as I walked back toward my truck. She answered after a couple of rings.

"Mom, I just left the ATM and there's over

twenty-five thousand dollars in my account!" I said.

"Then you must have a fairy godmother, because I didn't do that," my mother said.

"I guess the bank must have made a mistake," I said as I pulled out of the bank parking lot. I started to turn back to notify the branch of the mistake, but when I looked at my dashboard clock, I realized I had only ten minutes to find a parking spot on campus and get to class on time.

"Maybe they did, but don't worry about it. They'll catch it and work everything out. Just don't spend any of it. That's not your money," my mother said.

"Okay. Love you."

"Love you, too, baby. Oh, before I forget, I'm meeting with Basil Henderson of XJI. He's sent me a lot of information and is flying in from New York. I will keep you posted."

"Sounds like a plan, Mom," I said before hanging up the phone.

I took Barrett's hand as we strolled out of the Blockbuster near campus. I had been excited when she suggested we rent Spike Lee's *Inside Man*. I much preferred to see a crime thriller than one of the chick flicks Barrett loved. But even with two of my favorite actors sharing the screen, Denzel Washington and Jodie Foster, I couldn't focus. Not with the way Barrett put her head on my chest as we lay on her bed, and the way the fragrance of spring rain settled around her from the lotion she wore.

"I was thinking how I want you and my mother to be closer," I said as I wrapped my arm around Barrett more securely. "You are my girl."

"I don't think your mother likes me," Barrett said.

"Why would you say that? You've only met her one time."

Barrett sighed. "I'm a woman. We know things like that. I've dealt with women not taking to me all of my life, so it's really no big surprise."

"But my mother isn't like that. I mean, give her a chance to get to know you like I do," I said.

"I guess I understand, with you being her only son, but you should have seen the evil eye she gave me when I walked up to you after the game and held your hand. If looks could kill, then we'd be having this conversation with you looking over my tombstone." Barrett laughed.

"I bet your father is the same way about you."

"But he knows I'm no longer his little girl," Barrett responded.

"Because you're my girl," I said as I leaned over and kissed her deeply.

"Do you want to spend the night?" she asked seductively, her warm, sweet breath all in my face.

I thought for a few minutes about how wonderful it would be to wake up with Barrett in my arms. I could play with her hair and inhale her body's tantalizing scent and feel the amazing smoothness of her skin. I wanted to know what it would feel like to take my manhood and go inside her, knowing that it would be tight and wet. And then I saw Naomi's sad face when she told me that she was pregnant. I knew I could use a condom with Barrett, but I also knew they didn't always work. I wanted Barrett bad, but I told myself I could wait.

I held Barrett tight and whispered, "You don't know how much I want you, but I think I better bounce before I do something we might regret tomorrow."

CHAPTER 11
BARRETT MEETS HER MATCH

Barrett came out of the shower, her body moist and smelling like the lavender perfume she would spray into the air and then walk into nude, like she was walking toward the heavens.

She picked up the phone and called Brady.

"Hello," Brady said.

"Whatcha doing?"

"Just thinking."

"About me?"

"You know I'm always thinking about you," Brady said.

"Are you ready for the game this weekend?" Barrett asked.

"We're playing Kentucky, so we should be okay. I'm more worried about what to get my mother for her birthday," Brady said.

"What did you do this evening?" Barrett asked, ignoring Brady's mention of his mother.

"I had an interview with ESPN," Brady said.

"With who?"

"Stuart Scott," Brady said.

"The black guy?"

"Yeah, he was real cool."

"Have you decided who you're going to sign with? You need to make that decision soon, don't you?" Barrett said.

"My mom is meeting with one of the agents, Basil Henderson."

"Oh, so will your momma choose your agent for you?"

"Well, why don't you choose for me," Brady said.

"Are you serious? You would trust me with that decision? What if I picked somebody that neither you or your mother liked?"

"You want what's best for me, don't you?"

"Now, Brady, you don't even have to ask me that," Barrett said.

"I know. You make me so happy," Brady said.

"That's my job," Barrett replied.

"Good! I gotta go, Barrett! Talk to you later."

Barrett hung up and smiled as she read the interview "Brady Jamal Bledsoe — Heisman Contender." She'd purchased *Jaguar Illustrated* when she saw Brady's picture on the cover.

When she finished the article, she stood up, still naked, and glanced down at the photo of Brady on the magazine's cover, and smiled.

"You're going to go crazy when you get a piece of this," she said to the picture. Then she turned and sauntered into the bathroom.

Barrett picked up her cell phone and hit #1 on the speed dial. After a couple of rings, Nico picked up.

"Hello, beautiful," he said.

"Hey, Nico. Miss me?"

"You know I do. Now, what's going on with our boy?"

"He's fine, but it looks like his mother is meeting with some guy from XJI," Barrett said.

"It better not be Basil Henderson," Nico shouted.

"I think that was the name Brady said. Where have I heard that name before?"

"Oh, hell naw! You heard it from me. That was the faggot I used to work with. I think now's the time for you to close this deal."

"I don't know if he's ready," Barrett said.

"Make him ready," Nico demanded. His anger-laden voice seethed through the telephone; Barrett held her breath.

"Don't worry," she said finally. "I'll deliver."

Dear Diary,

I was expecting a cleaning lady courtesy of Nico, so when the doorman called to say that a woman was here to see me I told him to send her up. I didn't even bother looking through the peephole but when I opened the door, there stood Maybelline, making a wet, gray day even drearier.

I should have slammed the door in her ugly face. She walked into my condo like she owned the joint, checking out my fabulous furniture with an envious, evil eye. She was dressed tacky as usual — looking like a retired stripper, which I guess made sense, since that's exactly what she is. Maybelline or May, as we called her back then, was one of my mother's friends, and that certainly fit the saying "birds of a feather flock together." I didn't know if Maybelline had ever worked as a hostess, but I knew she was slutty like Lita and the rest of my mother's friends. When I was younger, they would sometimes spend the whole day just sitting around our kitchen table, drinking, smoking, and talking loud.

Maybelline told me she thought it was me when she saw me at the football game and asked what type of scam I was pulling by acting like a college cheerleader. I told her she needed to keep her weak little mind on her damn own business.

I asked her how she found out where I was staying and she told me Lita told her. I bet if I stopped those checks Lita's tongue wouldn't give out information so quickly.

She had the nerve to ask me why I didn't take better care of my mother and then the bitch called me "Raquel." I had to tell her that I don't go by that name anymore. Sick of this charade, I asked May why she had darkened my doorstep. She told me she was here checking on her son, who was going to be a big-time professional football player real soon. As she sat her fat ass on my sofa, May said he was going to take care of her when he got his signing bonus. I don't know why it took me so long to figure out that she's the mother of Brady's thug roommate, Delmar.

I lied and told her I was happy for her and then literally lifted the bitch off my sofa and led her to the door. Right before I pushed her out, she warned me she would be watching me.

She had me so flustered that I went straight to the kitchen and made myself a stiff drink.

CHAPTER 12
CARMYN'S NEW PLAY

"I hear you want to talk to me," Maybelline announced as she walked into the shop wearing skintight double-knit slacks stuck in boots with three-inch heels. "Yeah, I do," I said as I went over to greet her. I knew I hadn't been nice to her at the football game or when she came to the shop. Calling myself a good Christian woman while acting like a snooty bitch wasn't for me, so I decided to offer the olive branch of friendship, but I knew Maybelline wouldn't make it easy.

"Well, get to talkin'! You think I got all day to be standing up in this joint with all you uppity bitches and bastards?" Maybelline said as she eyed Zander. He put down the hot curling iron he was handling and started over toward the two of us.

"Who in the hell do you think you are?" he demanded.

"I'm Maybelline, May-Jean for short. Who

in the hell are you?"

"Carmyn, you betta tell this woman she fucking with the wrong one."

"You tell me. Aren't you man enough?" Maybelline said.

"I didn't know they still made double knit," Zander said as he turned his nose down toward Maybelline.

"I bet there's a lot you don't know. You just jealous 'cause you ain't got none," Maybelline retorted.

Before Zander could reply, I put my arms around both of them and said, "Why don't we take this into my office?"

"Why? You scared somebody might see me in this joint?"

"Carmyn, tell me this is not the Greta Ghetto you want me to work with," Zander pleaded.

"Greta? That ain't my name. Work with me how? I don't know nothin' about doing no hair. That ain't my field. Is that why you called me? To offer me a job? Well, honey, I ain't looking for no job. In case you haven't heard, my boy is going to be a millionaire very soon," Maybelline said.

"Let's go to my office," I repeated.

Maybelline and Zander followed me into my office, both acting like young children in the back of a car during a long road trip. I

273

could hear them calling each other names in whispers, and I thought maybe this wasn't going to work out.

"Have a seat," I instructed.

"Are you asking me or telling me?" Maybelline said.

"Aw, crazy woman, just sit your ass down," Zander said.

"Say one more word to me and I will teach you the manners your mama didn't," Maybelline said.

"Don't you use my mama's name in vain," Zander screamed.

"Children, children. Both of you sit down."

"I'm going to act like you asked me nicely, like a lady should," Maybelline said as she sat down and crossed her legs.

"Now, I have an opportunity here. The local ABC affiliate wants to do a makeover show using different salons. Both the stylist and client will be featured on the show, and I think it will be a great opportunity for both of you. Zander, you will get even more exposure, and Maybelline, you'll have the benefit of a super stylist like Zander and a new wardrobe."

"Who said I need new clothes?"

"Obviously, you don't have any mirrors in your house," Zander said, and laughed.

"Punk ass bitch," Maybelline retorted.

"Come on, folks," I said, now wondering if this was going to be worth it.

"So will I get a new weave?"

"Zander, what do you think?"

"I don't think Greta needs a weave," Zander said, looking at Maybelline as if for the first time. "I think we should cut it and layer it, giving focus to the face."

"You think my face is cute?"

"I didn't say that," Zander said.

"But that's what he meant to say," I interjected.

"She's all right. I might put some highlights here," Zander said as he touched Maybelline's hair. I was saying a silent prayer that she wouldn't pop him, and then her body language softened. Zander continued, "I'd like to bring down the makeup and go with a more natural look, highlighting her full lips and these eyelashes. Honey, are these real?"

"They sure are. I can't tell you how many times people ask me that," Maybelline said proudly.

"I know some bitches that would sell body parts to have these."

"I heard that! I'll sell body parts to have my hair a little longer with blond streaks," Maybelline said.

"We can do the blond streaks, but I tell you

short is in, you know, Toni Braxton–like. That look is back."

Maybelline looked at Zander, smiled and slapped him on the knee, and said, "Maybe you ain't a punk ass after all."

I took this as a sign that maybe everything would work out, and I excused myself as two new friends got acquainted.

I broke into tears after the Jaguars crushed the hapless Kentucky Wildcats 63–13 and Brady put in a herculean effort of 206 rushing yards in the first half alone. With that done, he was able to rest on the bench for the entire second half. I was upset the coach took him out, because Brady would have had the chance to add to his statistics and keep up with Darren McFadden from Arkansas, but I also understood that the coach didn't want to risk injury with big games against Arkansas, Florida, and Georgia Tech upcoming.

It was not the Jaguars' rout and Brady's success that had brought on the tears, but what happened after the game. I stood at the locker room door, waiting to greet Brady and that girl Barrett. I had hoped I wouldn't have to celebrate my birthday with Brady's new friend.

When Brady emerged from the complex,

Barrett was not hanging on to him as she had in the previous games, and I heaved a sigh of relief. Instead, his teammates, still in their uniforms, followed him like he was the Pied Piper. Each of them was carrying a single red rose. They all came toward me, surrounding me, and then when Brady signaled, they began singing "Happy Birthday." The thirty-eight football players each presented me with a rose until I stood there in tears, holding thirty-nine roses after Brady gave me the last one.

After a few seconds of total silence, Brady hugging me tightly, I looked toward the crisp, blue sky and said a prayer of gratitude. After all the trials and tribulations I'd experienced during my teenage years, God had seen fit to give me the most perfect son.

I thought for a second about the call from Daphne, but then thought that as the years had passed, my memory had been layered by the wonderful events of Brady's life. To me that was nothing but a blessing from God.

"I got you this time, didn't I, Mom?" Brady whispered.

"Yeah, baby, you got me," I said. I looked up, smiling into my baby boy's eyes just like I had the first time I laid eyes on him.

CHAPTER 13
BRADY FOR THE HEISMAN

It was one of those perfect days when I felt the world was at my feet. It was the beginning of October, the CGU Jaguars were 4–0, and coaches and fans alike were telling me to get my tux and speech ready for the Heisman Awards. The team was two games away from being bowl eligible for the first time in school history.

I had gained over 200 yards in the last game and was over 1,500 all-purpose yards for the season with over eight games left, plus a possible bowl game. The Wildhog formation allowed me to pass the ball, something I hadn't done since I played quarterback in middle school. With me throwing the ball the defense couldn't put nine men in the box to try to stop the run. Not only was I being heralded as a superstar, but so was Delmar for his blocking and running ability. Professional scouts were saying we were both certain to be first-round draft picks and instant millionaires.

While all this was exactly as I'd dreamed it would be, nothing made my heart race like when I had Barrett in my arms after a hard practice or a victory over a tough opponent.

On the first Saturday in October, the Jaguars' streak continued as we beat Florida 37–31 in a homecoming victory. I rushed for 267 yards in three quarters and was able to rest and watch Delmar finish his third 100-yard game, which was an amazing feat for a blocking back.

We had raced off to a 28–0 lead going into the fourth quarter, only to have Florida's quarterback, Chris Leake, throw four touchdown passes in eight minutes to bring the Gators back. A touchdown by Delmar in overtime saved the Jaguar victory.

My mother was in the stands in her normal spot, and she had told me she needed to talk with me alone after the game. Translation: Lose Barrett. I knew my mother didn't understand how I felt about Barrett, so I told Barrett that I would meet her at her apartment later in the evening.

When my mother and I walked into the Rib Shack, CGU fans started applauding as loudly as they had in the stadium earlier. Several fans started chanting, "Heisman . . . Heisman," as I blushed and my mother smiled proudly. Brando, owner of the restaurant, greeted us and escorted us to the private dining room my mother had requested.

"I wish I could say dinner is on me," Brando said. "But I don't want to get the next Heisman winner in trouble with the NCAA."

"No problem, Brando. We both understand," my mother said, sitting down after he pulled out her chair.

"Enjoy your meal, and if there is anything I can do, just tell your waiter to come and get me," Brando said before he left the room.

After we ordered, my mother seemed as if she was ready to start her speech, when she noticed that my ring finger was naked.

"Brady, where is your ring?"

"It's in my pocket," I said as I dug my hands into my jeans.

"Why aren't you wearing it?"

"Chill, Mom. I'm going to put it back on. I just didn't feel like having the fellas tease me today, so I didn't put it on after I took my shower," I said. The truth was that I didn't know how much longer I would be able to wear the ring. Barrett's kisses drove me wild and I knew my body wanted more. I knew I couldn't use the excuse I'd used the first time Chloe went down on me that it wasn't really sex. With Barrett I would make love like I had with Naomi.

"You sure you can still wear it?" my mother asked.

"What are you talking about, Mom? Of course I can still wear it," I said, looking away nervously.

"Well, I am certainly glad to hear that. I mean, ever since you've been spending time with *that* girl, I've been concerned that you might forget how important your vow was."

"Mom, her name is Barrett, and she knows how important the ring is to me and she respects that," I said.

My mother looked directly into my eyes to see if I was telling the truth. It was something she could usually count on, so she had to know that I was lying. After a few moments of awkward silence, she said, "You just make sure you both continue to respect your vow."

"I'm straight."

"Brady, you know how much I love you and how I want the best for you. I've made you my life's work, and I won't let anyone hurt my baby."

"Nobody's going to hurt me, Mom," I said.

"How much do you know about this Barrett?"

"I know she's the most wonderful girl I've ever met," I said.

"I'm sure you think that's true, but let's face it, baby, you're not that experienced when it comes to women and the tricks they play. Don't you know that there are young ladies who come to college just to snag someone like you?"

"Barrett's not like that. She cares for me," I said.

"Is she a virgin?"

"Does that matter?"

"Yes, it does. Not only is it important for me that you do well in school and football, but also that you keep the vow you made in church before God."

"Look, Mom, I'm not having sex, and if that changes I will do what you taught me, and that is get married. I will ask Barrett to be my wife," I said calmly.

"After several weeks? Brady, you're too young to be thinking about getting married. You have your entire life in front of you."

"How long did you know my father?" I asked.

"What does that matter?"

"How long, Mom?" I demanded.

"I met him in high school."

"When did you know you were in love with him?"

"Brady, that's in the past. This girl is not good for you," she said sternly.

"But I want Barrett to be a part of my life."

"Please tell me you're not serious about her, Brady."

"I can't do that, Mom. I think it's time for me to see what I've been missing."

"Think about this. Please!"

"I will, but I don't want to lose Barrett."

"If she is the right girl, then you won't lose her," my mother said.

"I need your support on this, Mom," I pleaded.

"Brady, I can't."

There was a long silence.

My mother looked like she was on the verge of tears, but she didn't let them fall. I touched her hand and looked lovingly into her eyes and said, "Mom, please think about this. I don't want to consider something as serious as marriage without you."

After a few minutes of silence, my mother finally said, "Then don't."

CHAPTER 14
BARRETT AND THE AKAS

Before Barrett walked into the Student Union, she tried to reach her mother one more time.

"What do you want?" Lita asked in the groggy voice that sounded like she'd just woken up from a deep drunken sleep.

"Where have you been? I've been trying to reach you," Barrett said.

"Mind your own damn business. I don't need you to keep up with me," Lita said.

"Who's watching Wade?"

"What in the hell do you want?"

"Why did you give that May-Jean woman my address? I told you not to talk about anything that concerns me. Do you know what could happen if Chris finds out where I am?"

"It would serve your ass right."

"Okay, be that way, but you won't get another penny from me if you give out my information again. Do I make myself clear?"

Barrett said.

Lita didn't answer, and a few seconds later Barrett heard a dial tone. "That bitch makes me sick," she said to herself as she walked into the food court.

After surveying her choices, Barrett picked up a chicken wrap and longed for the day when she could go back to eating caviar, roasted chicken, and a baked potato fully loaded. She hated this broke-down tired cafeteria food and the entire campus scene, but Nico told her she should put in an appearance on campus at least once or twice a week to make it look like she was a serious college student.

Sometimes Barrett tried to believe this was her life. She liked to imagine that she was a carefree college student, with rich parents paying her bills and putting unlimited funds into her checking account.

After paying for the wrap, Barrett spotted an empty table with only one chair. Then she heard Shante Willis call out her name.

"Barrett, why don't you join us?" Shante said.

Even though she hated to admit it after that phone call with Lita, Barrett did feel like a little companionship — but very little. She wasn't down for a female powwow, just some polite and quick conversation. Plus, she could always get up and go if they started working her nerves.

"Yeah, girl, come on over here," Shante said.

Barrett sat down with great fanfare, and then eyed the other girls suspiciously.

"Barrett, these are my sorority sisters — Whitney, Beth, and Amber," Shante said.

"Nice meeting you," Amber said.

"I haven't seen *you* on campus," Whitney said.

"Oh, I've been around," Barrett said as she took the plastic off her wrap. *This* Whitney obviously had herself confused with the one and only Miss Diva Whitney. Who did she think she was, questioning Barrett Elizabeth Manning?

"Where are you from?" Beth asked.

"Atlanta," Barrett said as she took the first bite of the wrap and thought,*These chicks are nosy, nosy, nosy.*

"What part?" Amber asked.

"What?" Barrett asked, raising her eyebrow.

"What part of Atlanta? I'm from Atlanta. Maybe we can share a ride the next time we go home," Amber said.

"I'm from Buckhead," Barrett lied proudly. The truth was that one day, she wouldn't mind having a second home in

Buckhead — the shopping was all that and then some.

"Fancy," Whitney said.

"So who is teaching the Chi Os?" Shante asked.

"Hannah, I think," Amber said.

"No, Hannah is teaching the A O Pis," Whitney said.

"Who's teaching the Kappas?" Amber asked.

"Sarah Beavers," Shante said.

"I didn't know Sarah was still in school. I thought she got married," Amber said.

"She gets married this summer," Shante said.

The incessant jabbering was making Barrett's ass hurt. What language were they speaking? The whole situation was getting on Barrett's nerves, and she wanted to finish her food and get the hell out of the Union.

"I bet the Pi Phis win again," Whitney said.

But since Barrett was on a college campus and she remembered the ad that said a mind is a terrible thing to waste, she figured she could at least ask a question or two. "What kinda mess are you girls talking about, Shante?"

"We're talking about the Unity Greek Show," Shante said, and laughed.

"What's that?" Barrett asked.

"It's one of the biggest events on campus. Our sorority, Alpha Kappa Alpha, throws the Unity Greek Step Show every year during homecoming. Our sorority and our brother fraternity, Alpha Phi Alpha, teach the white sororities and fraternities how to step. It's a large-scale multicultural dance show. It's a big deal. Everybody on campus comes out, but we usually have to turn people away," Shante said.

"You mean to tell me that the black students share their moves with the white students?" Barrett asked. "You teach them your stuff? Why can't they make up their own shit?" Barrett continued.

"That's why it's called Unity, silly," Whitney said.

Barrett cut her eyes at Whitney, wondering who this bitch was calling silly.

"Whatever," Barrett said, and sighed.

"You should come," Shante said. "I can get you a ticket."

"Don't think so. I have some big tests coming up," Barrett lied, then added, "Don't let me hold you girls." She'd had her fill of females for the day.

Shante, Whitney, Beth, and Amber stood up, grabbed their trays, and told Barrett it was nice meeting her and they hoped she would come to the show.

"Yeah, right," Barrett mumbled as she finished her wrap, not even looking up as they left the table.

Dear Diary,

It's taking me longer to get Brady in bed than I expected. I don't know where he gets his self-control from, because if he knew what's between my legs he wouldn't be such a gentleman. The last job I did like this was with NBA wannabe Chris Johns at the University of Washington.

On a rainy Seattle evening, Chris Johns eased into my bed sure as sugar, and he came back day after day and couldn't get enough of what I had between my legs. Almost two weeks later, he was proclaiming his love for me and telling me he wanted me to meet his mama. Every time he brought up meeting her I would whip some of my good stuff on him and he'd forget. Mamas don't like me and I should have remembered that before meeting Brady's mama.

Seattle was a cool place to live, but Nico insisted that I leave the minute Chris signed over his power of attorney to him and was locked in as one of Chris's clients. One of the first things he did was "invest" a lot of Chris's signing bonus with phony stocks he'd made himself on his printer. Chris with his dumb ass didn't have a clue because he was whipped and saw some sheets of worthless paper. Besides I was telling Chris how brilliant I thought Nico was every chance I got. It also helped that Chris was dumber than dirt.

After we got Chris and I got my share, I did what I always did after I finished a job: I took a great vacation, sent some money to my mother for Wade, and then waited for my next assignment and name change. I put aside almost half of my earnings in a savings account I opened using Wade's social security number. Nobody including Nico knows about my secret stash.

It seems that the stakes keep getting higher with each and every job, and I've been making Nico a lot of money, and when I finish with Brady it'll be my turn to really cash in. Aside from money, Nico usually gets me little gifts — after Chris, I got a pair of diamond studs. After Brady I'm expecting a big payoff, a little something for my ring finger and the ultimate prize of becoming Mrs. Nico Benson.

CHAPTER 15
CARMYN'S QUIET STORM

Kellis and I walked out of a stunningly beautiful Sunday-morning service through the doors of New Foundation Baptist Church. My heart was filled with joy because of the season my son was having during his senior year and because Kellis had agreed to join me for services. No small accomplishment. I knew the offer to take Kellis to brunch afterward at the Ritz-Carlton in Buckhead had a lot to do with why she agreed to go to church. I didn't care, because I missed attending services during the football season.

The day before, Basil Henderson, one of the partners of XJI, had flown to Atlanta and taken me to lunch at Jermaine Dupri's Café Dupri, off of Piedmont. It had been delightful, and not only was Basil one of the most handsome men I'd seen in a long time, but he was knowledgeable about what he would do for Brady and his professional career. I made up my mind that Brady would definitely visit his firm once the season was over.

We were waiting for the ushers to open the doors of the church when Sister Jolene approached us. She was wearing an incredibly unflattering yellow suit and an alarming shade of red lipstick.

"Good morning, Sister Carmyn. Praise the Lord," she said.

"Good morning, Sister Jolene. Praise the Lord," I said.

"I'm Sister Jolene," she said as she extended her hand toward Kellis.

"I'm sorry. This is my good friend Kellis," I said.

"Welcome to New Foundation," Sister Jolene said.

"Thank you, and nice meeting you as well," Kellis said.

Just as we were getting ready to go inside the church, Sister Jolene said, "So sorry to hear about our girl."

I turned and asked, "What girl?"

"You didn't hear? I thought you knew."

"Thought I knew what?" I asked, hoping Sister Jolene wasn't getting ready to deliver some mean-spirited gossip.

"Come over here, let me tell you," Sister Jolene said, using her ring finger to beckon me to the corner.

I leaned over and heard, "Your girl Shelby got herself knocked up." I felt the gust of her voice as she whispered and it felt like fire, and then I thought of a phone call and a few e-mails I'd gotten from Shelby that I hadn't gotten around to answering.

"Who told you that?" I demanded. I hadn't seen or heard from Shelby since I'd done her hair a few weeks ago. I had been worried about her the day I'd received that disturbing phone call and didn't pay attention to her rumblings about her boyfriend, Torrian.

"Her mother. I was over there yesterday, so not only did I hear it, I saw it. Yeah, Little Miss Thing is knocked up. I think she's going to give it up. Her mother is so upset. It was like a funeral over there, so I felt the need to take over one of my cobblers. That girl had so much potential," Sister Jolene said.

I suddenly felt nauseated and empty. It was another reminder that no one emerges un-scathed from youth, no matter how many groups they join. I thought about Brady and that girl Barrett and knew it was going to be hard for my son to resist her. And I thought about the last time I saw Shelby and how I brushed off her questions because I was wor-ried about someone finding out my secrets. I no longer wanted to go into church; I wanted to go home, where I could crawl into bed and eat chocolate.

"How is Brady doing? We've been hearing folk talk about him and that trophy," Sister Jolene said.

I didn't answer her, because my eyes were misting up. I blinked the tears away.

"Did you hear me, Carmyn?"

"I'm sorry. What did you say?"

"How's Brady?"

"Brady is doing well. Excuse me, Sister," I said. I touched Kellis and whispered, "Let's get out of here."

"Okay, we can leave. But does this mean I don't get brunch?" Kellis asked.

I didn't answer and just headed toward the door.

CHAPTER 16
BRADY'S MAILBAG OR FAN MAIL

On a glorious Saturday afternoon designed by God for college football, several of my dreams came true. Running like I was possessed, I rushed for 323 yards and four touchdowns as we beat the defending national champs, the Texas Longhorns, 38–25 in front of a record crowd of 82,329 screaming fans. The win gave us the longest winning streak in the nation for the year.

After the game, several University of Texas players came up to congratulate me and wish me well in the Heisman race. One of the linebackers who had charged me for much of the day told me, "Man, they just need to mail you that trophy."

While I was searching the sidelines for Barrett and the stands for my mom, I felt someone tap me on the shoulder. I turned around and a middle-aged white man, wearing a Texas polo jersey and a burnt-orange Texas hat, said, "Great game, Brady. You know, I don't think I have ever seen a performance like what you did out there on that field today."

"Thank you, sir. That's very kind of you to say," I said, extending my hand toward the man. "I'm Coach Dennis Watson. I'm the running backs coach and recruiting coordinator at the University of Texas. I have coached some great backs, including Cedric Benson and Rickey Williams, and you are every bit as great as they are."

"Coach, I appreciate you saying that," I said. "I used to follow you guys and I loved Rickey Williams, so I was upset when you didn't even send me a recruiting letter."

"Excuse me. Do I need to get the wax out of my ears? Did you say that we didn't send you a recruiting letter?"

"Yes sir, that's what I said. I never heard from you guys."

Coach Watson took off his hat and ran his hand through his hair with a perplexed look on his face. He looked toward the warm, metallic sky like he was searching for an answer and then turned back toward me.

"Son, you were at the top of our recruiting board. I know this because it's my job. We started sending you letters when you rushed for over 200 yards as a sophomore, but every letter we sent was sent back with "Return to

Sender" written on it. I even reached out to your coaches in hopes of setting up a meeting with your parents, but I was told you were not interested in the University of Texas and we should cease our attempts to contact you. I just figured your family had some connection with the University of Arkansas Razorbacks or Oklahoma Sooners. That happens a lot in recruiting."

"Are you sure it was me, Brady Bledsoe, you were talking about? Did you speak with my coach?"

"Son, I spoke with your coach on several occasions. I remember him telling me that your mother was specifically against you talking with Texas. Was your father involved in your recruiting process?"

"My father is dead," I said. Just as I was going to ask more questions of Coach Watson, I felt a small, delicate hand touch me. I turned around and looked down into the blue eyes of a little boy with hair the color of straw. He was wearing a jersey with my name on it; it fit him like his grandmother's nightgown. He had a pen and a program in his hand.

"Mr. Brady, will you sign my jersey and program?" he asked.

"Sure I will, little buddy. What's your name?"

Coach Watson patted me on the back and wished me good luck for the rest of the season, and especially with the Heisman voting.

"Thanks, Coach," I said as I got on my knees to become eye level with the boy and have my picture taken with him by his father.

After I finished taking the photo, I stood up and saw Barrett walking toward me with a huge smile on her face.

"There is my girl," I said, smiling at her.

"Does the star of the century need a kiss?" Barrett asked.

"I always need a kiss," I said as Barrett threw her arms around my neck, her pompoms still in her hands, and gave me a moist kiss.

When we finished, I looked around the stands, where fans were still celebrating the victory.

"Brady, what's the matter?" Barrett asked.

"Have you seen my mom?" I asked.

"I think I spotted her a couple of times from the sidelines," Barrett said.

"I need to speak with her," I said, squinting my eyes in hopes of seeing her. I knew she would meet me at my locker room door, but I also knew she would sometimes sit in the stands and savor my team's victories.

"Is everything all right?" Barrett asked.

"Sure. Sure. I just need to talk with my

mother about something. Can I get with you a little later?"

"Is it about that agent she met with?" Barrett asked.

"What? No, something else," I said.

"Okay. You want to meet at my place?"

"Yeah, after I talk with my mom."

"Okay, boo. I'll see you later," Barrett said as she gave me a peck on the lips and raced off the field.

After facing over fifty reporters, all with the same "how does it feel?" questions, I headed for the shower. I still hadn't seen my mom and figured she was at Lowell's. It was quiet in the locker room, since all my teammates had showered and headed home. As I lathered my body with soap and shampoo, I thought back to my conversation with Coach Watson and wondered why he would lie about recruiting me. I thought back on all the times my mother and I had shared over the kitchen table talking about what college I would attend. We even framed the first letter I had received, from Grambling University and signed by Coach Doug Williams.

My mother had bought a file cabinet especially for the hundreds of letters that came addressed to Brady Bledsoe and would put them in folders with a list of pros and cons of the programs. I kept an online journal that was run in my school newspaper, and the *Atlanta Journal-Constitution* even did a story on me when I narrowed my choices down to the five schools I would visit.

As I rinsed my body for a final time, I could picture that file cabinet and all the letters. I remembered the orange and white of the University of Tennessee and Clemson University, and the orange and blue of Auburn University and the Florida Gators, but I knew I had never seen the burnt orange and white from the University of Texas. If the letters really had been sent back, I wanted to know why.

"What are you two talking about?" Lowell asked. He was carrying a silver platter with a pitcher of strawberry lemonade, chips, and salsa. He sat it on the table in front of the swing on his porch. Lowell had sent me a text after the game telling me to come over and that he had solved my Chloe problem. I didn't ask how, but I was relieved. For days I had checked the Net scared to death I might see my erect penis staring me in the face.

"What Brady is going to wear to New York if he is invited to the Heisman ceremony," Mom said.

"Don't you mean when?" Lowell said.

"Come on, guys. I might not even get invited," I said.

"Not get invited? That is not going to happen," Mom said.

"How many players are invited?" Lowell asked.

"Five, I think. It depends on how close the vote is," I said.

"Then you're in for sure," Lowell said.

"I was thinking a three-button black tux and a light green shirt, with a gold tie," Mom said.

"Yeah, school colors. That sounds nice," Lowell said.

While Mom and Lowell loaded chips and salsa on plates, I thought back to the game and my conversation afterward with Coach Watson. I thought about how the current process of picking an agent would be similar to my high school recruitment. Maybe Coach Watson had made a mistake, but I still wanted to know what had happened.

"Mom, do you remember ever getting any letters from the University of Texas when I was in high school?"

My mother looked at me, startled. She became so rattled that she dropped her plate to the porch floor and chips splattered everywhere.

"Oh crap," Mom said as she bent down to

pick up the chips. "I'm so sorry, Lowell."

"Don't worry, I'll clean that up," Lowell said as he went into the house.

"Mom, are you all right?" I asked. I reached down and took her hand and lifted her up. I looked at her face, and her expression had changed from one of calm to an anguished look I had never seen.

"I'm fine, Brady. I don't know what came over me," she said. There was an impatience in her voice I rarely heard.

"So do you remember getting anything from Texas?"

"Brady, why would you ask me that?"

I told her about my conversation with Coach Watson after the game and that he had told me their letters were sent back.

"Why would he tell you something like that? Texas never sent you anything," Mom said.

"Are you sure?"

"Brady! What did I say?" My mother raised her voice at me for the first time in I don't know how long. It was obvious my questions about Texas were making her angry, but I didn't know why.

"I'm going in the house to see if I can help Lowell find that broom and dustpan," Mom said as she rushed off.

Chapter 17
Barrett Meets Mr. Big

Dear Diary,

Tonight Nico left me a message and told me to expect a surprise this evening at a certain time. Sure enough, almost to the minute there was a knock at my door. I looked out to make sure it wasn't Maybelline, and I see this really fine man standing there, so I open the door.

He asked me if my name is Barrett. I tell him "yes" and he hands me a silver box and tells me Nico sent him.

I can't stop staring at this man. His face is so smooth, almost too beautiful for a man, yet he was decidedly masculine. I asked him who he is and in a gentle voice he said, "Kilgore." And then he disappeared into the night.

I stood in my foyer and wondered who this mystery man was and then I remembered I had a gift to open.

I ripped open the box and out fell a

beautiful silk daffodil-yellow and pale pink peignoir set with a note from Nico that said, *Dear Love . . . This should do the trick . . .*

The next day, Barrett bounced through the lobby of her well-appointed condo building on the way to the gym and spotted a tall, handsome black man looking in her direction. He was smiling, which didn't surprise her because men always smiled when they saw her coming. Maybe it was her perfect smile? Or the perky twins? Barrett thought she would have a little fun before starting her workout, so she did a playful *drop it like it's hot* move with the towel she'd brought to use at the gym.

She could feel the man staring at her firm yet plump ass, so she remained bent over for almost fifteen seconds before turning around and asking him if he lived in the building.

"No, I don't, but I suspect you do. That boy always does things first class," he said.

"I just moved here," Barrett said, ignoring his last statement and moving in closer. The first thing she noticed, besides the expertly tailored navy blue suit, were his eyes. His steel-gray eyes with green rims were so piercing, she thought they could see right through and read everything that was going on inside her — the joy she got from flirting with good-looking guys, but also the pain she'd caused unsuspecting young men seeking their first serious relationship. From the way he filled out his suit, Barrett knew he'd been an athlete at some point in his life.

"What's your name?" he asked.

"Barrett. Barrett Elizabeth Manning," she said.

"Any relation to Archie Manning and his boys, Peyton and Eli?" he asked.

"You mean the professional football players. They're white," Barrett said.

"But you know who they are, which I find interesting but not surprising. Were you born with that name, or did somebody give it to you?" he asked.

"Excuse me? You're asking a lot of questions, so now I'm going to ask a few. What's your name?" Barrett said.

"John."

"Do you have a last name, John?"

"You're one of Nico's girls, aren't you?" His voice had changed from friendly to firm and businesslike.

"What's a Nico?" Barrett asked, wondering how the handsome stranger knew about the man she loved. Maybe he had been sent by Nico to check up on her.

"Don't toy with me, Barrett Manning. If that's really your name. You look like the type of young lady Nico would put on a college campus. I could have spotted you a football field away with your perfect breasts, long hair, flawless skin, and that unmistakable aura of a professional gold digger."

Barrett looked at him, puzzled and troubled. He did have Nico's MO down to a tee, and now she was determined to let him know he wasn't right.

"You must have me confused, John, but thanks for the compliments since you described me correctly, minus the gold digger part. I don't know who your friend Nico is," Barrett said.

"He's not my friend and I'm not his," John said. "And trust me when I say he's not yours either, but you'll find that out soon enough. But let me give you a bit of advice so you won't end up like Brittany and Katie. Get your shit and run before you end up in jail like some of his other girls. You're very pretty and won't last long in the joint. But if you don't stop what you're doing, I'll tell Brady and his mother what you're really up to, and I think you know Nico won't like it if you fail."

And then he walked out the door, leaving Barrett with her mouth open and her beautiful body visibly shaking.

Barrett took a few moments to compose herself. She was debating if she should go to the gym or up to her condo when John walked back into the building. Barrett quickly headed in the opposite direction, but she could feel him close by and wondered for the first time if he was dangerous.

"Barrett," he called out to her.

"What do you want with your crazy ass?" Barrett said as she turned around to confront him. One thing she'd learned from Lita was to never run away from a fight, even if it was with a man twice her size.

"Here's my card. And don't forget to ask Nico about Katie and Brittany — they should be up for parole real soon."

The man left again and Barrett stood holding a business card that read:

John Basil Henderson, XJI, Inc., President and Founding Partner.

CHAPTER 18
CARMYN'S CONFESSIONS

It was a beautiful Sunday afternoon. Lowell and I had just finished a brunch of fried chicken wings and waffles, scrambled eggs, and fruit salad. I was on my second mimosa when Lowell looked at me and asked, "So what happened between you and Brady last night?"

"What are you talking about?" I asked. I wanted to avoid this conversation, even though Brady's questions had caused me a restless night. All I wanted to do was get in my car and drive to Atlanta and get in my bed.

"Well, if I'm not mistaken, it looked like you two were having a disagreement. And then you dropped those chips like they were covered in cyanide. Do you want to talk about it?"

"There is nothing to talk about. A coach from Texas told Brady that someone had sent his recruitment letters back," I said, hoping Lowell would leave it at that.

"Why would someone do that?"

"I don't know what that man was talking about," I said as I sliced in half the single strawberry on my plate and then plopped it into my mouth.

"Can I ask you something else?" Lowell said as he poured hot coffee into his half-filled cup.

"What?"

"Do you think we're too old to fall in love?"

"Damn, Lowell, you make it sound like we're in our sixties. We haven't even made forty yet. Why the questions about love?"

Lowell sipped his coffee for a few moments, then turned and faced me directly and said, "If I told you something really hush-hush, would you keep it to yourself?"

"Of course I would. Lowell, how long have we known each other? Anything you tell me will stay between you and me," I said.

"You promise?"

"I promise. Lowell, come on. Tell me," I pleaded.

"I think I might be falling in love," he said.

"That's great."

"It might not be," he said softly.

"Why not?"

"Well, he's young."

"How young?"

"He's twenty-four, but he's very mature," Lowell said.

"Does he have a name?"

"Yeah, but his age isn't the only problem."

"I'm listening," I said as I poured more champagne into my fluted glass. I could tell this was going to be good, and a little buzz would make Lowell's news even better.

"He's one of my students."

"Stop it!" I shouted as I hit the dining table with my flat hand.

"I know. Isn't that horrible?"

"What about your rule?"

"Carmyn, he's is so damn fine I just couldn't stop myself," Lowell said with a swoon in his voice. "He came to my office at the beginning of the school year to get an override for my class. When I first saw him, my heart started beating fast and my neck and forehead started to sweat. He's built like an Adonis and has these blue-green eyes like Vanessa Williams. Matter of fact, they look like they could be kin."

"What's his name?"

"Kilgore Roberts."

"That's a different name," I said.

"Oh, he's something else. He came to class the first week wearing a tight-fitting shirt and slacks. He didn't wear those baggy jeans most of my male students wear. You know, hanging down on the butts. Kilgore would be the first one in class and the last one to leave. The one thing he did do, that the boys do, is hold on to his stuff."

"So how did you know he was gay?"

"I didn't. But during the second week of school he came to my office under the guise of asking what he could do for extra credit."

"Extra credit my ass," I said, laughing. I might have put too much champagne in my glass. I rarely drank, and when I did, it usually gave me the giggles or a loose tongue.

"Exactly. The next thing I knew, we were on top of my desk, kissing like we were supplying the other with lifesaving oxygen. If any of my other students had walked in on us, let's just say it wouldn't have been good. And then I just did something real silly."

"What did you do?"

"I gave him my address and asked him to come after ten. I told him the back door would be open. That evening, I heard the back door open and it was on. I felt like I was twenty years old again."

"So you think you're falling in love with him?"

"Carmyn, it might be too late. I live for the boy. As soon as you leave, I'll call or text him and spend the rest of the day in bed with him."

"I guess I should say I'm happy for you," I said.

"Thank you. But what about you? When are we going to find someone for you?"

"I'm fine, Lowell. Maybe I'll start dating when Brady goes to the league," I said, giving my standard reply.

"So how much in love were you with Brady's father?"

"I don't want to talk about that," I said quickly. Suddenly I didn't feel giddy, as memories I had tried to erase entered my mind. They must have shown on my face, because Lowell took my hands and said, "Carmyn, you can trust me. What really happened between you and Brady's father?"

Maybe it was the champagne, but I looked into Lowell's eyes and they looked like a safe place to leave some things I had tried to forget.

I took a deep breath. "It's a long story," I began. "A twenty-year-old story. It started when I enrolled at the University of Texas."

Lowell frowned. "I thought you graduated from Clark. I never knew you even lived in Texas."

"I told you a lot of things. Now I'm going to tell you the truth. My name is really Carmyn Johnson, but I was known by my childhood nickname, Niecey, until I had Brady.

"I went to the University of Texas in 1987, but left after . . ." I paused, wondering if I could really say the words aloud. "When I was a freshman, I was . . . I went to a party . . . had a few drinks." I stopped, not able to go on.

Lowell chuckled. "Girl, everyone has a night or two like that in college. You don't have anything to be ashamed of. Hell, I can tell you stories that are a lot worse."

I shook my head. "Nothing's worse than what happened to me. Nothing's worse than what I let happen to myself that night." I sank in the chair and faced Lowell, although my mind took my eyes away, back to that time, back to a night I had tried to pretend never happened.

"My boyfriend was a star football player for UT, and he invited me to the party for the prospective high school recruits. I didn't even want to go, but I wanted to please . . . Woodson." It was the first time I'd said his name aloud in more than two decades.

"At the party, I drank a little, smoked a little. I wasn't trying to get drunk or high. I'm the daughter of a preacher. I had lived a sheltered life, and I just wanted to have a good time. I wanted to fit in, be popular and make my boyfriend proud of me. I don't remember much about the party, but I remember everything afterwards," I said as tears formed in my eyes.

I continued unfolding the story as it glided from my memory: how I'd awakened in a room not knowing where I was, Woodson finding me naked, and then the smear campaign that Daphne, Woodson's former girlfriend, launched, and then the letter from Woodson that drove me from campus, back to my parents and Houston.

"Didn't your parents want to know why you came home?" Lowell asked.

"I told them I didn't like going to a big white school like UT."

"Didn't you have friends you could talk to?"

"No, not really," I responded. "Can you believe that Daphne called me the other day after all these years?"

"What did she want?"

"I didn't talk to her long enough to find out. I just hung up," I said.

"Good for you," Lowell said. "This Daphne sounds like a playa-hating bitch. Women can be so evil towards each other. But look at you now. You've done so well for yourself and Brady. I envy the relationship you two have."

Every time Lowell said my son's name, my

tears returned. "I haven't told you the real story yet." I took a breath. "I'd been in Houston about a month when I suspected that I was pregnant. Shortly after that, my family doctor confirmed that I was, and two months later my parents had me on a plane to Atlanta, so I could have the baby without anyone finding out.

"My parents were mortified. I couldn't answer any of their questions. They assumed that Woodson was the father. I couldn't tell them what happened. I couldn't tell them who the father was, because I didn't know. They looked at me with such disgust and disdain in their eyes and then told me I needed to disappear faster than ice in a hot drink. As a prominent minister, my father couldn't have a pregnant unmarried daughter. My mother was so embarrassed that she wouldn't speak to me, so she sent me a letter.

"But they were good Christians." I chuckled bitterly. "After a few days of tears from my mother and silence from my father, they told me they forgave me and that one day God would forgive me. And then they sprang into action. Abortion was never an option, but after some research, my mother found the Pure Life Home. It was a Christian home for girls in my situation."

"I can't believe your parents sent you away. That sounds like some shit from the fifties."

I nodded. "I cried every day for the first month I was there, but then I had to get on about the business of finding the perfect family for my baby."

"You were going to give Brady up?"

I nodded. "At Pure Life, that's what you're supposed to do. That's why my parents sent me there. The plan was for me to have the baby, give it up for adoption, and then return to Houston as if I'd just been away at school. I agreed. I was just eighteen. What was I supposed to do with a baby?

"Pure Life introduced me to five families, and I met an African American couple, Rex and Sophie Maddie. Both of the Maddies had Ph.D.s, and I was impressed with the beautiful home they had just built in an exclusive gated community. I knew they would treat my baby well, because Sophie couldn't have children and they wanted a baby so badly. I was six months pregnant when I met the Maddies, and for the rest of my pregnancy, they treated me like their daughter. They took me out to dinner, took me shopping; I even spent a couple of weekends in their new home. And they were different from my parents. There was never any shame in their eyes when they looked at me. All I ever felt from them was love. They thought I was a blessing.

"Sophie even encouraged me to write a letter to my baby explaining that I loved him but that I wanted him to have a better life.

"Sophie was in the delivery room when Brady was born. But I wasn't prepared for what happened next. When my baby was delivered, the plan was to take him out of the room right away. But I begged them to let me see him, let me hold him so that I could say good-bye. And although they hesitated, the nurse handed me the baby." I paused. "And I never let go. I felt such an immediate and intense love for him."

"You kept . . . Brady."

I nodded. "It was so hard. He was my reason for breathing. Sophie cried, and Rex threatened to sue me for all the money they'd spent. For days I pleaded with them to understand, but all they could feel was their own pain. Sophie told me that I might as well have snatched her heart from her. I cried for them, but I just couldn't give my baby away."

I smiled. "I held my baby's hand. I counted his toes and his fingers. And when he looked at me and stopped crying, he took my breath and filled my heart with love. I couldn't give him up.

"The nurses were happy for me. They asked me what I was going to name him. I hadn't considered any names, but I looked up at the television and *The Brady Bunch* was on. I always loved that show. I had registered at the hospital as Carmyn Bledsoe, using my mother's maiden name, and I liked the way Brady Bledsoe sounded. Also, by keeping my mother's maiden name I didn't totally lose my identity. That day, Niecey Johnson left the building."

Lowell exhaled a long breath. "I know your parents probably went crazy."

"That's one way of putting it. They tried to force me to change my mind, but when I didn't, they told me I couldn't come home. My preacher father and my mother, the first lady, told me to stay out of Houston so I wouldn't embarrass them. They told me they would welcome me back with open arms if I ever gave up my baby.

"I was in shock. I was a teenager, on my own, living in Atlanta, a city I didn't know. But it didn't matter. I kept Brady and made a life for both of us. I did get some help with diapers, formula, and other items from an organization called Brandon's Room that was started by a young woman who gave up her son but then regretted her decision and didn't have money for a lawyer to get him back. I'm still so grateful for the help I received that every year I send the organization a donation."

Lowell leaned forward and took my hand. "You made a wonderful life for you and Brady. You did what you had to do, but I think you should tell Brady."

"What? He might start to hate me. No, I can't do that."

"So you did send back those letters from the University of Texas," Lowell said.

"What could I do? Brady couldn't end up at the place where I ruined my life. I couldn't let that happen to my baby or to me. I sent back every one of those letters."

CHAPTER 19
BRADY TAKES ON BAMA

I walked into Coach Hale's office and noticed a strained look on his face. I knew the coaches were worried about the upcoming game against the University of Alabama, but Coach Hale never let the players see his concern. But when he asked me to come by his office after practice, there was something different in his voice. At first I thought this might be about Chloe, but Lowell assured me he'd taken care of that.

"Coach, you said you needed to see me," I said as I walked into the massive office overlooking the end zone of the practice field.

"Come in, Brady, have a seat," Coach Hale replied as he took off his baseball hat, revealing the receding hairline that the players often teased him about.

"Thanks, Coach," I said. I took a seat in one of the office's green leather chairs with a gold jaguar head emblazoned on the back.

"Great practice today, Brady," Coach Hale

said. "I can't tell you what it means to see a senior everybody's saying might be the best player in the country going full out in practice. It sets such a good example for the younger players. And those early-morning workouts you mandated are really helping, with our players still being fresh in the fourth quarter."

"Thank you, Coach. I'm just doing what I do," I said, thinking that the coach hadn't called a private meeting to compliment me on something that I did all the time.

"So how's your mother?"

"She's fine. She'll be in Tuscaloosa this weekend," I replied.

"Good. Good. We need all the fans we can get in that place."

"My mom never misses any of my games," I said proudly.

"I know, Brady. You're so lucky to come from good stock. I knew that when I recruited you. Good stock. I wish all of my players were like you, but I understand they can't be. Not everyone's as fortunate as you, Bledsoe. I think the NCAA should relax the rules and pay the young athletes who need money so they won't be forced to do things that are against the rules, like take money from boosters and agents."

"Yeah, Coach, I'm blessed," I said.

"How are you handling the agents?"

"I'm not, Coach, but my mom is. She'll know what to do."

"Great, Bledsoe. I did tell one agent, Basil Henderson from XJI, that I would give him his props when it came to you. He's a great agent, and he's done right by some of my players who signed with him."

"My mom has already talked to him," I said.

"Good to hear. Henderson follows the rules."

After a few nervous moments, I asked Coach if that was all he needed. The coach stared at me silently, then asked if I would shoot straight with him about one of my teammates.

"Sure, Coach."

"How are things at home?"

I was puzzled. He had already asked about my mother. What home was he talking about?

"Home? You mean in Atlanta?"

"No, I'm sorry, Brady. I mean here on campus. You and Delmar getting along okay?"

"No doubt — Delmar is my boi. We get along fine. Why do you ask?"

"I don't know any other way to put it, but I have been hearing some rumors that are bothering me. I know it might just be gossip, but we are not talking about a sorority here, we're talking about a football team. Men. You understand what I'm saying, Bledsoe?"

"I don't think so, Coach. What are you talking about?"

"Damn, I'm just going to flat out ask you. Is Delmar dealing drugs?"

"What? No, Coach. Delmar wouldn't do anything like that. Who told you that?" I asked.

"We don't have proof positive, but several of the coaches and even a couple of the trainers have been noticing that he has changed his wardrobe, started wearing better clothes. Then we heard from a couple other guys that he has been picking up the tab at victory celebrations for his teammates, paying for strippers and stuff."

I had noticed the extra money Delmar seemed to have, but I figured it was coming from his summer job. But what kind of job did he have in the summer? He didn't say, but I knew he'd gone to several smaller cities in Georgia. I couldn't imagine Delmar doing anything illegal to earn money.

"Coach, I don't believe Delmar would do something like that, and I haven't seen any evidence in our apartment."

The coach asked me if we had a lot of visitors and also what had happened to Delmar's baby's mother. He went on to tell me that in previous years they had received calls all the time from his ex-girlfriend, complaining that Delmar wasn't paying his child support, but that the calls had recently stopped.

"Is that girl still alive? You don't think he's gotten rid of her, do you?" Coach Hale asked.

"Come on now, Coach. This is Delmar you're talking about. He wouldn't harm a flea. He's all talk," I said. "Besides, he's always on the phone with her trying to get her to bring his son to games, so I know she's still around."

"Do you think he's taking money from an agent?"

"I doubt that. We're not talking to any agents yet," I said, knowing that was totally true.

"Yeah, but you're a straight shooter, Brady," Coach Hale said. "They know better than to offer you any money, but some of these agents have no morals, like the guy your mother had to report to the NCAA."

"Yeah, Nico Benson. But I'm just trying to play by the rules, Coach," I said.

"You guys represent the University and should be paid. Think about all that money we get from the conference and bowl games.

It's just not fair," Coach Hale said.

"Maybe it will change some day. I know all my teammates aren't as blessed as me. Do you want me ask Delmar where all the money is coming from?"

"No, don't do that. Hopefully, you're right and Delmar wouldn't be foolish enough to jeopardize his career. Both of you boys will be playing on Sunday. Just keep your eyes open, son."

"I will, Coach," I said as an image of Delmar drinking that expensive Champagne entered my mind. As I walked out of the office, I wondered if my best friend would risk everything for some quick cash.

CHAPTER 20
BARRETT GETS SOMETHING
TO CHEER ABOUT

Barrett was getting ready to walk into the complex for cheer practice, and felt her cell phone vibrate. She looked at the name on the tiny screen and decided to take the call. Some of the female squad members walked by, engaged in conversation and acting like they didn't see her. Before answering, Barrett muttered, "Bitches," and turned around, facing the parking lot so she wouldn't have to see any of them until she joined them for their two-mile run before practice.

"Hey," Barrett said.

"Are you sitting down?" the familiar male voice said.

"Actually, I'm standing up," Barrett said.

"I've got some startling news which might help our cause, but you've got to act on this right away. First of all, you're not going to believe this. Maybe I should catch a flight down and tell you in person. I would love to see your face when I tell you."

"Don't do that to me. Tell me," Barrett demanded.

"Okay. Well, it seems like Mother Bledsoe was a little slut puppy back in the day. Got herself knocked up with your boy while entertaining the football troops. She doesn't have a clue who her baby's daddy is," he said, laughing.

"What? Brady's father is dead," Barrett said.

"I wouldn't be so sure of that."

"How did you find out?"

"From the horse's mouth. You see, I'm thorough, baby, and I always cover all the bases, and I had a backup plan just in case your feminine power couldn't close the deal. You know I hire some good-looking guys who are just big-time freaks in case I'm trying to sign some faggot mofo. You'd be surprised how many of them there are in the league," he said.

"I'm sure Brady isn't gay, so what are you talking about?" Barrett asked.

"I'll explain that later, but this is what happened. It seems like Brady's mother had a 'come to Jesus' moment and shared her deep, dark secret with her best friend, that faggot professor who's Brady's godfather."

"So what do you want me to do?"

"You have to tell him."

"How can I do that without connecting you to this?"

"If you use the right acting skills, which means your I-hate-to-do-this-but-I'm-really-concerned act, I think it will send him over the edge."

"Do you have any more details, just in case he doesn't believe me?"

"Sure. Ask him if he ever met his grandparents."

"I've never heard him mention grandparents."

"Right, because his mother never told him about them and it seems the good preacher and his wife disowned their daughter the tramp."

"This is too wild. I guess that bitch of a mother is going to be sorry she turned her nose up at me," Barrett said as she noticed Frank, one of the male cheerleaders, running toward the door. Barrett knew she was at least ten minutes late for practice, since Frank was always late — so late that the squad members took bets on when he would show.

"I think you should tell him this evening."

"I didn't have plans to see him. I need to meet with this chick who's writing some comp papers for me," Barrett said.

"Change it. We need to get moving on this."

"Okay! Gotta run. I'll call you later," Barrett said as she clicked off her phone and raced into practice.

CHAPTER 21
CARMYN'S BELOVED

With thoughts whipping through my mind like autumn leaves in a breeze, I considered how Lowell was pressuring me to tell Brady. I didn't know if I agreed with him, but what if I did tell Brady? Would he understand why I had done what I did? How angry would he be over the missed chance at having a relationship with his father? Would he understand when I told him that I wasn't really sure who his father was and that I didn't even know if he was alive?

I shook my head, trying to discard those thoughts. But then my mind filled with new images — of Brady when he was five years old, starting school, wanting a "daddy" and a puppy badly. I remembered the look on his face when he watched his friends' fathers pick up their sons from football practice. How my heart had ached. But nothing was as bad as the time he'd come home crying after his first loss in a Pee Wee football game.

"Mommy," he cried. "I'm mad at God."

"Why would you say that, Brady?" I asked, concerned.

"Because I keep praying and praying and He won't send me another daddy. I don't know why. He took away my first daddy and He should give me a new one."

Tears had filled my eyes then, just as they did now as I remembered. All I was able to say was "God knows best."

I eased the car to the edge of the curb, glanced at the modest home, and then turned off the car's engine. As I walked toward the door, I pasted a smile on my face. I hadn't seen Shelby since the day I brushed her off, and I was sure she'd be happy to see a friendly face. I knew this wasn't an easy time for her. I knew this for sure, since it hadn't been easy for me.

"Hi, Ms. Carmyn," Shelby said when she opened the door. The tone of her voice told me that she was surprised to see me.

I hugged her, feeling the slight bulge of her three-month pregnancy. "You look good," I said, glancing at her. "How are you feeling?"

She shrugged as she closed the door, and then I followed her into the kitchen. "I'm okay. Do you want something to drink?"

"No, sweetheart, I'm fine." I settled onto

one of the bar stools at the counter. "So, how's everything?"

Again she gave me the standard teenage shrug. This girl was still a baby herself.

"Are you feeling okay?"

"I guess."

"Well, I wanted to stop by and see you and find out if there was anything I could do. I'm still willing to do your hair whenever you want."

She shook her head. "I won't be able to do that. Next week, I'm going away."

I raised my eyebrows. "Going away? You don't need to go anywhere. You need to stay here with your mom and brothers. Family is what you need now."

"My mom doesn't want me here, she's making me go. I'm going to Chicago to stay with my aunt" — she lowered her eyes — "until the baby is born."

"Oh," I said, and waited for her to continue.

She took a deep breath. "Mama says it'll be better this way because my aunt works for Social Services and she'll be able to find the baby a good home —"

"Wait a minute." I held up my hand. "Find the baby a good home?"

She nodded but still didn't look at me. "I'm giving my baby away."

I wondered if she noticed the way her hand moved to her belly when she said those words. She was already protecting her baby.

I stood, walked over to her, and held her in my arms for a moment. "Shelby, sweetheart. Giving away your baby . . . is that what you want?"

She nodded but didn't look like she meant it. "It'll be better for me . . . and the baby," she said, as if she had rehearsed the words.

"Come here," I said, taking her hand and leading her to the kitchen table. We sat next to each other, and when I looked at her and saw the tears in her eyes, my heart broke.

"Shelby, you don't have to do that."

"I do," she said, tears now crawling down her cheek. "It'll be better, because I'm only a girl and I can't take care of a baby. Besides, Torrian already has another girlfriend."

I took a breath. I knew it would be tough, but if I could do it, Shelby could too.

Shelby continued. "My mom said that I have to do it this way because she can't feed another mouth and she said I can still go to college . . . and . . ." She stopped as if she could find no other reason. "I have to do this."

Memories flooded back to me as I recalled hearing all the same things, except my parents weren't worried about another mouth to feed — they had the means, they just didn't want the shame.

"You don't have to give up your baby, Shelby. You can still go to college."

She waited a moment, digesting what I'd said, as if she needed time to believe me.

"I don't want to give up my baby," she whispered as if she weren't supposed to say the words aloud. "But my mother is so mad at me. Sometimes I think she hates me."

"Oh, sweetheart," I said, squeezing her hand. "Your mother doesn't hate you. She may be disappointed, but she loves you."

"That's what she said, but she told me that I have to give my baby away. She said I have to give my baby away, or else . . ." She stopped.

I raised my eyebrows. It wasn't like me to come into someone else's home and tell their children what to do, but I'd walked in Shelby's shoes.

"Listen to me, Shelby. What happens with this baby has to be your choice. Because you're the only one who has to live with it. And you don't want to grow up with regrets. You need to make the decision yourself."

"Ms. Carmyn, I want to keep my baby," she said, her voice stronger this time. "I'm scared, though. I do want to go to college and I don't want to ruin my life."

"You can't let one night ruin your life. Take that from someone who knows."

"You really think so?" She looked at me, her eyes pleading for reassurance.

"I know that you can take care of yourself and the baby."

"But how do you know? My own mother doesn't believe I can make it on my own if I keep the baby."

How could I explain all this to her? There was no way I could tell her my secrets. Not when my own son didn't know.

"I know because I know you can do all things through God. And God created your baby. So if you want to keep your baby." I paused and smiled. "God will give you everything you need to take care of her once she breathes her first breath."

It was such a simple answer, but it seemed my words were ones Shelby needed to hear.

Still, she said, "But how will I keep my baby and go to school? I'd have to get an apartment and job. How will I be able to do all of that with a baby?" She looked as if all those thoughts overwhelmed her.

Suddenly, Brady's empty bedroom popped into my head and I found myself saying a quick prayer, hoping I was doing the right thing. "Shelby, if you want to keep your baby, you can stay with me. I will see what I can do to help you find a job. Maybe you can work at the shop."

Her eyes widened. "I could live with you? Really?"

"Yes, sweetheart."

She gave me a grateful smile. "I thought you'd be disappointed in me, just like my mother."

I wanted to tell her that there was no way I could pass judgment. But instead I said, "This may not be what I wanted for you, but this is where we are. So we'll just deal with it." I leaned over and hugged her. "You still have some time to think about this, but I want you to know that you have choices."

She nodded.

"And if you want to keep your baby, I will help you do that, okay? Even if it means having to talk with your mother."

She nodded again.

I stood, grabbed my purse, and headed to the door.

"I'll give you a call in a couple of days, but if you need me before then, you know where to find me, okay?"

"Thank you, Ms. Carmyn. I hope Brady knows how lucky he is to have a mother like you."

After I left Shelby, I felt a sudden urge to

read something I had written over twenty years ago. Later, I found myself at the top of my home, nestled in a seldom-used room that reminded me of the inside of a jewel box. Brady had only been in the room once since we bought the house.

Natural light flooded into the attic through a bay window. I located a small, smooth wooden box that I had hidden behind a water tank and pulled it out. Inside were almost a hundred letters that were like photographs of my youth in an old scrapbook. Most of the letters were from Woodson, but there were a few from girlfriends, and one letter at the bottom of the box that no eyes had seen but mine. I recognized my handwriting and the words *My Beloved* on a dingy white legal-sized envelope.

I wondered if the words I'd written two decades earlier could be a comfort to Shelby now, and I was surprised by the wave of emotion that overcame me as I opened the envelope and began reading the letter.

October 17,1987

My Beloved Child,

If you're reading this letter, I guess you've finally turned eighteen. Happy Birthday, baby!

The first thing I want to say may sound

cliché since you're adopted, but I reallly did give you up so that you could have a better life. Even though it hurts me to say it, right now I'm just not capable of being the mother you need to thrive in this world. The best way I can love you is to give you to two wonderful people who will raise you as their own.

Please know that I will always love you.

Now that you're old enough, it's time for you to learn a little bit about your birth family. The Johnsons are a strong, proud family. Your grandfather hails from Waco, Texas. His parents were educators, and your grandfather followed their lead and is the dean of an historically black college where he is loved and respected. He is also a minister, a true man of God. People say his sermons can raise the dead. He calls me his princess, and until recently I felt that way.

Your grandmother comes from a long line of Texas beauties. She, as her mother before her, has devoted her life to helping others. Since ninth grade I've spent at least one month each summer helping un-derprivileged people right alongside my mother.

My darling child, I wish I were older, wiser, and up to the task of being your mother.

I want all your dreams to come true, baby. I dreamed of getting married one day and having my father, your grandfather, perform the wedding ceremony.

Maybe someday we'll meet and I can tell you all the things that escape me now. I'm fighting back tears with each sentence I write. I hope you can forgive me for giving you up for adoption, baby. One day, I hope, I'll get to hug and hold you.

My faith right now is fragile, but I hope you'll welcome God into your life and never let him go.

There's a scene at the end of the The Color Purple, one of my favorite movies. I won't give it away, but I cry every time I see it. It's a scene about hope that reminds me that family ties can never be broken. Maybe one day soon we'll get to mend ours.

With all the love in the world,
Your birth mother,
Niecey

I felt a pain in my heart, and I began crying tears of guilt over what might have been and the joy I would have missed.

CHAPTER 22
BRADY'S BOI

I walked up the granite stairs into Maynard Jackson Hall, where Lowell's office was located. The smell of fresh wax wafted off the floors and I heard the sound of the morning janitor buffing them before the first bell rang. I couldn't remember the last time I was up this early when it didn't have anything to do with football, but when Lowell had called me the night before and asked me to come by, his request had seemed urgent.

I reached the third floor, and when I walked into Lowell's office, I saw him looking out the window.

"Enjoying this beautiful day?" I said, startling Lowell.

"Brady, thanks for coming by on such short notice," Lowell said. He moved away from the window and toward me, giving me a bear hug.

"No problem. I only have one class today. I love being a senior and having all my hard courses out of the way," I said as I sat in the dark red leather chair facing Lowell's desk.

"So you've got your Heisman acceptance speech ready?" Lowell asked.

"I'm trying not to think about that, and I know you didn't call me over here to talk about football. You know, that's all anybody wants to talk about these days. I want to talk about something else, like American citizens being spied on. Or if Bush plans to withdraw the troops from Iraq, or continue to send more of my brothers and sisters over there to die."

"Sounds like you should come and sit in on one of my classes. Or maybe even teach," Lowell said.

"Maybe one day," I said.

"Do you want something to drink?" Lowell asked. He seemed a little nervous, and I wondered if what he needed to talk to me about was causing the apparent anxiety.

"No, I'm cool. How did you get Chloe to leave me alone?"

"Oh, that was easy. All I had to do was to remind her you were seventeen when you came to college, and while that's legal in Georgia, the president and dean don't look favorably on teachers doing whatever they want with young, impressionable students. I told her if she released one picture we'd sue her ass. By the way, I have the pictures."

"What are we going to do with them?"

"Already done. I shredded them."

"Sometimes she used a digital camera," I said.

"I wouldn't worry, Brady. She is not going to do anything. In a way I felt sorry for her, because it was obvious she had feelings for you, but she was in way over her head. How's your roommate?" Lowell asked, suddenly changing the subject.

"Delmar? He's cool. Why do you ask?" I quizzed. Had the rumors and the coach's concerns about Delmar reached Lowell, as well?

"I don't know what to do other than to just come out and say it. Did you know that Delmar has been dancing at a private club in Savannah?" Lowell asked.

"Dancing? What kind of dancing?" I asked, laughing at the thought of Delmar dancing for an audience.

"I guess you really can't call it dancing. I guess stripping is a better term," Lowell said.

"You mean like dancing with a G-string?"

"Yep."

"Are you sure it's Delmar?"

"It was him. No doubt."

Lowell told me about a private club he frequented in nearby Savannah called The

Living Room. He explained that it was an upscale establishment for professional black gay men who didn't want to go to the clubs populated by what Lowell called finger-popping sissies. He explained that on Tuesdays and Thursdays they brought in strippers from Atlanta and Jacksonville, Florida. He told me that one night he had walked into the club, only to see Delmar in a G-string and white cowboy boots allowing men to stick dollar bills in his skimpy undergarment.

"Did he see you?" I asked.

"I don't think so. But I talked to a couple of my friends after he finished his show and I found out this wasn't his first time dancing there and that he sometimes does private shows for clients away from the club."

"Private shows?"

"Yep, and even though I'm embarrassed to tell you this, I've had a private show or two in my day and it usually includes more than dancing," Lowell said. "Thank God I've met someone and don't have to do that anymore."

"What are you saying? Is Delmar gay or bi?" I asked.

"I can't say. I'm not concerned about that. I just want to make sure he doesn't get in trouble. I know a few other professors who frequent the club, and one who shall remain nameless is the NCAA faculty representative for Central Georgia," Lowell said.

"Maybe Delmar is one of those DL guys the females on campus are always talking about," I said, trying to get the picture of Delmar in a G-string, shaking his behind in front of a man, out of my head. For some reason the thought made me want to laugh, but then I thought of the ridicule Delmar would face if any of our teammates found out about his part-time job.

"Most likely he's part of the new GP wave," Lowell said.

"GP wave?" I asked. Sometimes when I asked Lowell questions, I got more information than I wanted to hear. I hope'd that was not going to be the case this morning.

"The down low is old news. Now it seems there are a lot of guys who are gay for pay," Lowell said.

"Gay for pay?"

"Straight guys who will go a little crooked for the right amount of money," Lowell said. "They usually target wealthy, older men, and some of them are very dangerous."

"So maybe that's where he's been getting all the extra money," I said. "At least he's not selling drugs."

"Will you warn him to be careful, Brady?

He only has a few months before the draft, and I know he doesn't want to mess up. Lord knows he won't be able to fall back on his education, since he never goes to class."

"Yeah, I'll talk to him. Good looking out," I said. I got up from the chair and shook my head. I couldn't wait to hear what Delmar had to say for himself.

After practice in preparation for the Ole Miss game, I did what I always do when faced with a dilemma — I called my mother.

After trying to reach my mother at both salons and her cell, I called her home number. I was surprised to find her there so early in the evening.

"Hey, Mom," I said.

"Brady. How are you?"

"I'm fine. Hey, Mom, that money is still in my account. Do you think I should go to the bank and tell them about the mistake?"

"Trust me, Brady, they are not in the business of giving away money. They will figure it out and take it back," Mama said.

"Okay, if you say so. Are you feeling all right?" I asked.

"I just needed a time-out," she said. "I'm feeling a little stressed lately."

"Is there anything I can do?"

"Just keep playing football and being the

perfect son."

"Mama, I'm not perfect."

"You're close to it."

"If ever there was a perfect mother, it's you," I said. I was thinking about all that my mom had done for me and the sacrifices she'd made. Even though having a father would have been nice, he would have to have been a cool dude to deserve my mother.

She didn't respond. I heard sniffles on the other end of the phone.

"Mom, are you crying?"

"No, baby. I just need to get some rest," she said

"I love you."

"I love you, too. Remember that, Brady."

"I always know that, Mom."

CHAPTER 23
FOR YOUR CONSIDERATION
. . . BARRETT MANNING

Barrett paced on her balcony. She had practiced over and over, but she was still nervous. This was the most important thing she'd have to do in her mission with Brady. Everything rested on whether she could convince him and how he reacted.

As she looked over the balcony's railing, she saw Brady's Navigator turn the corner and she jumped back out of sight. She watched as he parked, then she backed into her condo. Her heart pounded more as she dialed Nico's number.

"Is he there?" Nico asked.

"He just drove up. It should only take him a minute or two."

"I forgot to ask — how's he going to get into the building? The doorman has to buzz you, doesn't he?"

"Most times, but tonight I told the doorman to let him up without stopping him. I'm going to leave my door slightly open."

"Oh, great move. And what are you wearing?"

"Just one of my little silk robes," Barrett said. "I want it to look like I was just waiting for him."

"Okay, well, you've got it together. Now start talking, just in case he gets up there sooner."

Barrett walked into her living room and stood by the door. As soon as she heard the door open, she said loud enough for Brady to hear as he stepped into her apartment, "I cannot believe this. It doesn't make sense." She turned, facing away from him, knowing he'd follow her voice.

"Brady told me his father was dead." She paused for a moment, as if she were listening to someone on the line.

"Good job, girl," Nico said. "That acting class you took is sure coming in handy."

"Are you sure this is true about Brady?" Barrett asked, wanting to say his name as much as possible. "How can his father not be dead? I'm so upset. I could never tell Brady this —"

"Tell me what?" Brady asked from behind her.

Barrett took a moment to form her expression. She had to have just the right look. When she turned around, her face was filled with surprise and dread. "Oh, Brady . . . I'm sorry."

Brady stood with his hands tucked deep inside his jeans and his face wrinkled in confusion. "What are you talking about? Who are you talking to?"

"I'll talk to you later," Barrett said, then clicked off the phone, just as she and Nico had planned.

"Brady, sweetheart." She paused and then rushed into his arms. "Oh, Brady, I'm so sorry," she said, sobbing into his chest.

He held her tight for a moment, then released her. "Barrett," he said, still holding her by her shoulders. "I heard you say something about my father?"

"Brady, I don't want to say anything," she said, turning her back to him for dramatic effect. She could feel his eyes on her. She sniffed as if she were upset. "I'm still so shocked by this news."

He took her by the hand and led her to the sofa. She leaned into him as they sat, letting the hem of her robe rise up her leg. "Oh, baby, this is terrible."

"Barrett, you have to tell me what you were talking about. What is this about my father?"

She leaned away from him. She'd stalled long enough. "Brady, this is just so awful." She paused. "But maybe it's good news. Because your father . . . he may not be dead."

She watched as Brady's eyes glazed over, as if he didn't understand her words. "My father is alive?"

She nodded. "He could be. It's just that . . . your mother, she doesn't really know who your dad is."

"What?" Brady asked, jumping from the sofa. "That doesn't make sense. None of this makes sense. My father is dead!" he exclaimed.

"I know that's what your mother told you," Barrett said, moving toward him as he stood near the window. "Brady, it seems that when your mother was in college at the University of Texas —"

"The University of Texas? My mother never went there."

"There are a lot of things that your mother didn't tell you. But she was a student there, and then at a party or something, she had sex . . ." Barrett paused, wanting Brady to fill in the rest. Finally, she continued. "She had sex with several guys. The news spread all over campus, and then she left school. But nine months later, you were born." A part of Barrett felt sorry for Brady, but she thought back to how Carmyn had treated her and she felt this couldn't happen to a better bitch.

"Who told you this crap?" Brady asked,

breathing heavily.

"I know it's hard, Brady," Barrett said.

"Where did you hear this?" he demanded.

"I can't say. I think you should speak with your mom."

As Barrett leaned against him, she could feel him shaking. She wrapped her arms around him. "I am so sorry, Brady. So sorry to tell you this."

"So you're saying my mother lied to me?" he said, disgusted.

"Maybe she was trying to protect you." Barrett knew it didn't matter what she said about Carmyn. From what she knew about Brady, he valued the truth. He hated liars. He would hate his mother for this. Even though it might be temporary, it would be long enough for Barrett to seize the control she needed.

"Protect me?" Brady said. "How could a lie protect me?"

Barrett remained silent.

"Are you sure about this, Barrett?"

She nodded. "I'm sure. And I'm so sorry." She wrapped her arms around him again. "But maybe now you can find your father."

She felt him cringe. Maybe that was too much for him to digest right now. She could tell by the way he held her that she'd won. She didn't really have to add any more.

"I've got to talk with my coach, and then I need to see my mother."

"Do you want me to ride with you?"

"I need to see my mother," he repeated as if in a daze. "I've got to go."

Barrett watched Brady stumble out of the apartment, and for a moment she hoped he was going to be all right. She went to the balcony and watched as he walked slowly to his car and then sped off.

Inside her condo, Barrett collapsed onto the sofa. The acting had taken more out of her than she imagined. It wasn't that it was so hard saying the words to Brady. It was just hard breaking his heart that way. Even though she wasn't in love, she was beginning to care about this young man. She hoped that what she had just done was enough to finish this assignment.

"Hello," Barrett purred into the phone. She was smoking a joint.

"I thought I would have heard from you by now," a male voice said.

"Who is this?" Barrett asked, wondering who from her past might have finally caught up with her.

"This is Mr. John Basil Henderson. You kept my business card, didn't you? I thought you were smarter than Nico's other girls."

"I'm not one of Nico's girls. I'm going to be his wife," Barrett said firmly.

"You're joking, right?" Basil said with a hearty laugh.

"How did you get my number?" Barrett demanded.

"If I can get it so easily, then I bet it won't be long before Chris gets it as well," Basil said. "Athlete management is a very small world, Barrett. I know what happened to Chris Johns."

Barrett slammed down the phone and muttered to herself as she picked up the remainder of the blunt, "That nigga's tryin' to fuck with a lady's high."

CHAPTER 24
CARMYN GETS A CLUE

"What do you think of this?" Zander asked as he held out a beautiful chocolate-brown silk wrap dress with a geometric print.

"Is that for me?" I asked.

"So you like it," Zander said. His freshly shaved head looked like it had been polished with Wesson oil, and he was dressed stylishly himself in black form-fitting slacks and a black silk shirt. I guess I saw what some of his clients were seeing.

"Is that for Maybelline?"

"You think she'll wear it? It's not a miniskirt." Zander laughed.

"If she won't, I will. When are you going to let her try it on?"

"Let's call her now. I got some beige heels and a lovely scarf to go with it," Zander said.

"That'll look nice. It may be a little formal for a football game, but it's lovely for a press conference or a nice lunch with the ladies," I said.

"I'm going to put her on speakerphone so we can both talk to her," Zander said.

"Okay," I said as I looked over a Carol's Daughter order form. A few moments later, I heard Maybelline's voice: *"If this is a bill collector, I rebuke you in the name of Jesus. All others leave a message. This is May-Jean, unless you are a bill collector."*

I started laughing so hard I couldn't talk, and so did Zander for a second, but he quickly pulled himself together and said, "May-Jean, this is the new man in your life. Give me a call. I got a few things I want you to try on. Have a great day, darling. But you got to pay your bills, sweetheart. 'Bye."

Zander went to the back of the shop to get fresh towels when the phone rang. I thought for a moment of waiting for Zander to pick up with the strong, sexy voice my customers loved, but then I decided to answer.

"Back to My Roots, Carmyn speaking," I said.

"Mrs. Bledsoe?"

"Yes."

"This is Basil Henderson from XJI. Did I catch you at a bad time?"

"No, Mr. Henderson. How are you doing?"

"Great. I just called to see how things were

going and if you and Brady have decided when you're coming to New York."

"We haven't. I want there to be as few distractions as possible until the season is over. I know you understand," I said.

"Sure I do. Is Brady ready for this week's game? Every game is a big game for him," Basil said.

"Brady's always game ready," I said.

"Ms. Bledsoe, I hope I'm not getting into uncharted territory here, but I hope you know I have Brady's best interest in mind," Basil said.

"I know that, Mr. Henderson," I said, wondering where this was leading.

"Does Brady have a new girlfriend?"

"I wouldn't call her a girlfriend," I said quickly.

"Well, I only mention it because I know that a concerned mother such as yourself is very much aware that some girls will do anything to hook up with a potential NFL star like Brady. I had a client whose girlfriend took a used condom and conveniently wound up pregnant right after he signed his contract," Basil said.

I wanted to say that was just plain nasty, but instead I said, "Mr. Henderson, I appreciate your concern, but Brady was raised with the highest standards. He's saving himself for marriage and won't fall for a trick like that."

"Yes, I've read that Brady is celibate, but I wanted to warn you. Sometimes college athletes have to be as wary of their fellow students as they do agents," Basil said.

"Yes, but as soon as the season is over, Brady and I will sit down and map out a plan for his future," I said.

"Okay. I just hope my firm and I are a part of those plans," Basil responded.

"I think you've put yourself in a position to do just that."

"Thanks, Ms. Bledsoe. You have a good day."

"I will, and you do the same. Good-bye."

CHAPTER 25
BRADY'S THROWN FOR A LOSS

I parked my SUV in the garage of my childhood home, turned off the engine, and without pulling the keys from the ignition, slumped in the driver's seat.

Earlier, after a brief conversation with Coach, I had walked silently out of the locker room through a kaleidoscope of tattooed biceps and body parts. As I walked outside toward my truck in the parking lot, the clouds dissipated and the sun came down from a dirty sky.

During my drive back to Atlanta, I kept telling myself that what Barrett had told me could not be true. I thought of calling my mother on my cell phone during the drive, confronting her with the story, but decided I needed to wait until I could stand face-to-face with her, read her eyes to see if she was being honest with me.

But what if she wasn't?

What if she tried to lie to me? Or tell me

she didn't know what Barrett was talking about, that my father was dead and this was just Barrett's way of coming between the two of us.

I pulled the keys from the ignition and dragged myself from the car, walking up the stairs and using my key to open the door. I opened it cautiously, trying not to make a sound.

Once inside, I called out to my mother. When no answer came, I walked in and closed the door behind me.

I walked through the living room, then into the dining room, stopping at the table, resting my hand on back of one of the chairs. I remembered all the holiday dinners we would have there together, just me and my mother. Sometimes Kellis, Ramon, or Lowell would drop by after dinner for desserts and eggnog.

I remembered one Christmas when I was eight years old, sitting here and asking my mother why I didn't have a father like Ramon.

My mother would always avoid the question, putting me off by saying things like "Why, I'm not good enough for you?" or "All you'll ever need is me, baby."

I stepped back from the dining room table, making my way through the house again. I went into the study, where my mother did her reading, had her favorite chair, and shelves loaded with her favorite books.

On those shelves were also photos of me and my mother. I lifted one, an old framed snapshot of me in a Pee Wee league uniform. Staring at the photo of me with a huge smile on my face and holding a football, I remembered how happy I was that day.

I set the old photo down and glanced at another, one of me and my mother. My mother was squeezing me tight, planting a kiss on my cheek as I laughed and squirmed in her embrace. I felt a smile try to come to my face now, like it usually did when I saw this picture, but this time the smile did not surface.

My mother had deceived me. She'd lied to me.

But how did I know that? There was no proof. There was only what Barrett said. I reminded myself that I had only known Barrett for three months, but I also believed she had no reason to lie to me.

I turned and left the room, shaking my head, trying to rid myself of my negative thoughts. It wasn't fair to my mother, who had loved me as much as any mother could love her child. I felt ashamed of myself for already convicting her without giving her a chance to deny it. I needed to stop myself from doing that.

I ran up to my old bedroom, threw myself onto the bed, grabbed my pillow, covered my face with it, wrapped both my arms around it, and squeezed, trying to stop the thoughts from entering.

But I couldn't.

I ripped the pillow from my face, slung it across the room, where it hit the frame of the door and landed on the floor just in front of my mother's feet.

She was standing there, looking at me oddly. I wasn't sure for just how long she had been there.

"Is there something wrong?" she asked. "What are you doing home?"

"Coach let me off. I had some things to work out," I said as I got up from the bed and gave my mother a half-hug.

She looked at me like she knew there was something heavy on my mind.

She pushed me back from her and looked deep in my eyes and said, "Brady, what's wrong?"

"Mom, I need to ask you something and I need you to tell me the truth," I said, my voice cracking with emotion.

"Baby, I always tell you the truth."

"Even if it means telling me the real story

about my father?" I asked as I eyed my mother with suspicion.

My mother looked numb. She was shocked that I had asked her such a thing.

"Let's go downstairs to the kitchen. You look like you need something to drink," she said.

I nodded, and we walked downstairs in silence. When we reached the kitchen, my mother pulled out two bottles of water from the refrigerator and gave one to me.

"Tell me what's the matter, baby, you've got me really worried," my mother said.

"Is my father really dead?" I asked.

There was a long silence, and my mother seemed to have trouble forming her words. "I don't know, Brady," she finally said. "Why are you asking me questions like this?"

"What do you mean you don't know? Either he's dead or he's not," I said very slowly, trying not to raise my voice.

"Can you answer my question first?" my mother demanded.

"Somebody told me my father might be alive. They told me that you went to the University of Texas. Is that true, Mom?"

"Who is this somebody? Who told you that?" my mother asked.

I wanted to tell her to stop asking me questions and just tell me the damn truth. "Barrett told me," I said.

"Barrett? What does that girl know about me or my life?"

"So it's true?"

"Yes, Brady, I went to Texas my freshman year," Mom said.

"Why didn't you tell me that?"

"It wasn't important, Brady. I was only there less than a year."

"So my dad could be alive?"

"I don't know, Brady," she said, looking away from me like she was searching for answers and avoiding my eyes.

"You told me he was dead," I said. "What's the truth?"

"Brady, baby, I've lied all these years because I don't know who your father is," my mother said. She looked away and took her index finger to dab at her watering eyes.

"What do you mean you don't know who he is? You told me he was killed in an accident on the way to the hospital when I was born. What kind of woman are you to do this to me?" I said. My heart was beating fast, adrenaline was flowing like a sprinter on the verge of winning a race, and yet it felt like something was collapsing inside me.

"Brady, let's go into the dining room and talk. Let me explain," my mother said, her eyes pleading with me to understand.

"Explain what? How you lied to me all my life? Told me my father was dead and now you tell me you don't know who he is? Why should I believe you? Why should I listen to anything you have to say?"

My mother took a long gulp of water, looking as though she was trying to sort this all out in her head. "Brady, I need to take a nap. Can we talk about this later?"

"We don't have to ever talk about it," I said as tears started to stab at my eyes.

"Brady, come back," my mother screamed. She rushed toward me and tried to hold me, but I pulled away.

"I'm going back to school."

"Brady, talk to me, baby," she cried.

But now it was me who couldn't look at her, and so I bolted for the back door and raced for my truck.

CHAPTER 26
BARRETT'S BALLET

Dear Diary,

If Paris Hilton ever decides to do a sequel to that little sex tape of hers, the bitch needs to come and take a master class from me.

Brady came to see me after he returned from seeing his mother. When I opened the door, he stood there, his eyes red-rimmed and his body slumped over as if he carried a dead body the size of himself on his shoulders. His eyes were blank. Without a word, he dragged into my apartment and collapsed onto the couch.

When I took his hand and asked what happened, it took him a moment to look at me. He told me I was right and that his mother wasn't perfect like he thought she was all these years and that maybe she was just too good to be true. Then tears fell down the length of his face. When I brushed them away, I was surprised at how warm they felt.

I didn't expect the lump that filled my throat and the ache that grabbed my heart. I knew Brady was in a lot of pain and there was nothing I could do to soothe it. I had to once again remind myself that this is business. Any feelings had to be put on hold.

When Brady stopped crying and used his sleeve to wipe his face, I told him to take off his shirt and offered to get him a warm towel. Brady didn't say a word. He just stood up in front of the couch and removed his pullover with one swoop. His upper body glistened with sweat.

When I returned with the towel, I couldn't help but admire his six-pack abs and broad shoulders. Despite his grief, Brady was oozing masculinity and the alluring smell of sexual promise that young men have without knowing it.

I wrapped my arms around him, and when he responded by squeezing me tighter than I'd ever been held before, I closed my eyes, knowing now was the time.

Pressing into him, I held Brady like a baby, letting him release his emotions into my chest. After a little while I began to plant delicate, wet kisses on his flat stomach and then up toward his chest, shoulders, and finally his lips. My tongue met his, gently at first, but then he started kissing me hungrily.

I told him to stand up, and he obeyed and stood directly in front of me, and I took my hands and touched his already stiff manhood through his sweatpants. I was cautious, remembering the times he had pushed me away. But this time was different, and I became aggressive with my strokes.

Brady's eyes seemed to track my every move like he was a wild animal. I slipped his sweats from his waist, removed his boxer briefs, and took his full manhood into my hands. It was so big and beautiful.

When he whispered he needed me, I reached up and placed my finger over his lips and then I kissed the head of his manhood. I took it whole into my mouth. Brady's sigh was full of pleasure, and I was afraid he'd explode before I could take it out.

I knew the rolling movement of my tongue gave Brady a sensation that was beyond his belief, and I could almost feel every muscle in his body quivering. Then suddenly I stopped.

I took his hand and led him toward my

bedroom. The seduction I had originally planned included candles, new lingerie, and perfume, but my maroon silk pajamas and pink thong underwear would have to do.

Inside my bedroom, I leaned into him and pushed him playfully onto the bed and spoke the words he needed to hear: "I'm going to make everything better," I said softly.

I removed my pajama top and his eyes admired my beautiful, firm breasts. He told me how beautiful I was as I dropped my pajama bottoms and climbed on top of him. When I put my arms around his neck, he took one of my breasts into his mouth and sucked it like it was fresh fruit. I felt his snake of a dick flop against my thigh, totally hard, and felt the taste of his mouth, the touch of his hands.

He positioned himself on top of me and pressed his body into mine. When we kissed, I turned so that I was on top. I needed total control, and I saw surrender in his face. His eyes told me that he wanted me more than words could ever say. Holding his stare, I slid onto him and relished the sound of his moan. Slowly, I began to move in a circular motion, staring at him and controlling him with my eyes and hips.

His moans became whimpers, and I rode him faster and deeper until suddenly I felt a piercing jolt of warmth as he screamed out, "Barrett, Barrett. Oh, my God!"

I wanted to tell him the good Lord couldn't help him now.

That stupid little boy didn't even ask for a condom.

Got him.

Game over.

Time to move on and collect my prize.

CHAPTER 27
CARMYN'S ORANGE CRUSH

Around 5:30 a.m., I was awakened from a restless sleep. The first thing I did was call Brady, but my call went straight to his voice mail. I wondered if he had slept at all and when I would see him.

Over my black coffee I felt like a wreck, as memories of the conversation the night before played over and over in my head. As I got up for a second cup of coffee, I was suddenly back in Houston, walking down the hallways of Jack Yates High School. In my mind's eye I saw him, Woodson Crutchfield, dressed in all white, which made his ebony-smooth skin look even better. He looked like a black prince when he flashed a smile of bright white teeth that could put a set of the finest bone china to shame.

I was a sophomore in high school when I first met Woodson, and my mother and father didn't like the fact that he was a senior. They also weren't fond of the fact that he had dropped his steady girlfriend, Daphne, to date me. Throughout our first years of dating, my very strict minister father and mother watched us like wardens in a maximum-security facility, but when I entered the University of Texas all bets were off: I lost my virginity to Woodson the first night I spent on campus. My first time was kind of painful, but by the end of September I was pushing Woodson for sex. I loved Woodson and I loved sex. It was like a drug, and I would neglect anything in my life that didn't have to do with Woodson or sex. I rarely went to class, and I wouldn't miss a football game or a party for all the money in Oprah's bank account.

Woodson loved me deeply, but all that changed after a night that has lived inside my memory like a ghost. And I realize how the aftermath of that night has also haunted the one person I promised never to disappoint: Brady.

I tried to reach Brady again before I went to the shop, and all I got was his voice mail. I called his apartment. After a few rings, Delmar answered the phone.

"Yo, thanks for callin' the house of beauty, speaking to Cutey."

"Good morning, is this Delmar? Has

Brady left for class yet?"

"Yo, what's good, Ms. B? Let me check his room," Delmar said.

A few moments later, he came back and said, "I don't know what's up, Ms. B, but Brady ain't here. It looks like his bed hasn't been slept in."

"Are you sure, Delmar? Brady always makes up his bed," I said, trying not to think the worst. Had Brady had an accident or something?

"He just makes up his bed when he knows you're coming," Delmar said, laughing.

"Okay, Delmar, please tell him to call me. I'm worried," I said.

"Aw, don't be worried. I bet Brady is with ole girl," Delmar said.

I started to ask him who ole girl was, but I knew, so I just ended the conversation by saying, "Have a good day, Delmar."

"You too, Ms. B."

When I hung up, I tried Brady's cell phone again without success. Then I called Lowell, and when he answered I started crying.

"Carmyn, calm down. What's going on?"

"That girl told him. How did she find out? You didn't tell anyone, did you?"

"Carmyn, now come on. Who would I tell? I don't know Barrett like that. Besides, I would never betray you," Lowell said.

"Are you sure?"

"I should be pissed off at you for even thinking that, but I know you're upset. What did Brady say?"

"I don't really remember. All I know is he's really upset with me. He rushed out of the house, and I haven't been able to reach him since," I said.

"Have you called him?"

"Like a stalker. I even had Delmar check his room. He said Brady didn't come home last night. I know he's with that little tramp. I still can't figure out who told her."

"I'm the only one you've told?" Lowell asked.

"Yes."

"I don't think she knows where I live, so she couldn't have been at the door listening to our conversation," Lowell said.

"Right now I'm not real concerned about her. I'm just worried about my baby. Will you go up to the football complex this afternoon and make him call me?" I asked.

"What time does he practice?"

"Around three P.M., but Brady always gets there around two-thirty."

"I can do that. You need to stop worrying. Carmyn, everything will be just fine."

"Thanks, Lowell. I pray to God you're right."

A little after 2:30 p.m. Kai walked into my office carrying a blow dryer. I hadn't been able to work all day. I just played solitaire at my computer and listened to my iPod. George Benson's "This Masquerade" played over and over again, and finally I realized that that song described my life the last twenty years. My tears would not stop falling.

"Ms. B, there's a lady out front to see you," she said.

"Who is it, Kai?"

"Some white girl who says she was a skin-care saleswoman and that she'd talked to you about carrying her line in the shop," Kai said.

I raised my eyebrows and vaguely recalled talking to someone about a new line of makeup developed for African American women and told her to bring by some samples. My cell phone rang as I walked to the door, and it was Lowell.

"Kai, tell her I will be out in a few minutes. I need to take this call. Hey, Lowell," I said.

"Carmyn. Hold on a second," he said as he passed the phone to my son. "Hello." It was Brady. My stomach suddenly filled with nervous energy. "Brady, where have you been?" I asked.

"I been here," he said.

"Why haven't you returned my calls?"

"I don't feel like talking. I have a lot on my mind," Brady said.

"I just want to make sure you're all right. I was worried you might have had a wreck or something."

"I'm cool," Brady said. He didn't sound like my son.

"When can we talk?"

"I don't know. I just need to sort things out."

"I understand. Maybe we can talk in Fayetteville," I suggested.

"Mom, I don't want to talk before or after the game," Brady said.

"But I'm going to be there, and we have to talk sooner or later," I said.

"I don't think you should come to the game."

"What? Brady, I never miss your games," I said. Tears were forming in the corner of my eyes again.

"Things are different now. Please don't come to Arkansas. I got to go. Practice is getting ready to start."

The next voice I heard was Lowell's. He asked me if I was all right.

"Are you sure that was my son?"

"Yes, even though it didn't sound like him. Even his body language was different," Lowell said.

"What am I going to do?" I cried.

"Stop crying, Carmyn, please."

But my tears wouldn't stop.

CHAPTER 28
BRADY GETS HOG TIED

Another Saturday arrived. Game day. I walked through the tunnel with Delmar at my side and my other teammates crowded around me, but I felt so alone.

As we neared the exit, I heard the roar of the crowd; I kept telling myself to put the stuff with my mother out of my head so it wouldn't mess with my game. But I couldn't seem to do it. I thought about how my mother had lied to me and if Barrett hadn't been there for me I might not have made it to the game.

Coming out from the tunnel, my entire team started to yell, trying to get hyped for the game as we ran out onto the vast and beautiful green field for pregame warm-ups.

It was a perfect November day for football. The sky was a deep blue canvas; it looked like one of Chloe's paintings had come to life. The air wasn't cold, just brisk, but a nervous chill ran through my entire body as me and my team took our place on the side-lines.

We looked up into the stands and there seemed to be nothing but a deep sea of frenzied Razorbacks fans, all wearing red, shouting, screaming, and pumping their red pom-poms in unison.

This would be one of our hardest games of the season. The Razorbacks were undefeated in conference play and ranked in the top five in the country. But I knew that a week ago and I wasn't worried; I never worried, because I always knew my mother would be up in the stands supporting me. Going back to Pee Wee football, in all the games I've played, if I ever got nervous or ever made a mistake, my mom always had my back and all I had to do was look up in the stands. She would be looking down on the field telling me with her gentle smile to calm down, mouthing to me that everything would be just fine. But now — I scanned the stands again, hoping that I would spot her, even though I knew she wasn't there.

My team started hitting shoulder pads, banging helmets together, getting themselves psyched for the game. We started our calisthenics and my body felt unusually tight.

"Yo, B, you ready for this or what!" yelled

Reggie, one of my offensive linemen.

I yelled back, "You know I am!" But I didn't believe myself. He slammed the flats of his fists down hard on my shoulder pads, almost knocking me to the grass.

"Yeah, boy!" he yelled, then started yelling at another player.

I felt lost all of a sudden. I looked up one last time — no sign of my mother. I glanced back toward the tunnel leading to the lockers. The thought of turning back there darted through my mind. I felt queasy all of a sudden. Not since my first Pee Wee game had I felt like this. I didn't know what was happening.

"Brady," someone said, grabbing me, spinning me around. It was Delmar. "You all right, bay-bee?"

"Yeah."

"You sure? You look like you about to fall out. This is a big game and I want you in there, but if you ain't right, you know I'll run the rock for you. I got your back."

"I'm straight, D," I said, trying to find the strength I needed to convince not only him but myself.

"All right, then, fool! Let's go out there and whoop some Razorback ass!"

"Jags on three," I shouted.

"One . . . two . . . three . . . Jags," my teammates shouted.

All my teammates roared around me as we took off, running onto the field, chasing our cheerleaders, and pumping our fists at the 3,000 CGU fans located at the ten-yard line. The sounds of boos from the Razorback fans were thunderous. I didn't think I'd ever been in a stadium where it was so loud.

I walked to midfield with the other two captains for the coin toss. I called heads, and when it landed on tails, Arkansas captains Jamal Anderson and Chris Houston chose to defend the north end zone and kick off to us. I was ready to get it on.

Arkansas kicked it out of the end zone, so we started on the twenty. As the kicking team came off the field, I tapped Delmar on his backside and said, "Let's do this, D."

As I got into my stance, I glanced over at the Jaguar fans and felt sick again because I knew my mother wasn't there. She had never missed one of my games. We wouldn't get to talk about how loud Razorback Stadium was or what a beautiful place it was. She wouldn't be able to tell me about how the popcorn, turkey legs, or hot dogs were. I had been very clear about not wanting her to come to the game, but just before the first play I suddenly wished I hadn't been so tough. This loneliness was my fault, because I had told my mother to stay away. I took a final glance into the stands, but I knew she would respect my wishes.

Blaine West, the quarterback, handed the ball to me and I looked for the hole. There wasn't one, and I was tackled by Jamal Anderson for a two-yard loss. The crowd roared even louder.

Back in the huddle, Blaine pointed out that Arkansas had eight defensive players in the box, a formation designed to stop the run. He looked at me and said, "I guess they heard about you, Brady. I'm going to throw."

"It's whatever, dude, let's just move the ball," I said.

On second down Blaine threw an incomplete pass, so Coach called an I-left twenty-eight toss on third down. I got the ball on the toss and again I was surrounded by cardinal jerseys with *Arkansas* stretched across the chest. Just as I felt myself being pulled from behind, the ball came out of my grasp and rolled behind me. I tried to recover it, but the Razorbacks surrounded the ball like it was hog slop. Arkansas defensive end Marcus Harrison recovered on our eleven. I walked dejectedly to the sideline. I had not fumbled since my sophomore year.

Arkansas running back Felix Jones scored a touchdown after two plays and we were down 7–0. We got the ball back on the twenty, my number was called again, and I gained five tough yards following the left tackle. The second play, Blaine passed short for three yards. It was third down and two and again my number was called. I was determined to find a hole and outrun the Arkansas defense, but again something didn't feel right and the Razorbacks' safety, Michael Grant, stripped the ball from me for a second turnover. This was a nightmare and I had to wake up.

As I walked toward our sideline, Delmar came up to me and hit his helmet against mine. "What's up, B? Are you all right?"

"I'm cool. You just need to block that dude wearing number fifty-two," I said as I took my helmet off. When I reached the sideline, Coach Hale came running toward me shouting, "Come on, Bledsoe. What the fuck is going on? Get your head out of your ass!"

Another first and it wasn't even halftime. Coach Hale had never cursed at me.

As the game went on, things went from bad to worse. Our dreams for an undefeated season were spoiled by an inspired Arkansas team as we lost 31–3. Hog running back Darren McFadden, also a Heisman candidate, riddled our defense by running for 231 yards. Good-bye, SEC Championship game.

Good-bye, Heisman Trophy. I couldn't do anything right, and Coach benched me in the fourth quarter after I had gained only 22 yards. If it hadn't been for freshman running back Koi Minter, we would have been shut out. He gained 63 yards in the fourth quarter alone against Arkansas's second-team defense.

I sat in the visitors' dressing room with just my Under Armour bottoms on and cried like a baby who needed his mommy. But I was too stubborn to make that happen.

CHAPTER 29
BARRETT'S BABY

Barrett had just finished a blunt and a naked shot of vodka when her cell rang. She looked at the number and heaved a sigh of disgust. It was her mother.

"Hello."

"I need more money," Lita said without even a simple greeting.

"What?"

"You heard me. I need more money!"

"For what?"

"I don't need to tell you how I spend my money. Just tell your business guy to send me at least a thousand dollars more," she said.

"I'm not going to do that until I know that you're using the money I give you to take care of Wade and not for alcohol or drugs," Barrett said.

"Well, I can't wait for you to do your little research. I need that money and I need it now. Don't act a fool with me, girl. Sometimes I don't think you got the sense that God gave a dog, but you think you're so damn smart."

"Are you going to use it to gamble?"

"Naw."

"Drugs. Are you using again?"

"Why in the hell are you asking me all these questions?"

"I got to go. I don't have to take this shit from you," Barrett said. The liquor had given her a dose of courage.

"Don't you talk to me like that, you no-'count bitch," Lita said.

" 'Bye, woman," Barrett said.

"Don't you hang up on me, little girl. I will tell you when this conversation is over," Lita said.

"If you don't stop talking to me like this, I can certainly make sure you don't get any more money," Barrett said.

"Yeah, you do that and I will be down at that basketball boy's place and I'll bring him to your ass. Not only will you get a good ass whupping but you and your friend will spend some time in jail. I'm not as stupid as you think. So don't mess with me," Lita said.

"Don't you dare," Barrett said.

"Then just try me. *Now,* this conversation is over, Raquel," Lita said and she clicked off the phone.

Dear Diary:

One of the things that I've learned from Brady is that it's easy and natural for boys to love their mothers unconditionally. If I ever have a baby boy with Nico, will the hatred I have in my heart for Lita prevent him from loving me the way Brady loves his mother?

I wonder.

I don't hate Lita because she's a whore and was a lousy mother to me. I hate her because of what her addictions did to Wade.

My baby brother was born with Fetal Alcohol Syndrome and it has haunted him his entire life. He won't get to play football or date beautiful girls like his big sister. Wade's almost twelve years old, and still can't read. Can't really communicate. He'll never have friends. He didn't ask to be born this way.

Would Wade still love Lita if he knew what she did to him?

I don't think so.

Chapter 30
Carmyn's Texas Tears

It's raining. But that's not the reason I can't seem to get out of my bed. I'm so depressed that I called both of my salons and told the assistant managers I wouldn't be in because I wasn't feeling well. Of course, the truth was I couldn't bear to face anybody. Not just yet.

There would be questions about why Brady had played so poorly on Saturday, and I didn't have the answers. While watching the game on television, I started several times to get on the first thing smoking and go comfort my baby. But Brady made it perfectly clear he didn't want me in Arkansas.

I just lay in bed with the television on mute, gazing at Martha Stewart and Patti LaBelle cooking and acting like they were best friends.

I turned my face into the pillows, and my mind wandered back to Texas and Woodson as a helpless sadness covered me. I couldn't stop thinking about that night, and I felt like I needed to get professional help to be released from my bad dreams and real-life memories.

I remembered the form-fitting red dress I wore and the string of pearls my parents had bought me for my debutante ball. Woodson and I had made love right before we left for the party, and I was so proud walking into the Renaissance Hotel on his arm. It was close to Christmas and the hotel had lights that adorned the entryway, twinkling and welcoming us and the season.

We walked into a beautifully decorated two-bedroom suite where there were only two other women and about fifteen young men. Woodson greeted a couple of his teammates before he turned to three young men who lingered by a huge window that overlooked the state capitol.

During the drive to the hotel, Woodson had told me how this was the most important recruiting weekend in Texas Longhorns history. As team captain, it was crucial for him that everything went well. Seven of the top ten players in the country were visiting Austin, they needed to make a good impression on them, and he needed my help. When I asked him what he wanted me to do, he simply said, "Just be nice to them, Carmyn."

As the evening wore on, some of the high school boys looked at me as if they were lions and I was a tasty piece of meat. I wanted to leave, but instead I had a couple of drinks to relax and even took a couple of puffs of a joint — something I'd never done. I remember a glass of a creamy brown liquid that tasted like a milk shake and how I sipped it and felt the muscles in my shoulders relax as I fell back into the sofa and its feather-filled pillows. I held court with the handsome young men and listened to their dirty jokes and stories of off-the-field exploits with girls just like me. I laughed at every one of them, sipping and puffing like I did this every day.

Woodson smiled and winked at me, then went out the front door. When I asked one of his teammates where he was going, he told me Woodson was making a liquor run and poured me another drink. It tasted different and I told him I shouldn't mix my liquor, but he smiled and told me everything would be okay. And that is where my memory ends.

The next morning, I woke up nude in the hotel suite, Woodson staring down at me. The most disgusted look I'd ever seen in my short life was on the face of the man I loved.

That was the start of the worst day of my life.

Now here I was twenty years later, still paralyzed by that night. By not telling Brady the truth, my life once again became a nightmare.

For three days I'd been wearing the same black silk pajamas, and all I'd eaten were smoked almonds and orange slices. Even Whitney Houston's *Greatest Hits* couldn't pull me out of my mood, so I knew I was going to have to do it myself.

I dragged myself out of bed and went to the kitchen to cook breakfast, but just before I reached the kitchen, I heard the doorbell ring. When I looked out the peephole, Sylvester was standing there holding flowers. I didn't feel like flowers or Sylvester.

I decided to ignore him and then heard Sylvester say, "Carmyn, if you don't answer the door, I'm going to call 911." The last thing I needed was EMS at my house, so I opened the door.

"Carmyn, I was so worried about you," Sylvester said as he tried to hug me.

"I haven't been feeling well," I mumbled pathetically, staring down at the dusty teak floor in my foyer. I looked a hot mess.

"What's the matter? Have you seen a doctor? Do you want me to take you to the emergency room?"

"I'll be fine," I said.

"I've been sending you text messages for days. Why haven't you answered them?" Sylvester asked.

"I turned my phone off," I said.

"Carmyn, I'm so happy you're okay, but please don't scare me like that again. I was afraid something bad had happened to you."

"Sorry, Sylvester," I said. "I've just had a tough couple of days."

He came close to me and put his hands around my waist, but I pushed him back.

"You know I care about you," he said.

I lowered my chin, shook my head in shame, and said, "Not if you knew what I did."

"What are you talking about?"

After a heavy silence, I said, "I've been living a lie and now it's come back to haunt me."

"What's going on? Does it have to do with Brady? I noticed he didn't play well on Saturday. I always check out his statistics on my computer," he said.

That surprised me, because Sylvester didn't strike me as the computer type.

"I know, and it's my fault entirely," I said as tears began to spill down my face.

"Let's sit down, and tell me what happened."

We sat at my dining room table, where the easy flow of tears continued and I struggled for the right words.

I told Sylvester about Woodson, that awful night, and how he treated me the next morning. I told him about the letter Woodson wrote to me and that I'd kept it all these years like some form of punishment. I also told him how my parents reacted and that I felt I needed to protect Brady from their judgment.

"Carmyn, time has passed. This guy might not feel the same. He was a young guy, and sometimes they make rash decisions. It sounds like it's just as much his fault as it was yours."

"He had every right to be upset with me. I mean, who wants a slut for a girlfriend, especially when the whole campus knows what happened?" I said.

"You're not a slut. Anyone who meets you can tell what kind of woman you are. Besides, he's the one who left you in the room with those guys. And even if it's true, it's only one night of your life, Carmyn."

"I should have known better. I wasn't raised that way," I said.

"Have you ever tried to get in contact

with him?"

"No. Why?"

"To tell him he has a son."

"Sylvester, don't you hear me? I'm not certain that Woodson is Brady's father. It could be any of those guys," I said as shame covered me again.

"You think he's still in Texas?"

"I don't know. When my parents made me leave Texas, I promised myself I would never return."

"If he continued to play sports, he could be found easily. I bet you could also get a list of names of the guys who were there for the recruiting trip that weekend. The university has to keep that type of information."

"Why would I do that?"

"So that you can find out once and for all who Brady's father is. He has every right to know."

"I don't know," I said sadly.

Sylvester took my hands, looked me straight in the eyes, and said, "Don't you want your son back?"

"Of course I do."

"Then you have to find his father."

"How am I going to do that? I would need to find every guy who was in that hotel suite that night."

"I can help," Sylvester said.

"How are you going to do that? I mean, you work all the time."

"I know people," he said confidently.

"What people? What are you talking about?" I asked, wondering how an hourly worker could help me with all the expense and time it was going to take to find Brady's father.

"Look, Carmyn, I haven't been totally honest with you."

"What?"

"There are some things about me that I haven't shared," he said as he looked away.

"Are you going to tell me? I've just told you the biggest secret in my life."

Before Sylvester could answer, a female voice called my name. It was Kellis. She walked into the kitchen and looked shocked at seeing me there with my nightclothes on and Sylvester holding my hands.

"I used the key you gave me. Is everything okay?"

"Hey, Kellis. I'm sorry I haven't called you back," I said.

"Yeah, I understand. Looks like we've been busy," she said in a teasing voice.

"This is Sylvester," I said.

"And I was just leaving," he said as he got up. He extended his hand toward Kellis and said, "Nice to meet you."

"Likewise, I'm sure," Kellis said.

"Carmyn, I'll call you later. Promise me you'll take care of yourself," he said in a voice full of concern.

"I will. Thank you."

Sylvester walked out of the kitchen and down the hallway. Kellis sat down with a smirk on her face and said, "So, Carmyn, what have you been keeping from me?"

"Nothing really," I said. "He's just a friend."

"Yeah, right. So this is why you don't have time to meet any of my friends. Looks like you're doing fine all by yourself. He's real handsome. He looks like someone I saw in a magazine or something. Is he a model?"

"No, he works as a clerk at the Croissant Corner," I said.

"A what?"

"A clerk, and before you say anything, please don't." I didn't need Kellis judging Sylvester.

"Who, me? Honey, if he's rocking your boat, then that's all that matters. But he just looks familiar."

"Maybe you saw him at the Croissant Corner," I said.

"I don't ever go in that place unless I'm with you, but I'll figure it out. Is he married?"

"No, I don't think so."

"You mean you didn't check? Honey, I get the social security number of every man I meet and run a credit and background check before I get serious about him," Kellis said.

"It's not that serious," I said.

"Looks that way to me."

"Trust me, it's not."

"So where have you been? I've called and called. Is everything okay?"

"How much time do you have?"

"I ain't got nothing but time," Kellis said.

"Then let me put on a pot of coffee and make you some breakfast. I got a story to tell you."

CHAPTER 31
BRADY'S BATON ROUGE BEAT DOWN

Don't you think you're being pretty tough on your mother?" Lowell asked.

"I don't know, what do you think? She's lied to me my entire life," I said. I didn't want to sound sarcastic or ungrateful. I was halfway through a double cheeseburger Lowell had cooked for me after practice. I knew he had invited me over so that we could discuss my current relationship with my mother, but I just didn't want to talk about it. Right now my main concern was getting my football mojo back after running for only fifty-five yards against LSU. The second straight game where I'd failed to run for a hundred yards and we'd lost.

It was one of those November evenings that was neither hot nor cold. Lowell and I sat on his deck with only long-sleeved T-shirts on. If my mom was here she would tell me to put on a jacket.

"Have you sat down and tried to find out

why she decided not to tell you? She's had a really hard time," Lowell said.

I took another bite of my burger and said, "Lowell, I know you mean well, but I have to work this out by myself. I got other things on my plate."

"Like what?"

"You've heard how badly I've been playing the last two weeks. We only have three games left, not counting a bowl game, and I got to get back on track and help my team."

"What do you think the problem is?"

"I don't know. Well, yeah, I do. The stuff with my mom and then trying to keep up with Barrett," I said.

"How's that going?"

"I'm a goner. So sprung," I said.

"What is 'sprung'?"

"It means I'm in love. Real talk," I said.

"How do you think she found out that information about your father?"

"Does it matter?"

"Yeah, it does. Your mom only shared that with me, and I didn't tell anyone," Lowell said.

"Would you have told me?"

"That's not my place, Brady."

"Do you think I should try and find my father?"

"Do you want to?"

"I've wanted a dad my whole life," I said.

"I understand that, but be careful what you pray for," Lowell warned.

"I got something to tell you, but you can't say anything to my mom," I said.

"What is it?"

"You got to give me your word first."

"I don't know about that," Lowell said.

"But you would do it for my mom. What kind of crap is that? You're my godfather and you're supposed to have my back," I said.

"Is it something that puts your life in danger?" Lowell asked.

"No," I said quickly.

"Okay, so I won't say anything. What is it?"

I just held both of my hands up in front of Lowell's face.

"What?" he quizzed.

"Do you notice anything different?"

"Not really," Lowell said.

"Dude, come on, now. Work with me. No ring. I'm not claiming to be celibate anymore," I said.

"Oh shit. Carmyn ain't gonna like this," Lowell said.

"She don't need to know," I said.

"It won't be the first time you've kept something from her," Lowell said, eyeing me with a serious look on his face.

"Are you talking about Chloe?"

"Yes."

"You didn't tell her about that, did you?"

"I promised you I wouldn't, but that situation could have gotten out," Lowell said.

"Thanks for having my back on that," I said.

"What are you going to do when you two reconcile?"

"I don't know if that's gonna happen too soon if Mom doesn't accept Barrett," I said. "I think I'm going to ask Barrett to marry me when the season is over."

"Brady, get over yourself. You haven't known this girl for more than three months, and just because she gave you some pussy doesn't mean she'll make a good wife. Maybe your mother was right about her," Lowell said.

"My mother doesn't know Barrett," I said.

"And you do? Where is that 'real talk' you're always saying?"

"That's what's up."

"I guess you're saying the Brady your mother and me tried to raise is gone."

"Long gone, sir. I'm a different man now," I said.

"Brady, getting a piece of pussy doesn't make you a man. Did you talk to Delmar about the stripping thing?"

"Not yet."

"Why not?"

"I don't know, I'm still trying to figure that out. If it's true, I don't know if he wants to talk about it. Besides, I've been spending most of my time with Barrett, so we haven't been talking as much," I said.

"Okay, but he's your friend. You can't forget about everybody and everything just because you got a girlfriend," Lowell said.

"I've lived my entire life to please my mother and she kept from me the one thing she knew I wanted. Now it's about Brady," I said as I beat my chest.

"I don't believe that, and you don't either," Lowell said.

"I'm telling you, man, I ain't the boy I used to be. That Brady is gone," I said as I took a last bite of my burger.

"Well, just let me know when the old Brady comes back," Lowell said.

CHAPTER 32
BARRETT'S WHIP APPEAL

Brady fell back on the pillow exhausted, slightly bewildered, and limp. Barrett had just served up some after-practice sex and was getting ready to work Brady over once and for all. A John Legend CD played softly in the background, and Barrett smiled mischievously. "That was amazing, girl. I could stay in bed with you twenty-four/seven," Brady said.

Barrett just smiled and said, "I bet you say that to all the girls."

"You know that's not true," Brady said.

"I know," Barrett said as she leaned over and gave him a kiss on the cheek, using the sheets to cover her breasts.

"What was that for?" Brady asked.

"Because you're so good," Barrett purred.

"Am I really?"

"Yes. How was practice?"

"It was okay," Brady said.

"Are you going to be ready for Georgia?

That's an important game,"

Barrett said. "Yeah, we got to win if we want to go to a bowl game. It would be a shame if we seniors never made it to one," Brady said, a look of concern covering his face.

"You will do just fine and then get ready for the next phase of your life," Barrett said.

"What phase?"

"The NFL, dummy."

"The way I've been playing lately, I don't know if the NFL is still interested," Brady said.

"Don't be silly. Of course they want you. Didn't you get invited to the combine?"

"Yeah," Brady said.

"Then you'll get the chance to show them what you can do. But you got to be ready," Barrett said.

"True. True."

"I know how I can help," Barrett said.

"By making love to me like we just did," Brady said as he moved closer to Barrett.

"I think my dad can get you in with The Thoroughbreds training company if you sign a three-month contract," Barrett said.

Brady leaped up from the pillow and screamed, "Could he really do that? Could he get me in?"

"Now calm down, but I was telling him

about you, and since he is a charter member he mentioned he thought he could get you in."

"Oh, Barrett, that would be so cool. It means I could work out close to home," Brady said.

"Well, don't thank me yet. But my daddy usually gets me what I want," Barrett said.

"What would I do without you?" Brady asked.

"Just make sure you never have to find out," Barrett said. Then she kissed him so deeply, it felt as though she were tickling his tonsils and toes at the same time.

CHAPTER 33
CARMYN TAKES A STEP

Today I had an amazing breakthrough, thanks to one of my loyal clients, Angel Beasley. As I was applying color to her hair, she turned to me and said, "Carmyn, I can feel the stress coming from your body. I need to pray for you."

Angel got out of the chair right then, grabbed my hand and pulled me to my knees, and prayed for me. It was a powerful prayer, and I bawled my eyes out. When she got ready to leave, she told me about a secret place that gave her peace. I asked Zander to take my 4:00 appointment so I could go right then.

I followed Angel's directions and found myself in the Ainsley Park area of Atlanta. I got out of my car and, under the shelter of a perfectly blue sky, I walked through a gate and into a maze of beautiful green shrubbery.

I was in the Labyrinth, a maze of shrubbery and a spiritual retreat where I could leave all my burdens so that I could begin to lead the life God had planned for me. A gentle wind swayed around me as I prayed to God to take all the things from my life that were causing me great pain.

I had given up that night in Austin when I allowed my youth to ruin my life. I forgave those young men who took advantage of the situation I presented them. I forgave Woodson for the hate-filled letter he left under my dorm-room door. As I walked through the Labyrinth, I forgave my parents for turning their backs on me when I needed them most. I forgave myself for the mistakes I had made, the lies I had told, and the people I'd hurt because I feared they would harm me. I told God I was ready for whatever He had for me and that I needed for him to return Brady back to my protective arms.

As I walked out of the meditation park, I felt my guilt and anger slowly lift like a wedding veil once the bride has made her vows.

CHAPTER 34
BUCKWILD BRADY

Barrett and I had just finished up a meal of mushroom ravioli at the Olive Garden when I felt her hands touch my stuff. It was beginning to thicken, and I suddenly wished I had worn boxers instead of the tight-fitting boxer briefs Barrett loved.

"Hey, girl, I'm not going to be able to get out of this booth," I said to her with a smile. Thanks to Barrett, I was transformed. I loved the fact that she wanted to make love as much as I did.

"I want you," she whispered into my ear. Her breath on my ear tickled me and increased the intensity in my boxer briefs.

"Wait until we get back to your place," I said.

"I don't know if I can do that," she said.

"Then I need to find that waiter," I said as I looked around the restaurant for our server. Suddenly, I saw Chloe walk into the restaurant with a potbellied guy who looked to be about fifty. It must have been her husband. Our eyes met for a quick second and I diverted mine back to Barrett. I felt a surge of guilt but quickly dismissed it.

"So what are you thinking about?" Barrett asked.

"Thinking about what we can do when we finish eating," I said.

"Brady, come on. We've already done it twice today," Barrett said.

"But they say that three times is the charm."

"For somebody who claimed to be a virgin, you sure do know your way around a woman's body," Barrett said, eyeing me with suspicion.

"Always been a fast learner," I said, and smiled.

Barrett reached into her purse and pulled out some papers.

"Here is the contract for training with The Thoroughbreds. I need to get it back right away so they won't give away your spot. I've read it. It's all pretty plain and simple. They agreed to help you improve on all your speed and other skills, and you agree to pay them once you sign with an agent," Barrett said.

"Okay, I still need to read it over, though. What happens if I don't get an agent or get drafted?" I said. When the season was over, I knew, the chances of that happening were slim to none, but my mom had always told me I could never take anything for granted.

"Now, we both know that's not going to happen. Just sign it and let me get it back. I told my father I would get it back to him tomorrow. Don't you trust me?" Barrett quizzed.

"Of course I trust you, but let me see it," I said as I took the three pages from Barrett. I scanned over the document and it looked like she was right. I took the pen she was holding, signed the last sheet of the contract, and handed it back to Barrett.

"Thank you very much, sir. Now, that wasn't so hard. So what's the first thing you're going to splurge on when you get your signing bonus?"

I started to tell Barrett a beautiful diamond ring for her, but instead I told her that I had everything I wanted.

"So you're going to be frugal? Why am I not surprised?"

"I used to think that I would buy my mom a new car or a house," I said sadly. It had been over two weeks since I talked to my mom. We'd never gone that long without talking. I missed my mother and our conversations, but she needed to be reminded of what she had taught me all my life: to be honest and truthful about everything. Which for me meant once we did start talking again I would tell her that I was no longer a virgin. I knew that wasn't going to make her happy.

"I hate that I came between you and your mother," Barrett said.

"It wasn't your fault. Where is that waiter?" I said. I noticed a tall black guy who looked like an athlete of some kind walking toward us.

"Sup, dude. Aren't you Brady Bledsoe?" he asked.

"Yeah, that's me. How you doing?" I asked.

"It's all good. Hey, dude, I was wondering if you'd sign this poster for my girl. I got a Sharpie," he said.

"Sure, dude. What's your name?"

"Erick Winston, but my girl's name is Amanda, so make it out to her. She's a big fan. And, man, don't let the fans and people from the sports boards get you down," Erick said.

"I don't read the sports boards or visit the chat rooms," I said.

"Good. Thanks to the Internet, everybody thinks they're a coach," Erick said. He told me he had walked on the football team at the University of Washington but had used up his eligibility and was now in law school at

CGU, where he'd met Amanda.

I signed the poster to Amanda and gave it back to Erick. I was getting ready to introduce Barrett to Erick, and when I looked over, she was reapplying her makeup. When she closed her compact, she looked up at Erick with a smile that suddenly turned into a frown.

"Hey, I know you. Bethany, right?"

"You must have me confused with someone else," Barrett said.

"Naw, I don't think so. Bethany Lewis. You used to go to the University of Washington for a minute, 'cause you dated one of my boyz, Chris Johns," Erick said. I looked at Barrett, and she didn't look happy.

"Chris Johns, the NBA player?" I asked.

"Yeah, that's him. He plays for the New Orleans Hornets now."

"My name is Barrett Manning and I don't know any Chris Johns," she said firmly.

"Well, girl, you got an evil twin and she ain't nice. She and some crooked agent swindled Chris out of over a million dollars of his signing bonus with some phony stock scam and then booked the hell out of town. Like, poof. Chris is still looking for her ass," Erick said.

"Dude, for real? That's wild, but I guess stuff like that happens all the time," I said.

"Brady, let's go," Barrett said as she suddenly pushed me out of the booth. I had never seen her so flustered.

"Are you all right?" I asked as I gently took her hand.

"Yes, let's go," she said.

I gave Erick a handshake and got up from the booth.

"Hey, dude, I didn't mean to upset your girl," Erick said.

"It's cool. You just made a mistake," I said.

I led Barrett by the hand and started out of the restaurant, when I heard Erick mumble, "Dude, for your sake I sho do hope so."

I walked into my apartment and Delmar was sitting on the couch with his hands down his boxers, wearing a wife beater, and drinking a beer.

"Should you be doing that during the week?" I asked.

"Is there a law against scratching my balls during the week?" Delmar quizzed.

"I'm talking about drinking that beer. Dude, this is a big game week," I said.

"Nigga, I'll be cool by game time, don't worry 'bout me."

"If you say so. You better hope Coach don't have us running sprints tomorrow."

"What are you doing here? You not spending the night with shawty?" Delmar asked.

"She wasn't feeling well," I said. I was thinking about how jumpy Barrett was as I drove her home.

"I know you be beating that pussy down. That's my boy. I knew you had it in you. All we had to do was get that monkey released," Delmar said as he slapped my hand.

"Hey, dude, I signed with The Thoroughbreds to train after the season is over," I said.

"Those dudes are off the chain. How did you pull that off?"

"Barrett's dad had the hookup and he got me in. Do you want me to try and get you in?"

"That would be sweet. I see Miss Nose in the Air is good for sumthin'."

"So where's Maybelline been?" I asked, changing the subject to something else.

"Don't ask me. I ain't her keeper," Delmar said.

"Are you inviting her to Senior Day?"

"Oh, hell naw," Delmar said.

"Dude, that's your mother," I said.

"B, she just gave birth to me."

"That's cold," I said. Even though my mother had disappointed me and I was still upset with her, I knew she had done more than give birth to me. In many ways, she had given up her life for me.

"That's real talk, fam," Delmar said as he got up and walked over to the computer. He hit a few keystrokes and then shouted, "Fans ain't shit."

"What you looking at?" I asked.

"Just looking at this shit the fans be writing on Jaguars Illustrated board, talking 'bout how we gonna lose the rest of our games, the coach ain't shit, you ain't shit, the team ain't shit. At the beginning of the season, all of these mofos had man-crushes on all us. Now they just hatin'."

"Why do you read that stuff?"

"I don't know, but sometimes I want to go on there and cuss out all their asses. They don't have a clue about how hard we work for this school, and we don't get shit, but maybe a tired-ass letter jacket."

"You have a scholarship," I said.

"What the fuck's that gonna do for me if I don't get no degree? We both know I'm going to be in big trouble if I don't play on Sunday," Delmar said. "I got to make it into the league and stay awhile."

"You can still get a degree."

"Yeah, right. If you believe that shit, I got a swimming pool in Alaska I want to sell you."

"So what are you going to do if you don't make it to the league or don't stay in that long?"

"I don't even want to think about that. I guess sell this body of mine." Delmar sighed. He sounded serious, and I took this as my opening to bring up what Lowell told me.

"You sure you're not doing that already?" I asked in my best non-judgmental voice.

Delmar took a swig of Gatorade and an expression of uneasiness crossed his face.

"What the fuck you talking 'bout, Bledsoe? You got sumthin' you want to say to me?"

"You know, I was talking to Low—"

Before I could finish, I heard Delmar's booming voice yell, "I knew that faggot couldn't keep his goddamn mouth shut. They like bitches, always gossiping."

"Look, D, don't disrespect my godfather," I commanded.

"What did he tell you?"

"You knew what you were doing?"

"Just 'cause I let a fag suck my dick don't make me one. I do it 'cause the paper's long. You know I'm not no faggot, B," Delmar said.

I was in shock. What was Delmar admitting to? I began searching frantically for the right words to say, but all that came out was "I know that, D," and I turned and went into my room.

CHAPTER 35
BARRETT'S READY TO ROLL AGAIN

Barrett was all packed and ready to leave when the doorbell rang. She thought it was her driver, so she didn't look through the peephole, just opened the door.

"How did you get up here?" Barrett asked when she saw Maybelline standing there puffing a cigarette.

"It seems that your little doorman is from New Orleans and we know some of the same people. Hmm, it looks like we're going on a trip," Maybelline said as she walked into the foyer of the condo.

"I didn't ask you to come in," Barrett said as she followed Maybelline closely.

"I don't need an invite from a tramp like you. We just got a little business to conduct and then you can be on your way."

"What kind of business?" Barrett quizzed.

"You're going to give me five thousand dollars," Maybelline said frankly.

"The hell I am," Barrett said.

"Okay, suit yourself. When I get through talking with your little make-believe boyfriend and tell him who and what you are, you'll think giving me what I asked for was the wise thing to do," Maybelline said.

"You don't know anything about Brady and me," Barrett protested.

"I know you're running a scam and he doesn't know how old you are. I know that."

"Get out of my house, you skanky bitch, or I'll call the police."

"Call 'em. I'm sure they will be just as interested to know where you live, just like that basketball player. You see, your mama, God bless her, told me everything. I saw her a couple of weeks ago when I went back to New Orleans to check on some things. After a few vodkas, Lita can't shut her trap. She told me she had even thought about telling that basketball player Chris where you were, but she didn't want to have blood on her hands in case he came here and killed your ass."

"Lita doesn't know anything about my life. She's just an old delusional drunk who's jealous of me because of my looks. No one will believe anything she has to say," Barrett said.

"I believe her. Now, let's talk about that five thousand dollars, and don't even think about giving me a check. May-Jean wouldn't take a check from Oprah, so you know what I think about any piece of paper with your name on it. Damn, you don't even remember what your real name is." Maybelline produced a pack of cigarettes and lifted one out.

"I should slap your face," Barrett said.

"Come on, bitch. You feelin' frisky? Slap me, but let me warn you, stitches might not look good on that pretty little face."

"You better be glad I know it's against the law to hit old people. I'll need some time to get the money," Barrett said.

"You got twenty-four hours. Meet me this time tomorrow at the pancake house near the campus. And please don't keep a lady waiting. Or else I might have to make a few calls back to New Orleans myself," Maybelline said, looking down at Barrett before walking out.

After Maybelline left, Barrett rushed to the kitchen and was happy she'd left a bottle of wine in the fridge. She poured herself a glass and then called Nico. When he didn't answer, Barrett left a message telling him that she had accomplished what she'd been sent to do and was ready to come home.

Barrett paced nervously in her living room. She had tried to get in contact with Nico several times on his cell phone, without success. Barrett didn't want to call his home, because she knew his wife hardly ever left there. I mean, why would she leave her huge mansion when she had a staff to provide her every need? But Barrett knew that was going to end soon when she became the new lady of the house. Nico had promised her that.

In the huge mansion Barrett would be protected from people like Maybelline and Chris.

Barrett tried his cell one more time, then grabbed her red leather bag with the small silver triangle on it and pulled out an amber bottle of pills. She took one of the pills, popped it into her mouth, and chased it with a glass of wine.

She poured herself another glass of wine, then picked up her cell phone and dialed Nico's number again. After a few rings, Nico's answering machine came on. This time Barrett decided to leave a message: "Hey, Nico, I did what you wanted. Now you got to come through for me. I got Brady's signature. So now do your thing. Get that woman out of my house. I'm scared Chris might know where I am or Lita might tell him. I'm leaving here first thing tomorrow. My work is done. Call me."

Chapter 36
Carmyn's Blast from the Past

I was staring at the phone again, agonizing about Brady, wondering when, if ever, he was going to call me back. I had called him three times this morning, once at home and twice on his cell phone.

I left him a message saying I would explain everything. I didn't want this mess between us to spoil Senior Day. We'd both waited so long for that day. But his not calling me back made me think that maybe he didn't want me there either.

Tears came to my eyes, and I had to cry at the thought of not being there for my son on the day we had both talked about and dreamed of for so long. But I told myself to toughen up.

I picked up the phone again and was preparing to call Brady to let him know just what the deal was going to be, but then I set the receiver back down. Maybe it was best that I surprise him. That way he would have no choice but to hear me out. I would tell him everything that happened, why I never told him about his father, why I lied.

But I sat there a moment and wondered what Brady's reaction would be. Would he tell me how much he had missed out, how his life could have been different if he had only met his father? Then I would say something like "Yes, different. But who's to say better?"

All of a sudden, I picked up the phone and started dialing Sylvester, thinking that maybe it wasn't too late to find Brady's father. Whoever Sylvester said he could hire would have to work hard and fast, but maybe Brady's father could still be found before Senior Day. But I couldn't let Sylvester pay for it. He didn't have that kind of money.

As I punched in the first number, the doorbell rang. I reluctantly hung up the phone and went to answer the door.

I looked out the peephole and was surprised to see Sylvester standing there. I smiled, swung open the door, and said, "Speak of the —" but the last word hung in my throat when I saw who was standing beside him.

The first thought that ran through my head was *It can't be.*

"There's someone I want you to meet,"

Sylvester said.

I stood there in shock, my eyes bulging wide, my mouth hanging open. "That's not —"

"It's Woodson, Carmyn. I said I would locate him for you and I did," Sylvester said as he urged Woodson forward.

He was as handsome as I remembered him. His skin was still as smooth, his eyes as bright. But there was a maturity in him now that he didn't have then. A calmness that a college boy could never possess.

"Carmyn," he said, speaking my name like he had done twenty years ago. I was transported back. I heard the melancholy love songs of my college days. Back to the way he loved me, the way he made me feel. But then the memories of that night came back, and afterward, when he abandoned me and broke up with me in a hate-filled letter.

Tears welled up in my eyes and threatened to fall. An anger started to burn in the core of my body. "No, I don't want to see you," I said as I stepped back in and slammed the door shut.

"Carmyn," I heard Sylvester calling through the door. "If you knew the trouble I went through to find him, you'd at least hear him out."

"I said I don't want to see him. Get him

out of here, Sylvester," I said as tears poured from my eyes. I slid down and sat with my back to the door.

"Sylvester," I heard Woodson say through the door. "Let me talk to her alone."

"Are you sure?" Sylvester said.

"If she doesn't let me in, I'll catch a taxi back to my hotel."

"Just call me on my cell. I'll come back and get you."

"Thanks, brother," Woodson said.

"No problem. I hope you two can work this out. Call me on my cell if there's anything I can do."

After that, I listened but didn't hear anything for a moment.

"Carmyn," I heard Woodson say all of a sudden. His voice was strong and very clear, like he was leaning on the door, pressing his mouth to where he thought my ear was. I could see him doing that, because that's what he used to do twenty years ago when he would come to my dorm-room door and I was mad at him. "You know I never meant to hurt you."

"But you did!"

"I'm sorry. I've been trying to find you to apologize. There is something I need to tell you."

I wiped the tears from my face with the

sleeve of my blouse and opened the door.

"You tried to find me?"

"Carmyn, please. Let me in, and I'll tell you everything."

"Okay," I said as I opened the door.

Woodson walked in as I stepped back from the door with my arms folded over my chest. It had been over twenty years since I'd seen him, but like Sylvester, he'd aged well. He looked like he could still fit in his burnt-orange and white football uniform.

"Carmyn, it's good to see you," he said.

"Where did Sylvester find you? How did he find you?" I asked.

"He tracked me down on the Internet and then he just called me. The first call, I blew him off because I thought he was a nut. I didn't know anyone named Carmyn Bledsoe. The Carmyn I knew was Carmyn Marie Johnson. The girl everybody called Niecey. That's the Carmyn I knew. Did you get married?"

"No. It's my mother's maiden name. I couldn't be a Johnson anymore, since my father and mother were so embarrassed by me," I said.

"Can we sit down and talk?"

I reminded myself that I had been cleansed by my talk with God in the Labyrinth and even though I had released the demons from my past

I could at least give Woodson a chance.

"Let's go into the breakfast nook," I said.

Woodson followed me through the family room and kitchen into the small area off the kitchen that leads to the deck. I didn't know if I should offer him something to drink or how long this conversation was going to last.

We sat down, and for several moments and I avoided looking into his eyes. I looked instead at his hands and noticed the gold band.

"So you're married," I said as I finally looked into his eyes.

"Yes, for fifteen years. I met her in Seattle when I was playing for the Seahawks. We have a set of twin girls, Madison and Miller, who are nine, and Andrea, who just turned thirteen. Sylvester tells me I might have another child."

"He had no right to tell you that. I'm not certain Brady is your son," I said.

"His name is Brady? Is it Brady Bledsoe? That couldn't be," Woodson said in disbelief.

"Yes, my son is named Brady Bledsoe."

"Does he play football?"

"Yes, at Central Georgia. He's a senior."

"And a very fine football player. He's at the top of our draft board," Woodson said.

"Your draft board? What are you talking about? "

"I'm an executive vice president and in charge of scouting for the Houston Texans. That's your son? He could be my son. That's wild, because a few weeks ago I was coming to see him play against Texas Tech but my plans changed at the last minute," Woodson said, shaking his head.

"After what happened that night, I can't be certain he's your son."

"What do you mean, what happened?"

"You know," I said.

"Carmyn, that's why I've been hoping for years to find you. I got the story wrong," Woodson said.

"What story?"

"Carmyn, a few years ago I got a visit from Daphne. She had just survived a bout with breast cancer and had a "come to Jesus" moment. Daphne told me she had a secret from all those years she wanted to share with me. She told me that when she got to the hotel that night you were already drunk and passed out. She had the guys put you in bed, but she took off all your clothes. Then she convinced all these recruits to lie and tell me that they had sex with you. Daphne was trying to get me back and would do anything. It was all a big lie. She set you up, Carmyn.

She hated you and thought you'd stolen me from her. She promised me she would find you and tell you. I didn't know anything about you having a kid."

"Why did you stay away so long that night? And didn't you want me to sleep with them?"

"Hell no. Why would I want my girl to do that?"

"You told me to be nice," I said.

"Come on now, Carmyn, I would have never asked you to do something like that. Back then, you could be a little tough on guys. And as far as being gone so long, I had stopped by my line brother's house and had a couple of drinks and watched a little football. I didn't want to get stopped for drunk driving, so I waited until I sobered up. I fell asleep."

So many emotions swirled through my head. All these years I had carried this secret shame with me when all I had done was get drunk and pass out.

"Are you sure about this? Do you believe Daphne is telling the truth now?" I asked Woodson.

"As sure as a man can be, and yes, she's a different woman. I'm sure she tried to get in touch with you."

"Then Brady has to be your son. You and I

made love right before the party. I'll never forget that. I didn't sleep with anyone after I left Austin. I was too upset. If what you're telling me is true, then you have to be Brady's father," I said as tears began to stream down my face.

"I'll take a blood test and do whatever you want me to do. Does he know anything about me?"

"I told him his father died in a motorcycle accident."

"So you had me in mind," Woodson said.

"What do you mean?"

"Carmyn, don't you remember my motorcycle and how you and Coach used to get on me all the time about riding it? When can I meet him?"

"I don't know. He's not speaking to me now," I said.

"Why? Don't you two have a good relationship?"

"We've had a wonderful relationship until this girl he met told him that his father might be alive. I don't know how she found out. All I know is that Brady has wanted a father all his life and he feels that I took that from him."

"How old is he?"

"Twenty. He turned twenty-one in October."

"A twenty-one-year-old son. Wow, that's

crazy," Woodson said.

"I have to be sure," I said. "He'd kill me if this wasn't true."

"I understand that. Besides, I need to talk to my family as well. I have seen press photos, but do you have a picture of him when he was a little boy?"

"Yes, in my office. Let me go and wash my face and I will bring you his picture and his baby book," I said.

"I'd like that."

"Do you want anything else?" I asked.

"It looks like I might be getting a son soon. I think that's quite enough for one night."

CHAPTER 37
BRADY BLEDSOE . . . PRIVATE INVESTIGATOR

Late Thursday night, I found myself in the one place my mother always prayed I would never be: I was at the Scarlet Springs police station. I couldn't find Barrett. I didn't see her at cheerleader practice, and when I asked her coach where she was, he told me no one had heard from Barrett.

When I got home, I called her cell every five minutes, to no avail. Finally, I got in my truck and went to her condo and convinced the doorman to let me go up. There was no answer as I rang the doorbell for about ten minutes. I started knocking on doors and calling out her name. I even looked in the windows, and still no signs of Barrett. I looked in the parking lot and her car was gone.

I went back to my apartment and convinced Delmar to come to the station with me, even though he thought I was making too big a deal of this. He told me, "Bitches do crazy shit all the time. She'll be back. That bitch is a gold digger for sho."

We got to the station closest to campus and I went to the information desk. "How can I help you, young man?" asked a thin, white, uniformed woman with wire-rimmed glasses.

"I need to file a missing persons report," I said.

"Who's missing?"

"My girlfriend, and I'm really worried," I said.

"When is the last time you saw her?"

"Last night around nine-thirty."

She looked at her watch and said, "Well, it hasn't been twenty-four hours. Do you think she could be avoiding you? Maybe you two had a fight or something?"

"No, we didn't have a fight, and she has no reason to be dodging me," I said. This was making me mad. Something bad could be happening to Barrett and this woman was making up things that weren't true.

"We can't file a missing persons report until after forty-eight hours. Is she a student at the university?"

"Yes. And forty-eight hours might be too late."

"Did you contact campus police?"

"No, she lives off campus."

"Why don't you go home and keep trying to reach her. If you don't hear from her, then come back tomorrow," she said.

"That's not good enough. Can I speak to your supervisor?" I asked.

"Suit yourself," she said. Then she got up and went through a door behind her desk.

I walked over toward Delmar, who was leaning against the wall drinking a bottle of water.

"What did she say, fam?"

"Some crap about having to wait forty-eight hours," I said.

Delmar shook his head and smiled. "Boy, oh boy. That girl got you whipped something bad. Look at you, sweat popping from your forehead like bullets from a gun. Four months ago, you didn't even know this girl. Damn, four months ago you didn't know what good pussy was."

"Dude, shut the F up," I said as I wiped my forehead with the back of my hand. I looked over at the desk and saw the woman and a tall policeman. She pointed toward me and I walked back to the desk.

The male officer extended his hand toward me and said, "I'm Sergeant Fontana. How can I help you, young man?"

"Yeah, my girlfriend is missing and I'm worried. This is not like her," I said.

"That's what Officer Mathis tells me. We really can't do anything until forty-eight hours," he said.

"There's got to be something you can do. I'm really worried," I said.

"What's your name, young man?"

"Brady. Brady Bledsoe."

"Are you *the* Brady Bledsoe?"

"I'm the only one I know," I said.

"Don't you play running back for the Jaguars?"

"Yes, sir," I said.

"Man, you sure can run that ball. My son and I go to all the Jaguar games, and you're his favorite player. Can I get you to sign an autograph, or better yet, take a picture with you?"

"Sure we can do that. But do you think you can help me out?" I asked. I figured I might as well use my local celebrity for something good.

"Where does your girlfriend live?"

"In Jaguar Gardens."

"That's a pretty nice condo, and I just happen to know the resident manager because she and my wife are sorority sisters. Let me give her a call and see if she'll go inside the apartment. What is your young lady's name and her apartment number?"

"Barrett Manning, and she lives in apartment two thirty-nine," I said.

"And you have tried to reach her on her cell phone?"

"Yes, sir, I have."

"Okay, give me a few minutes. Why don't you take a seat over there and I will be back in a few."

"Thank you."

I walked back over where Delmar was standing and tried to reach Barrett once again. This time her cell phone was full and I couldn't leave another message. Maybe her parents were looking for her as well.

About twenty minutes later, Sergeant Fontana walked over to me carrying a camera.

"I don't think I have any good news for you, young man. She went into the apartment and said there wasn't anybody there. She said there was furniture in there but no clothing or personal items. Did your girlfriend drop out of school and maybe not tell you?"

"That can't be," I said as I shook my head in disbelief.

"What did you say your girlfriend's name was?"

"Barrett Manning."

"I thought so. My friend said the place was owned by a Nico Benson. Does that name sound familiar?"

"Nico Benson? That's the agent out of Atlanta who tried to sign me last year," I said. What was going on?

"If you don't locate her by tomorrow, then come back and I'll see what I can do. Now can we take that picture?"

I stood there in a daze for a few moments, wondering why Nico would buy a condo for Barrett. How did she know him? Where were all her clothes and all the other things I knew she treasured?

"Brady," Sergeant Fontana called out, breaking me from my trance.

"Yeah, I'm sorry. Let's take the picture," I said.

CHAPTER 38
"UGLY BARRETT"

Barrett lay in bed watching *Ugly Betty* in a sumptuous Ritz-Carlton suite. The Ritz in Buckhead was her favorite hotel, with its unsurpassed service, five-star dining, and every spa-related service she could dream of. It was about time she got back to living the way she was accustomed to, she thought.

Barrett sat up as Nico walked back into the bedroom wearing nothing but black silk pajama bottoms. "I'm still mad about having to give that bitch five thousand dollars," Nico said.

"Yeah, I know, but we really need to blame Lita for opening her damn mouth," Barrett said.

"We need to do something about Lita. Her crack whore ass is getting out of control," Nico said.

"Is there any way we can get her committed? Then Wade could come and live with us," Barrett said.

"That might be difficult. We should think of something to do with the both of them."

"I will take care of Wade," Barrett said firmly.

"If that's what you want," Nico said as he got out of bed and rolled the room-service cart and dirty dishes from the dinner of lobster and steak they had just finished into the living room.

He crept back into the bed with Barrett. She wore just a thin, thigh-length, silk purple nightie. He crawled up and over her body like a panther and held himself there, looking into her eyes, his lips almost touching hers.

"Now that dinner is over, I think it's time for dessert."

Barrett wanted him, could feel that he wanted her by the way his manhood throbbed against her thigh, but dimple or not, she would not be a fool for him until a very important matter was taken care of.

"Is she gone?" Barrett asked.

"Is who gone?"

"Your wife. Did you tell her you wanted a divorce?"

"Barrett, it's not that easy. I told you that," Nico said as he lowered himself all the way on top of Barrett and tried to press his lips against hers.

"Get up. Get up!" Barrett insisted.

Nico rolled off of her. Barrett jumped out of the bed, grabbed her robe from the chair, threw it on, and tied it at her waist. "You said when this job was done we'd be together. You told me to get Brady and you'd leave your wife. Do you know that if that guy I ran into tells crazy-ass Chris where I am, I could get beaten up or, even worse, killed?"

Nico stood. "I know, but I want you to ask yourself a question," he said as he stepped toward her.

Barrett extended her arm, raised her palm. "I can hear you fine from there."

Nico stopped. "Fine. But ask yourself, do you really want to marry me, or are you just in love with the fairy tale? Barrett, to be honest with you, what I have with my wife is shit. What you and I have is beautiful. We understand each other. We work so well together."

"If what you have with your wife is shit, why won't you divorce her?" Barrett said, crossing her arms over her breasts.

Nico didn't answer her, just stared, then said, "Don't ruin this. You're so good at what you do. What? The money isn't good enough? Places like this and a different house every year?"

"It's not that."

"Do you want a nicer place next time? You

want me to buy you more clothes, a better car? Name it, I'll get it for you," Nico said.

"None of that," Barrett said. She was so frustrated that she was near tears. "I'm tired of sneaking from place to place, changing names, and telling lies. I can't keep expecting people to believe that I'm twenty years old when I'm almost thirty. I don't want to keep on having sex for money when I want something else. I might as well go back to how I was living with my fucked-up mother. I don't want that life anymore."

"What do you want, Barrett?" Nico said as he approached her again.

"I want real love. And I want it from you." Nico halted in his tracks.

"You said you'd give that to me when this was over. You said you'd leave your wife. Now I want you to do it," Barrett said.

"What about one more job? There's a running back at Arkansas — actually, there are two. Darren McFadden and Felix Jones. I haven't decided which one yet. That will be our last job for a while. I'll be the biggest black sports agency and they'll be lining up to sign with me."

"Hell no! You want me to do two at one time. Oh, hell naw, I'm not moving to fucking Arkansas. I've done my last college town."

"All right, baby. You got me. I'll do it,"

Nico said, smiling that dimpled grin that would normally have Barrett melting, spreading her legs. But now she didn't budge. "Let's just make love tonight, and I'll break the bad news to my wife tomorrow."

"Hell no," Barrett said, grabbing the phone receiver from its cradle off the nightstand. She held it out to Nico. "If you're serious, call and tell her now. I want to hear you say it."

The smile disappeared from Nico's face. "Hang up the phone, Barrett."

Barrett didn't listen.

He walked over to her, took the phone from her hand, and set it down in its cradle. Then he turned to her and said, "Look, this is what it is. It's a nice situation. You really can't beat it. Now, I said I'd leave my wife and be with you, and I meant it. I don't need you telling me when that has to happen. It'll happen when I say so. Right now, I want you to crawl in that bed, because I want some ass. If you ain't feeling this anymore, if you can't stay with the program, you can pack your little shit and get the fuck out. Otherwise, lie down and we'll talk about this marriage business another time. What's it gonna be?" Nico's arms were crossed over his bare chest.

Barrett looked at him and saw that he was

serious. This was not the situation she wanted to be in, not how she wanted to be treated. She thought about the love that Brady had tried to give her, the way he treated her better than any man she had ever met. Now a part of her wished she could go back to him, go back to being his twenty-year-old, cheerleading sweetheart. But that could never be, because it never really was. That life was a lie. Her life was a lie. The life that was in front of her now — Nico, the bed he wanted her to crawl into, the money he would give her tomorrow — that was her life, what was real for her now.

So when Nico said, "You in or out?" Barrett slid the straps of her nightgown off her shoulders, let it drop to the floor, said, "Yeah, I'm in," then crawled into bed as she'd been told.

CHAPTER 39
CARMYN BREAKS UP A PLAY

"Well, this is a surprise," I said as I swung open the door. "What are you doing here?"

"Get dressed. I need to take you to dinner," he said. Lowell didn't look happy.

"Where?"

"Let's go to Morton's," he said.

"Are you all right? I mean, I didn't even get a hug," I said.

"I'm sorry," Lowell said as he hugged me halfheartedly. I could feel the tension in his body.

"Lowell, what's going on? You just decided to drive to Atlanta to take me to dinner on a school night? Is everything all right with you? Is Brady okay?"

"Yes, he's fine, but it's a little bit of both," Lowell said.

"Why don't we go in the den and talk? If you still want to do dinner after we talk, then fine. I have something I need to tell you as well."

We moved into the family room and took a seat on my avocado-green sofa.

"So tell Carmyn what's the matter," I said as I patted Lowell on the knees.

"I can't believe I'm this old and stupid," he said.

"Is it something about . . . what's his name, Kilgore?" I asked.

"How did you know?"

"It's all in your face, hon," I said, touching his smooth cheek.

"I owe you a huge apology," he said.

"For what?"

"I don't even know where to start."

"Come on, Lowell, talk to me."

"I know how Barrett found out about our conversation. A couple of nights ago, I was awakened in the middle of the night when a metal device fell from the ceiling and just missed my head. It was so weird and it scared the shit out of me. I turned on the light and saw what I would later find out was some high-tech listening device. Kilgore was there, and when I asked out loud what it could be, the look on his face told me he had something to do with it. I mean, no one else has been in my place but you and Brady, and I know you're not trying to wiretap me. I got up and poked around my house and found three other devices — in my living room, office, and in the breakfast nook where we had brunch the day you told me about Woodson."

"Who do you think put them there?" I asked.

"Oh, it was Kilgore. I got him to admit it."

"Why'd he do it?"

"Apparently, I'm not the catch I thought I was. It seems some agent hired him to seduce Brady because his celibacy might be a cover for being gay."

"What? Are you making this up?" I asked in amazement.

"I know it sounds like the CW network gone Lifetime, but it's true. An agent hired this kid whose name turns out to be not Kilgore, but James. They call themselves runners and they insinuate themselves into the lives of top players, become friends or lovers with them, and then convince them to sign with a particular agent. When the agent found out Brady was straight, he sent in Barrett and left Kilgore there to seduce me, because he knew I was Brady's godfather and thought I might be good for information or influence."

"Tell me you're kidding. This is something else! Barrett was sent to seduce Brady?" I asked. At first I was angry, but then I felt a sense of relief that I had been right about

Barrett. She was a little bitch.

"Yeah, James spilled the beans when he thought he might be able to get some money out of me for being so loyal. When I found out as much as I could, I kicked his ass out and told him I was going to turn him in to the authorities. It seems they got false college transcripts for Barrett and Kilgore and they've been doing all kinds of shit just to get Brady to sign with a particular agent."

"I knew there was something about that girl I didn't like. Have you told Brady?"

"No, I haven't. I wanted to talk with you first and see if you wanted to tell him," Lowell said.

"Is she still with Brady? I still haven't talked to him — I didn't want to distract him any more than he's been distracted, but I really need to speak with him soon because I have some news for him," I said.

"What?"

"I found his father!"

"Carmyn, that's great news! How?"

I knew now was the time to come clean about everything, and that included my relationship with Sylvester. I took a deep breath as one beat of silence passed and then started talking.

"It turns out I didn't do what I thought. Remember I told you about my boyfriend

Woodson?" I said.

"Yes," Lowell said.

"Well, it turns out he was the only person I slept with. Woodson is Brady's father."

"Are you sure?"

"I'm pretty sure, and Woodson has agreed to take a DNA test. But Lowell, if what he told me is true, then it turns out I didn't sleep with a bunch of guys but only the man I was so in love with."

"Brady will be excited enough for this to ease the blow about Barrett. He was pretty close to falling in love with this girl," Lowell said.

"I hope that little witch hasn't ruined my son," I said. I noticed Lowell blink his eyes and then look away.

"What was that look for?"

"What look?"

"Lowell, I know you. Is there something you aren't telling me?"

"I think you need to talk with Brady. When are you going to tell him about his father?"

"I'm waiting to see when Woodson can come back to Atlanta, and then I'll take him to Scarlet Springs. He needs to talk to his wife and family in Houston. He also travels a lot with his job, but I'll be able to tell Brady real soon," I said. "Oh and get this: Woodson works for the Houston Texans, so he knows all about Brady.

"How did you feel seeing him after all these years? Were there any sparks?"

"At first it was a little strange, but after we started talking it felt fine and no sparks. What we had was good, but it was just a case of young love. Woodson seems very happy with his life, and I'm finally beginning to feel good about my life. Every aspect of my life."

"So did you go to Houston? I mean, how did you find him?"

I told Lowell about Sylvester and how I'd been seeing him undercover for over a year. I shared how supportive Sylvester was and how much I enjoyed having him around.

"You little tramp. All this time you've been pretending you weren't interested in getting a little loving," Lowell said, and laughed.

"Yeah, I guess I've been pretending about a lot of things in my life, but that is going to change," I said.

The next morning when I got to the shop, Maybelline was waiting outside the door. She was wearing a new wrap dress as colorful as the early days of autumn. Her Mary J. Blige-like transformation continued, with Zander at the helm.

"Maybelline, what are you doing here so early?" I asked as I gave her a quick peck on her cheek. I noticed that her makeup was so light you could barely tell she was wearing any.

"I got an appointment with Zander, and you know how he is. Don't want him getting mad at me and sending me packing," Maybelline said with a laugh.

"Come on in," I said as I opened the shop. When I got inside, I looked at the book and saw that Maybelline's appointment was at eleven o'clock. I knew Zander's clients didn't risk being late, but four hours was a bit extreme.

"Can I be honest with you?" Maybelline asked.

"Sure. About what?"

"I really need to talk to you," Maybelline said.

"Okay. About what?"

"That woman your son is dating."

"You mean Barrett? Oh, honey, that's over," I said.

"Good. By the way, her name is Raquel and she is bad news. I know I should have said something sooner, but I wanted to be sure it was her. To call her a ho would be showing disrespect for women who work hard at being a ho, but in many ways she can't help herself."

"How do you know her?"

"I knew her mother from my 'hosting' days back in New Orleans. We used to work together. A part of the past I'd like to forget. But I lived it, so I have to claim it," Maybelline said.

"I knew there was something not right about her when I first met her."

"Like with me?"

"Maybelline, I misjudged you. I thought we were over that."

"Yes, but I've made so many mistakes with my life and I just hope it's not too late to correct some things."

"Like with Delmar?"

"I don't know. I might as well face the fact that I wasn't a good mother. He may never forgive me for that, and that's okay. He's too much like his father to be forgiving. I did come back into Delmar's life because I thought it was a way to make some quick money, but I think seeing the way you raised your son and how much he loves you . . . well, it just made me rethink my plans."

"Maybelline, I'm not perfect when it comes to raising Brady. I have made some huge mistakes." I thought about how I had tried to give Brady so much but had kept so much from him, like his father and grandparents. That was wrong.

"I appreciate you trying to help me and

taking me under your wing. No lady like yourself has done that for me."

"I don't think I did enough," I said softly.

"Do you have a favorite charity?" Maybelline asked.

"Yes. Why do you ask?"

"Because I'm going to write you a check as a way of showing you how much I appreciate you."

"You don't have to do that."

"I won't take no for an answer. What's the name of the charity?"

I thought for a minute, and then suddenly Shelby's face popped into my head and I said, "Make it out to Brandon's Room." Maybe the couple of hundred dollars that Maybelline was going to give me would help some new mother.

Maybelline pulled a checkbook from her purse, went over to the counter where I kept the hair-care products, and wrote out a check.

"Here you go," she said, and handed me the check. I looked at it and gasped. "Five thousand dollars. Can you afford this?"

"Let's just say I can't afford not to do this," Maybelline said as she winked with an easy smile.

CHAPTER 40
REALITY BITES BRADY

Lowell's words chilled me, and I shook my head in disbelief. The woman I had given myself to and fallen in love with was a fraud. I wanted to believe it was a bunch of lies, but I knew Lowell would never joke about something like this.

"How could this be true?" I asked.

Lowell looked at me sadly and said, "I know this is tough to understand now, but you will get over this, Brady. People do crazy things for money and power."

"I mean, I've heard of schools doing this when they're recruiting a player, but it's usually just some college girl who is easy," I said. My mind was spinning with confusion and frustration. Could Barrett really have played me just to get me to sign with an agent? An agent my mother had already dismissed. I thought about the guy at the restaurant and how he seemed so certain he knew Barrett. Why hadn't I paid closer attention to what he was saying?

"Are you going to be okay? Why don't you call your mother."

"So she can tell me 'I told you so'? Naw, I don't want to do that. I guess I can thank Barrett for bringing out the truth about my mother," I said.

"Brady, get over yourself! That's nothing to thank her for. Look at the wedge it put between you and your mother," Lowell said.

"I might never have found out that my father might really be alive. I may never meet him, but I don't feel so alone in the world."

"How can you ever say you felt alone? Your mother gave up her life for you. That's very selfish of you, Brady."

"I know . . . I know, but do you understand how this feels? The two women I trusted the most betrayed me. How would that make you feel?"

"Your mother loves you," Lowell said. "Barrett doesn't count. She's worthless."

"I thought Barrett might love me one day," I said. Tears were forming in my eyes, but I was determined not to cry. And what was I crying for — being the biggest fool in the world? It felt as though my insides were softening like ice cream left out in the sun.

CHAPTER 41
BARRETT PICKS A FIGHT

"Now!" Barrett told the limo driver from the back seat.

"Ms. Manning, I don't think we're supposed to tail another car into this gated community without first calling someone and asking permission to enter," the driver said, turning to her. After three days, Barrett had got sick of waiting for Nico to return to the hotel and decided to take things into her own hands.

Barrett and the driver sat on the street just outside the gate of The Country Club of the South, a posh, upper-crust settlement of mansions in Duluth, thirty minutes outside of Atlanta.

The only reason Barrett knew where he lived was that Nico had had balls enough to bring her here once when his wife and children were out of the country.

Nico had driven her into the curved driveway then, as she looked up at the five

Corinthian pillars that stretched high into the sky and supported the home. It was beautiful, built on two acres of sprawling green land, with a four-car garage and both a fish pond and an Olympic-size in-ground swimming pool in the back.

Nico took Barrett's hand then, pulled her out of his yolk-colored Maserati, and led her through the marble-floored house with the high white ceilings.

"This is where you'll be living someday, baby," he said, Barrett's head spinning at all she would soon have.

She found herself upstairs in the master bedroom, being undressed by Nico. As she felt her zipper coming down behind her, her eyes remained wide, her mouth slightly open, as she gaped at the huge flat-panel TV that hung from the ceiling above the elegant king-size four-post bed.

Barrett fell in love with what would be her new home. As her dress fell from her hips and she was pushed over onto the bed with 1,000-thread-count sheets, allowing Nico to enter her from behind, she smiled, knowing that soon the bed, the linen, and the blankets she was getting done on that very moment would all be hers.

"Drive through that damn gate now, before it closes," Barrett ordered the limo driver now as she leaned on the back of the seat, big sunglasses on her face, a silk scarf pulled around her head.

"Ms. Manning, better sense is telling me to stop and punch the code for the residence and request permission first."

Barrett rifled through her purse, dug out a hundred-dollar bill, and held it out to the man.

"What is better sense telling you to do now?"

The man took the bill from Barrett's hand. "It's telling me to drive, ma'am."

The driver sped the long, black car through the gates just before they closed.

"Take a left there, then straight ahead. It's the big house with the five pillars."

Once there, Barrett opened the car door.

"Shall I wait for you, Ms. Manning?" the driver asked.

"No, you can leave and I'll ride my bike home. Of course you're to wait, fool," Barrett snapped, slamming the door after stepping outside the car.

Barrett walked up to the door, wearing her beige, designer tea dress with matching shoes and bag. She wore a scarf around her neck, the tails thrown over her back. She approached the house with the confidence of a woman who would one day own it.

She rang the doorbell and impatiently tapped her foot until the door opened.

A middle-aged Hispanic woman, wearing a house servant's uniform, opened the door. With a thick accent she asked, "May I help you?"

"Yes. Fetch Nico for me."

"Mr. Nico not home," the woman said.

Barrett sighed, frustration evident in her voice.

"Then who is home?"

Before the woman could answer, Barrett heard another voice deep in the house. "Lucy, who is it?"

The Hispanic woman said, "She no say."

The other woman smiled and said, "That's okay, Margoly. I'll take care of it. May I help you?" the woman now said to Barrett.

Barrett did not say a word, simply pulled down the front of her sunglasses with the tip of her finger to get a better look at this woman. She assumed this was Nico's wife, but then again, it couldn't be. She looked much younger than she was supposed to — her skin less wrinkled, her figure too girlish. Her hair was shoulder length, black, shiny, with perfect auburn highlights. Her eyes were hazel, and a mole dotted the space just above the corner of her mouth. She was cute, Barrett thought, but Barrett wasn't fooled. She knew the woman standing before her was assembled like a cheap piece of IKEA furniture straight out the box. Plastic surgery, a hair weave, fake contacts, and an eyebrow-pencil mole could make any woman look halfway decent.

"You Nico's wife?" Barrett huffed.

"Yes." The woman smiled. "And who are you?"

"I'm your replacement," Barrett said as she tried to step into her new home. "You should probably start packing."

"Excuse me."

"Yes, your days in this house are numbered."

"You're a crazy woman," Nico's wife said, stepping back and closing the door. But before it closed all the way, Barrett said, "Then I'm the crazy woman your husband has been sleeping with. Nico is in love with me."

The door stopped, opened again, there was a woman standing there, a blank expression on her face.

"What did you say?"

"Don't act like you don't know. It's been five years that he and I have been making love the way it's supposed to be made. Don't act like you don't know. You've been played. He's leaving you."

"I don't believe you. Do you know how many women claim to be sleeping with my husband? You're just one more, gold-digging, groupie ho who's trying to get between me and Nico. Find your own man."

"Groupie ho!" Barrett said, almost hyperventilating. "If I wasn't sleeping with him, how would I know that you have a four-post bed in your room and a Phillips forty-two-inch plasma glued to the ceiling?"

"He could've told you that," the woman said, seeming uneasy.

"Then how would I have known how to get here?" Barrett said.

"We're in the book."

"Okay," Barrett said as she smiled a devilish grin. "Then how would I have known that the only time you give Nico head is on Christmas and his birthday, and even then you don't know what the hell you're doing? That he always tells you to watch your teeth."

Barrett didn't see the wild slap coming. It appeared from nowhere, knocking her glasses to the ground and sending Barrett stumbling. As she rose up, she touched the spot on her cheek where she'd been struck, felt it stinging. Barrett turned toward the woman and was about to lunge for her — when she was suddenly grabbed from behind.

Barrett spun her head around to see who was manhandling her. It was Nico.

"What the hell is going on? What are you doing here?" Nico said, obvious anger on his face.

"Looking for you and getting what's mine!" Barrett said.

"Nico, what is she talking about?" his wife said, tears in her eyes.

"Pressley, go back in the house. This doesn't concern you," Nico said as he tried to drag Barrett back to the limo.

"I'm not going anywhere," Pressley said. "I want know if what this woman says is true."

As Barrett continued kicking, fighting, trying to free herself, Nico whispered in her ear, "Just go back to the hotel and we'll talk about this later. You hear me?"

"I ain't going anywhere!" Barrett shouted, pulling free from Nico.

When he went to grab her again, his wife said, "No! I want to know the truth. Are you just trying to get his money, or are you really sleeping with my husband?" Tears still spilled over her cheeks.

Barrett knew this was the moment of truth. She looked at Nico, and he was doing everything short of shouting to her that she was supposed to lie. Lie and say that none of what she had said was true, and they would work this out. He would make sure Barrett got everything he had ever promised her. His eyes also said that if she told his wife the truth, they would be through. He would never speak to her again, never lay eyes on her.

Barrett stood there, her chest heaving, tears in her own eyes.

"No, I'm not just trying to get his money. I'm in love with Nico and he's in love with me," she said.

Nico's wife started wailing, looking as though she was about to faint. Nico grabbed her in his arms and yelled at Barrett, "Get the hell out of here and don't bother my family again!"

"But Nico," Barrett said, rushing toward him.

He shot a cautionary finger at her as he dragged his wife into the house. "Leave us alone, and if you bother my family again, I'm calling the police!"

Nico slammed the door in Barrett's face just as Barrett reached it. She began banging at it, kicking it, as more tears fell from her eyes.

"Nico, open this goddamn door! Please! I love you. What about your promise?" She begged for ten minutes after that.

He never came.

Now Barrett had no choice but to do what she had vowed to do if things ever came to this.

CHAPTER 42
CARMYN OPENS HER HEART

I finished cooking a meal of chicken Marsala, rice pilaf, and asparagus for Sylvester. I wanted to show him how much I appreciated his help finding Woodson, which I still hadn't quite figured out how he'd accomplished with his limited means.

I put on a Mary J. Blige CD, went into my bathroom, and sat at my vanity to put on my makeup. I had on peach silk pajamas over a black thong with a matching bra. I planned to serve dessert in bed.

The phone rang, so I pressed the speaker button and said hello. "What are you doing on this wonderful Sunday evening?" Kellis asked.

"I just cooked a little dinner and I'm waiting for Sylvester."

"Cooking? *You* must really like him."

I thought for a moment and said, "I think I do, and I'm very lucky my evil twin didn't run him away."

"He is nice-looking, but before you walk down the aisle, I hope I figure out where I know him from. I still can't get over how many secrets you've been keeping from me. I thought I was your girl, and here you are hiding your current man and your old man."

"I know, and you're my girl. But a lot of that stuff was so painful, I really wanted to forget it and act like it never happened," I said.

"Well, from what Woodson told you, some of it didn't," Kellis reminded me.

"And isn't that wonderful," I said.

"Yes, it is. Have you talked to Brady's daddy again?"

"We've talked a couple of times. He wants to talk to his family before we tell Brady," I said. "I'm holding out hopes he'll get to see Brady on Senior Day or in a bowl game."

"It would sure be nice if he could see Brady play," Kellis said.

"Yeah, I thought about that, but Brady has so much pressure on him, and with that girl gone I just don't want to put any more on him."

"How are you feeling about Woodson?"

"What are you talking about?"

"Do you think there is a chance something could happen between you two? Like maybe reuniting and being a real family," Kellis said.

"That man is happily married," I said.

"What if he wasn't?"

"Kellis darling, we have all moved on. Hold on," I said. I heard the call waiting beep and a Texas number flashed across the caller ID. I pushed the button on the phone and said hello.

"Carmyn." It was Woodson.

"Yes."

"Are you busy?"

"I'm on the other line. What's going on?"

"I just wanted to see if you've talked to Brady and when I might be able to meet him. I've talked things over with my wife, and we'd like to invite Brady down to Houston so he can meet his sisters," Woodson said.

"I don't know, Woodson. I don't know if Brady can get away until the season's over."

"It's your call, but I want to meet him soon. I'm really nervous about this. What if he doesn't accept me?"

"Don't worry, he will," I assured Woodson.

"Do you have all my numbers?"

"I do," I said.

"So just call me when you're ready, then. I'll be on the next plane out."

"I will. Have a good night."

"You do the same," Woodson said softly.

I clicked back over to Kellis. "Sorry 'bout

that, girl. That was Woodson. He's talked to his wife and he wants Brady to come and visit him in Houston. He said he's nervous and anxious to meet Brady."

"Can you blame him?"

"You're right," I said. I looked at the clock on the counter and told Kellis I had to finish my dinner prep.

"Get some for me, girl."

"Some what?"

"Some good lovin'," Kellis said.

"Go out and get some for yourself," I said, laughing.

After dinner, Sylvester and I retired to my bedroom. He laid his body down the length of my bed and gave me the most beautiful, gentle smile I had ever received from a man.

"What is that look about?" I asked.

"I was just admiring how beautiful you are," he said. "Why don't you come over here and let me give you a massage." I knew that was code for *let me undress you,* so I decided to turn the tables.

"Why don't you let me give you a massage," I said.

"Have I hit the jackpot tonight? I mean, first that wonderful dinner, a movie, and now a massage. What's going on, Carmyn?"

I moved toward him and pushed his body

over slightly so that I could sit next to him. I looked into his tea-brown eyes and said, "You're always doing things for me. Tonight is my time. Turn over and let me unbutton your shirt."

Sylvester smiled, and I began to slowly unbutton his light blue cotton shirt. As I reached the bottom of the shirt, I pulled it open, raised his T-shirt, and kissed his navel.

"Hmmm, that feels great," he said.

I looked up and said, "I never really thanked you for finding Woodson."

"Yes, you did."

"I know I can be . . . well, a bitch at times, but I hope now that you know my story, you understand why I didn't want to get close to a man. But you never faltered. Why?"

"Because I think you're worth it. I could tell that when I first met you," Sylvester said.

"So you're saying you could see right through me?"

"Well, sorta. It's been a while since I've been in a relationship, because I'm always working," he said.

"You said you were married once. What happened?"

Sylvester was silent for a moment. He looked up at me and started playing with my hair and said, "Do we really have to talk about my ex tonight?"

"Not if you don't want to," I said.

"This feels so nice. Just lying here looking at you."

"Very nice. May I ask you something?"

"Shoot."

"Would you like to go to Brady's last game? It's Senior Day and it's time you two met," I said.

Sylvester looked at me like I was speaking a foreign language, then asked, "Are you sure about this?"

"Yes, I am. Do you think you can get off work?"

"That's not a problem. That's really nice, Carmyn. I'd love to meet Brady."

"He's still not talking to me, but I'm going to surprise him. Brady has had enough time to sulk."

"I think you did the right thing by giving him some time to think things over. When are you going to introduce him to Woodson?"

"After the season's over."

"Why are you waiting so long?"

"Do you think that's too long?"

"Carmyn, this man has missed his son's entire childhood. I say the sooner you get them together, the better."

"I still don't know how you were able to find Woodson. I mean, I know it had to cost a lot of money. I'd like to pay you back," I said.

"No, Carmyn, I just got one of my employ—" Sylvester suddenly caught himself and stopped speaking, then looked around the room like the next word he wanted to say was on the wall.

"What's the matter?"

Sylvester looked at me and started rubbing my arms in an up-and-down motion like he was trying to keep me warm.

"Come on, now, we're heading in a new direction, but you've got to talk to me," I said. "Don't worry. I can handle it." But could I? What if Sylvester was getting ready to tell me that he wasn't divorced but had a wife and five kids?

"Carmyn, I haven't been totally honest with you," he said, looking down at the floor.

"About what?"

"Well, about who I am."

"Why not? I know you don't have a lot of money, but I've decided that doesn't matter to me. You're a good man, and that's what I'm going to focus on," I said.

"So even if I don't have a pot to piss in or a window to throw it out, that's cool with you?" Sylvester asked. I thought about it and braced myself to hear him tell me he lived in a homeless shelter or an SRO hotel and that's why he'd never invited me to his house.

"Yeah, that's what I'm saying. You were right when you said I might pass up a good thing. I make enough money for the both of us," I said.

Sylvester smiled and touched my face. Then he said I would never have to do that.

"You can't be too proud," I said. "Let me help you. Look what you've done for me."

He looked at me and shook his head and started laughing. I was being serious and didn't understand what was so funny. When he finally stopped laughing, he moved his body so he was sitting next to me. He took my hands and said, "Carmyn, I haven't been totally truthful with you. You don't have to take care of me. I'm really doing okay financially. In fact, I'm doing damn good. I don't just work at Croissant Corner. I own it."

"What?" I asked as my mouth dropped open.

"I started the business. I own the franchise and also Playa Rental Cars," he said.

"Playa Rental Cars? Are you kidding me?"

"Playa Rental Cars is a company I started after the Croissant Corner was really running itself. We rent luxury cars like Benz, Lexus, and others. We even have a Rolls we lease out provided folks put down a hefty deposit."

"Why didn't you tell me this before?"

"I didn't know where this was going, and most of the ladies I met before you were . . . how shall I say it? Gold diggers. I was even set up on a date once with your girl Kellis. I don't think she realized it when we met the other day."

"She said you looked familiar."

"She drank a lot of Dom that night." Sylvester laughed.

"So you're telling me you're rich?"

"I ain't got Bob Johnson and Bill Gates money, but I do okay," he said.

I shook my head and said, "I must be dreaming, because I don't believe this."

Sylvester pulled me close to him and whispered in my ear, "Believe it, baby." Then he gave me a long and tender kiss.

Chapter 43
Brady Prepares a New Defense

I walked to my truck after practice and there was a man standing nearby. He walked up to me and extended his hand and said, "I'm Nico Benson and I'm looking forward to making a lot of money for the both of us, Brady Bledsoe."

What was this fool man talking about? My mother had told him over a year ago I wasn't signing with him. I ignored his hand and prepared to unlock my truck.

"Did you hear me, Brady?" I didn't respond. I needed to get in my truck and out of the steady drizzle that was coming down. "You can ignore me now, but you're still going to be one of my top clients."

"That ain't never gonna happen," I said.

"Well, this says quite the opposite."

He handed me what looked like a signed contract. I looked at the heading with "The Great Ones," Nico's agency, and then, at the bottom, I saw my signature. I stared at him

471

in disbelief, then Barrett's face popped into my head — the day we were in the restaurant when I thought I was signing a contract for training with The Thoroughbreds, not representation by Nico.

"I didn't sign that," I said.

"But that's your signature, isn't it?" Nico said. "Take a look at the date you signed it. And if you don't intend to honor it, I need to call the NCAA and your compliance director about your breaking the rules, or better yet, talk with your coach. Your team will have to forfeit all the games you played and they'll be fined heavily. That would be so sad after the season the Jags have enjoyed this year."

"I haven't broken any rules," I said.

"You don't consider accepting gifts and money against the rules? You don't think *signing* with an agent before the season is over is against the rules?"

"I haven't signed any kind of contract with you."

"So why don't you call your mother and tell her you've found your agent."

"I'm not doing that," I said, looking at him with a brooding gaze.

"I know your mother is doing well, but I don't think even she can afford that ten-thousand-dollar Rolex watch you're wearing," Nico said as he looked at my wrist.

"This isn't a violation. I checked. It was a gift, and at the time I was under the impression that Barrett was my girl," I said.

"How could she be your girl when she's been fucking me since she was eighteen? I'm sure when they audit your checking account and see all the unexplained money, that will at least get you suspended. The hair business is good, but not twenty-five thousand in your son's bank account good. Like I said before, your team will have to forfeit all the games you've played in. No Senior Day, no bowl game, and you end your career tarnished. Nobody likes a cheater, Brady. Didn't your mother teach you that?"

"You do what you want. But you and your company won't ever see a dime of my money," I said. The fine drizzle had turned to rain, and my face was now covered with raindrops.

"Be smart, Brady. Even if you can prove that I did a few unsavory things, you'll still be suspended while they investigate. All I have to do is make one phone call. You'll miss the bowl game and that invitation to New York for the Heisman Awards will never arrive. Besides, I'm going to take good care of you."

"In case I haven't made myself clear, you can do whatever. My coach and teammates know me. I have my good name to stand on. What do you have, Mr. Benson? Some girl that's good in bed with anybody you tell her to lie with. I wouldn't brag about that."

"I have a whole lot of money to look forward to thanks to you, Brady," Nico said. "Despite the few bad games you've had lately, you'll still be a first-round NFL draft pick."

I pressed the button on my key to open my truck door, pushed Nico out of the way, and said, "We will see about that."

When I got home, Delmar was walking out of his room with a black leather duffel on his shoulders. I figured he was going to do another one of his strip shows, but first I had to tell him about my visit with Nico.

"Man, you want me to bust that nigga up?"

"Nah, I'm not worried about Nico. Don't need to have your butt in jail. We need you for the last two games if we're going to make it to a bowl game," I said.

"I heard some of the coaches talking that we might be going to the Cotton Bowl to play Nebraska if we win the last two," Delmar said.

"That would be nice. A New Year's Day bowl, and in Dallas, a place where I never been," I said.

"Son, I can't believe all the shit that bitch Barrett has caused. You think she's done this before?"

"I'm pretty sure she has," I said, recalling the guy in the restaurant talking about Chris Johns.

"What are you going to do if you run into her or hear from her?"

"I don't know. I doubt if that happens," I said.

"You gotta admit, she did do a few things that were good," Delmar said.

"Like what?"

"Now you know how good pussy is, and she got you to loosen up," Delmar said. "So are you going to tell Coach?"

"What do you think?"

"If he doesn't know, then shit won't happen. People do stuff on the team all the time and Coach don't find out. I hope you're gonna keep the watch and money," Delmar said.

"If Nico does go to the coach, I'll just tell Coach what happened and return the stuff."

"I think old dude is bluffing. Word will get out on an agent doing stuff like that. We both know schools do that stuff when they recruiting players, but I ain't never heard of this type of shit."

"You really think I shouldn't say anything to Coach? I mean, he might suspend me, but I could get reinstated before the game when I prove I didn't know what was going on."

"Don't be a Boy Scout. Just let things flow. This might hurt your draft position and getting invited to New York for the Heisman finals."

"You think so?"

"I don't know for sho, but I think you should chance it. What time you got?"

I looked at my watch and said, "Nine-thirty."

"I got to bounce. Hey, why don't you let me wear that watch? I mean, unless you're sentimental about it."

I took the watch, gave it to Delmar, and said, "This don't mean nuthin' to me."

If only that were true, I thought as Delmar headed out the door, admiring the expensive gift.

Chapter 44
Barrett Leaves the Building . . . Raquel Returns

Dear Diary,

It finally occurred to me that I don't need to use brute force with Nico. Despite what's happened, I'm a survivor, and I still have my brains, as well as all the secrets about the wrong he's done to so many college athletes.

I have receipts. And more important, I have you, my faithful diary.

That night at Nico's home, all of my dreams disappeared like melting ice. There won't be any Buckhead mansion, fancy cars, unlimited charge accounts, and private planes. No more kisses filled with tenderness and desire. Nico isn't coming back. He isn't going to call and beg my forgiveness. Like all the people in my life, Nico used me, and I still feel chills at the nape of my neck when I remember the look of disgust in his eyes.

I had stashed away a little money, but I

knew it wasn't going to last long. I had to come up with a plan for my future so I could continue to provide for Wade and then also maintain my lifestyle. I have to confess I also had a strong desire for revenge, so I picked up the hotel phone and got the number for the *Atlanta Journal-Constitution.*

I got the number and called and asked to speak to the sports editor. Instead of a real person, I got voice mail. At first I started to hang up, but then I decided to talk to the machine.

"I'm Raquel Murphy and I have a story I *know* you'll be interested in . . ."

CHAPTER 45
CARMYN'S FINAL TICKETS

Jaguar Senior Day was a beautiful, sun-dappled autumn day. Driven by his driver Cecil, Sylvester and I arrived in a Silver Shadow Rolls from his fleet of cars.

I was still getting used to Sylvester the businessman as he made phone calls and barked out instructions on the drive up. I nibbled on fruit and cheese and drank cranberry juice as we shared teasing glances, and I enjoyed the cool touch of his hand as he assured me that he was almost finished making calls.

After we arrived at the stadium, I showed Sylvester around the campus. We walked hand in hand like college students as I pointed out Brady's first dorm and where he took most of his classes. We were having such a good time that we almost missed the players' Jaguar Walk. The crowd for Brady's last game was larger than any I had ever seen.

I couldn't wait until the game was over and

hoped I could hug my baby again and introduce him to Sylvester. As we walked to the ticket window, my cell phone rang. I looked at the number and saw that it was Shelby. "Hello, Shelby," I said.

"Ms. Carmyn, I'm going to need to take you up on your offer. My mother said I can't stay here if I don't go to Chicago," she said. It sounded like she was crying.

"Are you all right?"

"I will be fine once I get out of this house."

"Okay, but I'm not in Atlanta right now. I'll be there later tonight. If you need to leave now, just go to the shop and tell Zander to let you stay there until I get back," I told her.

"I will. You sure this is going to be okay?"

"It will be fine. Everything will be just fine," I said.

"Thank you, Ms. Carmyn."

"No need to thank me, baby. Just take care of yourself and I'll see you later tonight."

"Okay."

I was a little nervous when I approached the will call window to ask for my tickets. What if Brady was still mad at me and had changed our permanent arrangement? Just in case, I'd spoken to Lowell and he'd offered seats in the dean's box.

"I'm here to pick up two tickets for Bledsoe," I said nervously.

A middle-aged white lady looked at me and smiled and said, "Oh, you're Brady's mom. We sure are going to miss him next year. What a fine young man you've raised."

"Thank you," I said as I offered her a weak smile.

"I can't find your tickets. Let me check with the manager."

"Okay, but please hurry — I don't want to miss anything." Maybe Brady had given my tickets to someone else. This was going to be so embarrassing. Still, nothing and nobody was going to keep me out.

A few minutes later, she returned and said, "I'm sorry, Ms. Bledsoe."

I didn't let her finish. "What do you mean you're sorry? Where are my tickets?"

"Here they are. I was going to tell you someone put them in the wrong place."

"I'm sorry. I guess I'm just nervous about the game. You know, if we win we go to our first bowl game."

"If Brady plays the way he usually does, then I'm not worried. Enjoy the game. We'll miss you next year."

"Don't worry, I will be back. Once a Jaguar, always a Jaguar," I said.

I left the ticket window and spotted Sylvester with his cell phone pressed to his ear. I walked over and stood directly in front of him and folded my arms across my chest. He got the message and said, "Got to run."

"Promise me you'll turn that thing off," I said.

"I will. Are we all set?"

"Ready to go," I said as I held up the two tickets.

We turned around and started walking toward Gate 5, when I heard a familiar voice call my name. When I turned around, there was Woodson about five feet from me.

CHAPTER 46
RUN, BRADY . . . WALK, SON

I slammed my locker door shut and then it just hit me. This was close to the end of college for me. Last night, me and the team did our usual thing before a game. We all went to a movie, went to dinner afterward, ate like pigs, and then made it back to the hotel just before curfew.

Me and Delmar shared a room, and after he turned out the lights, he lay in bed, staring up at the ceiling before he said, "After Senior Day tomorrow, that's it. No more CGU, no more hangin' out with our boys, no more college. It's gonna all be over."

"Look at you, getting all nostalgic. I'm not thinking about any of that. I'm only thinking about winning this game tomorrow so we can go to the Cotton Bowl."

"You ain't gonna miss all of this?" Delmar said as he continued to gaze at the ceiling through the dark room.

"Not really."

"Nigga . . . quit playin'," Delmar said, then rolled over and went to sleep.

I sounded crazy, but lying there at that moment, I truly thought I wouldn't miss college football because of all that was happening. This was supposed to be about having fun and not business like the NFL. There would be plenty of time when playing football would be a job.

After everybody woke up this morning, the day moved like a dizzying blur. We were all in our warm-ups, out of the hotel, and on the bus, driving toward campus, before it seemed we had fully awakened.

Some of the guys on the bus were joking, laughing, and roughhousing with one another. Others were off in their own little worlds, their skullcaps pulled low over their eyes, foreheads pressed against the windows, staring at all that passed us by for the last time.

I was somewhere in between.

Delmar was up out of the seat he shared with me, traipsing up and down the isle, talking to everybody like he was hosting a party. I had my iPod on, my hood over my head, staring out the window. I was listening to the new Lyfe Jennings joint, trying to hold at bay the thoughts I feared would surface sooner or later. It would be a hard day, but I kept telling myself to just stay focused.

We could see the hordes of people tailgating in the parking lot, wearing school colors, barbecuing, drinking, and dancing around the cars and trucks that crowded into every space. Some people even danced on the roofs of their cars and trucks.

"Look at all those fools out there, getting crunk for us," Delmar said.

"It's like they're having a party!" Rojo, the skinny redheaded punter, said.

When the bus pulled to a stop in front of the stadium, so many fans crowded the bus that security had to push through and make a path so the team could get off and head to the locker room.

As we made our way through the people, they grabbed us, held signs, and yelled our names. I saw signs that people had made for me that read, "We LUV YOU B.B.!!!" and "BLEDSOE, DON'T GO." I smiled and shook the hands of some of the fans.

Once we were inside, Delmar said, "Man, you hear all those women out there yellin' my name? Usher ain't got shit on me! I thought they was about to start tossin' panties, fool!"

All of the team members were feeling themselves, thinking that the insane crowd out there was just for them, until Coach walked in and said, "All right, everybody settle down. You got a taste of the pandemonium going on out there and now you all think you're Elvis. But have you all forgotten that there's a hell of a team out there in Georgia Tech, waiting to whoop knots on your heads? Suit up, get out there, focus on the game, and then we can talk about making school history and reservations in Dallas. You hear me?"

"Yeah, Coach," the entire team answered.

"I said, did you men hear me!" he yelled.

"Yes, Coach!" the entire team roared back.

"Good," Coach said. He stood around for a moment longer, looking at some of us dead in our eyes, then he said, "And congratulations to you seniors. We're all going to miss you around here."

After Coach left, there was no more laughing and joking. Everyone dressed quietly, caught in their own thoughts. Everyone except me. I thought about my running plays, I visualized carrying the ball for three hundred yards, anything to keep those thoughts of Barrett and my fighting with my mother from getting into my head.

When I looked up again, everyone was dressed and leaving the locker room, and Delmar was pulling me by the jersey.

"Yo, you ready?"

I looked up at him, about to pull my helmet off the top of my locker, and said, "Yeah, I'm cool. I'll be out in a second. Just let me lock up."

"Don't take all day. You know we can't start this party without you."

I grabbed my helmet, slammed my locker door, and then it all just hit me like a kick in the stomach. I had no choice but to lower myself onto the bench in front of my locker. The entire locker room was empty, and quiet except for the echo of shower drops hitting the cement floor.

I looked at my locker, saw the piece of tape that Coach had put there four years earlier and on which he had written my name. I thought about all the times I'd spent in this room, in this very spot, both good and bad. I saw the smiling faces of my teammates, heard their laughter, the jokes we all told, and realized only now that those things would never happen again. At least not here, because it was Senior Day — the end of it all.

I grabbed my helmet and stood. My knees felt wobbly as I walked out of the locker room, because I had thought of this day so many times in the past and it was turning out nothing like I had hoped.

My mother was supposed to be here. But

she wasn't.

I hoped I was doing the right thing by not talking to her, by avoiding her calls. *I told myself I was teaching her a lesson,* I thought as I stepped out of the tunnel and onto the field, *but the only person that was being punished was me.*

The stands were as full as I've ever seen them. The fans were all screaming at the top of their lungs, waving signs, dancing to "Money Maker" by Ludacris, which was banging out of the loudspeakers.

I tried to stop myself from looking up at my mother's seat, but I couldn't. She wasn't there, and that made me feel worse.

Coach gathered us all for pregame drills. We warmed up by doing jumping jacks, some stretches, some screen passes, and then it was time for the parents and seniors to meet in the middle of the field.

A line of senior players formed, waiting to greet our parents, receive a commemorative ball from Coach, and then have a picture taken.

I leaned a little out of line, like the rest of the players, to see Reggie, the linebacker, hugging his mother and taking a picture with Coach.

That wouldn't happen with me. My mother wouldn't be here, and only now could I admit to myself why. She had told me to stay away from Barrett, but I didn't listen. I got caught up in the love I thought I had for her, got turned out because she opened her legs for me and I couldn't handle it. Now my mother was missing one of the most important days of my life.

"I'm up next," Delmar said, nudging me with his elbow. "You know my pops will greet you when it's your turn."

"Yeah, I know, but I'm cool," I said.

"You know we family anyway. You're my brother."

"It's cool, Delmar, and that means the world to me," I said as I placed a hand on his shoulder pad. "Do your thang, fam."

He stepped onto the field, hugged his father, received the ball from Coach, and then I saw a tear come to his eyes. He was so happy, and his father looked so proud of him. They had talked about this day for a long time, just like me and my mother had.

I continued to watch, knowing I would soon be heading to the field, alone. I couldn't do it. My mother was supposed to be here with me. If it weren't for her, none of this would be happening.

As I walk from the sideline to the middle of the field to meet Coach Hale, my mind starts to torment me over the mess I've

made of my life. I looked up at the motion-
less clouds that dotted a steady blue sky and
it was so beautiful.

When I reached Coach Hale he was holding the football. He looked at me and asked,
"Brady, where is your mother?"

"It's a long story, Coach," I said sadly.

"Okay," Coach Hale said quietly. "Thanks
for four great years, son," he added as he
rubbed my shoulders gently and handed me
the commemorative football.

"No, thank *you,* Coach," I said, fighting
back tears.

When I left the field I found myself turning, and running as fast as I could back into
the locker room.

When I got there, I threw open my locker,
dug out my cell phone, and dialed my
mother's number. I got her voice mail on
every one of her numbers, but I left her a
message saying, "Ma, I'm sorry. I'm sorry
for how I treated you. If it's not too late, can
you come today?" Tears started down my
face. "It doesn't matter if you miss the game.
We can go to dinner after, have fun, do how
we always dreamed we were going to do on
this day. Please, Ma. Okay."

I hung up, knowing she wouldn't get the
message until it was too late, and that even if
she did, she wouldn't come because she was

disappointed with me. I felt like I didn't even want to play anymore.

I walked out onto the field with my head held low, toward the sidelines to get ready to meet Coach Hale.

I walked past people, not looking them in their faces, wondering what I would do after the game without my mother, when I heard someone say, "Brady."

When I spun around, I was shocked to see my mother, standing there, holding her arms out to me, tears in her eyes. I ran so fast to grab her that I almost knocked her down.

"I'm sorry, Ma," I said, crying. "For everything."

"Me, too, baby," she said as she tried to wipe the tears from my cheeks.

When we separated, I noticed a man standing beside her, smiling, staring at me.

I looked back at him and there was a familiarity about his face.

"Brady," my mother said. "This is someone I think you should know."

Then my mother started crying uncontrollably and I tried to console her.

The man came closer, extended his hand, and said, "Brady. My name is Woodson. I'm your father."

I felt my knees buckle, and it took all of my power to remain standing.

"What?" I asked as I looked at him and then back at my mother. She wiped her tearstained face and shook her head in affirmation.

Just as I was going to ask them both if this was true, Coach Hale barked out my name, "Bledsoe, git your ass in my office now."

I looked at my mother, shook my head, and darted toward the athletic complex.

I walked toward the coaches' office carrying my helmet, wondering what could be so important that Coach needed to speak to me now. Kickoff was less than fifteen minutes away. I knocked on his door and heard him tell me to come in. When I walked in, I discovered why he couldn't wait. Sitting in a chair across from Coach was Nico, grinning arrogantly.

"Brady, have a seat. This man tells me he has some information about you that would make me keep you out of the final games. Is that true?"

"Yeah, Brady, tell him what we've been up to," Nico said. He opened up a leather binder, pulled out some papers, and put them on Coach's desk. Suddenly, his phone rang. Nico looked down at his cell and said, "I need to take this."

"We don't have much time, Mr. Benson. If

you've got something I need to know, then put up or shut up," Coach said.

"What do you want, bitch?" Nico shouted into his phone. "I'm conducting business." Nico's eyes suddenly grew larger and he continued his shouting. "What kind of book? Don't threaten me, Raquel. You know I can have you silenced forever. And what do you know about Basil Henderson, and what does he have to do with me? Hey, let's deal with this now. Where are you? Raquel!"

Coach and I exchanged glances like we were dealing with a man straight wildin'. Nico slammed his phone shut, grabbed his papers and binders, and just as he bolted from his chair another man, dressed in a nice suit, walked into the office.

"Sorry to bother you, Coach Hale, but I heard there might be a little trouble here."

Coach Hale got up and extended his hands. "Basil, good to see you. Where did you hear that from?"

"Motherfucker, what are you doing here?" Nico asked.

"Looking out for a young man who you're trying to screw over," Basil said.

"You got me confused with yourself. You're the one who likes to screw over, or shall I say *screw*, young dudes. Does the good coach know that?"

"Dude, move on and get out of my face. I think you need to be getting ready for your meeting with the Securities Exchange Commission to explain all the fake stocks you sold your clients," Basil Henderson said.

Then he walked over to me and said, "Brady Bledsoe, it's so nice to meet you. I wish it would have been under better circumstances. Your mother is a lovely woman who loves you a lot."

"Yes, sir, I know that. Thank you," I said.

"Coach, I just want you to know that your top player here has become the victim of this slime who passes himself off as an agent. But he's just a crook, and in a few days the entire sports world will know," Basil said.

"So it's safe for me to play Brady today?" Coach Hale said.

"Without a doubt," Basil said.

Coach looked at me, smiled, and said, "You hear that, Bledsoe? All we have to do now is kick some Yellowjacket ass!"

"Then let's do it," I said as my coach and I trotted out of the office and down to the field.

For me, the game was filled with firsts and finales. It was the first game I rushed for over

300 yards. I shredded the Georgia Tech defense for 322 of them, not only a school record but an SEC mark as well. I felt elevated by the crowd, and as I ran, I felt as though my feet never touched the ground. We crushed the Yellowjacks by a score of 28–7.

When I closed my locker, I knew it was for the final time and was painfully aware that some freshman would be calling the locker his next season. It would be the first and last game my father would see me play at Jaguar stadium. But we still had a game in Nashville and now a bowl game in Dallas, and I hoped he would come.

I walked out of the dressing room into a throng of well-wishers and autograph-seeking fans. When I spotted my mother, she was surrounded by three men. There was Lowell, my father, and a man I'd never seen. I walked over and hugged my mom and Lowell.

"I'm so proud of you, Brady, and I love you," my mother whispered.

"I love you back," I said.

"Great game," Lowell said. "What a way to go out in Jaguar Stadium."

"Thank you," I said.

"Brady, this is Mr. Sylvester Monroe," Lowell said.

"Nice meeting you, Brady."

"You, as well," I said as I eyed Woodson, looking at me with what seemed to be pride.

The five of us made small talk while I signed a few more autographs. Finally, Woodson came closer and put his arms around my shoulders. It felt like the most natural thing in the world.

"I asked your mother if it would be okay if the two of us went somewhere to grab a bite to eat. Would that be okay with you?"

I looked at him and studied his face, his eyes, his nose and lips. There was no denying how much they looked like my own. The day I had prayed for had finally come.

"Yeah, that's whatsup," I said.

"Great. We have a lot to catch up on," he said.

As we walked away, I looked back at my mother and the men who surrounded her. Both Lowell and Mr. Monroe had their arms on her shoulders, and she held her hand over her mouth. She was crying, but she looked like I felt. Happy.

As I began my first walk with my father, I realized that magic happens so few times in life. As we reached my truck, I thought of the joy I felt when my mom had surprised me with the Navigator at the beginning of the season. Now she had gone out and given me the gift I'd always thought inconceivable. I guess when magic happens, dreams that once seemed impossible really can come true.

CHAPTER 47
THE JOCK WHISPERER

Dear Diary;

Guess what? I'm about to become famous. I'm writing a book about my dealings with Nico and the famous and not-so-famous athletes I've dealt with over the last ten years. A publisher who read about me in the *Atlanta Journal-Constitution* contacted me and then offered me a whole lot of money to tell my story. When I showed them all the entries I'd been writing, well, they increased the offer substantially. I got me an agent and a publicist, and I'm going to talk like a parrot.

I'm going to call my book *The Playbook: The Secret Diaries of a Jock Whisperer*, and I think it's going to make me rich. Finally I will be calling the shots and making enough money to take care of Wade and live the life I've become accustomed to.

I guess I owe a lot to Mr. Phine-Ass John Basil Henderson. He told me about all the women and young men Nico had used. He convinced me to go to the authorities before Nico double-crossed me and I wound up in jail like some of the other women who had loved Nico and fallen prey to his schemes. He told me he knew a lawyer who could help me if I decided to go against Nico.

One of the first things I'm going to do is change my name back to Raquel, because it was the one thing Lita gave me that I liked. I think I'm going to move to Miami and maybe buy me a condo on the beach. It will be nice to be close to water, and I think that will be good for Wade. I guess Lita will keep her ass in New Orleans, but really that's not my concern. She's like a roach; nothing will kill her.

Brady came in third for the Heisman Trophy, and I even watched it on television. Some guy named Troy Smith from Ohio State won (I'm glad Nico didn't send me to lovely Columbus, Ohio). The guy he wanted me to go after next, Darren McFadden of Arkansas, came in second.

Brady's mom, who I still think is a bitch, was all smiles (but she was fly and looked good on television), and when they told the story in an interview about Brady finally meeting his father . . . well, it brought tears to my eyes. I've given up hope of ever meeting my father, since I've finally accepted the fact that he was just some trick my mother met on a day she forgot her birth control.

Brady looked handsome in a black suit, and when he spoke you could tell he wasn't your ordinary jock. He was articulate and confident. He was humble, yet strong. He gave his mother all the credit for bringing him up right and said he looked forward to forming a relationship with his father after his Cotton Bowl game. Maybe if I were closer to his age I could have found true love. But I know true love is not promised to all — only a select few. His father is handsome, and I'm sure if they'd met even before I told Brady he was alive they would have still realized the connection. They look so much alike. I'm happy for Brady and hope that he'll find a girl worthy of him.

I'm cooperating with the government and the Securities Exchange about Nico's shady business deals and what he did with a lot of the money he stole from athletes. I told them about all the accounts he had in different names at banks here and abroad. His lawyer tried to threaten me by telling me all the money Nico had given me was income and therefore taxable, but my lawyer said that's not true. What Nico gave me was a gift because I was his girlfriend, and I didn't have to claim it. But that old low-down Nico said I was an employee and that I was never his girlfriend. I know better and so does he. So I guess we will let a judge decide. I'm just glad that I stashed away some money for days like this.

Poor Nico. I heard his wife left him and is getting more than half of his money (I guess his team of lawyers will use the other half to keep his ass out of jail), which is estimated at almost seventy-five million dollars. She is one lucky bitch, but I think if I tell everything I know and go on a book tour, I will sell as many books and maybe more than that Video Vixen girl, who by the way I really like. I think she's very pretty and smart. Maybe one day I can meet her and we can swap stories about how we used our female powers for good.

Well, Diary, I don't know how much I'll get to write to you anymore, since I'll be writing this book, but I'll visit you often and think of the comfort you've brought me so many nights. At first I thought keeping a diary was silly, but I've learned that you were the only one I could trust, so I'll miss you. But I'll put you in a safe place just in case I need you, if only to see how far I've come.

CHAPTER 48
MESSAGE TO MAMA

Spartanburg, SC
August 9, 2007

Dear Mom:

Since PCs are banned the first couple of days of training camp I thought you'd like a real letter better. When was the last time I've handwritten you a letter? Was it in the third grade when you told me to write you and tell you what I wanted for Christmas? That was the year you told me there wasn't a Santa Claus. What did I ask for? Most likely what I asked for every year: a daddy and a dog.

That's why I'm writing you, because I now have them both and I have you to thank for that. I want to thank you for being the most wonderful mother any son could ask for. One of the things I've learned during my two years of playing professional football from some of my new teammates is how good I had it, even though I spent

503

most of my life with one parent. I share that with a lot of my teammates. But what makes me different and so blessed is that I had you, a woman who was willing to give up her entire life to love and protect me. I thank you for that.

Although my experience with Barrett damaged me for a while, recently I have been on some dates with some pretty nice young ladies. Because of you, Mom, I still have a heart that is willing to hold love. I'm just a little careful about which girl is worthy of meeting my mom and dad.

When I think how you went against your own parents demands, my body shudders at what you gave up for me. How difficult that must have been for you. That's real love, Mom. And even though you say your parents are old-school black people and will never budge on their stubbornness, I still hold out hope that one day I can meet them. And that we can complete our family. You deserve to be loved and cherised by them and I will keep praying the prayer of forgiveness will come to us all.

How are Shelby and her beautiful baby, Rhianna? Has she heard from Torrian or is he still refusing to pay child support? I'm so happy the NCAA allowed me to donate the money Nico put into my account to

Brandon's Room to help young ladies like Shelby. I just don't get dudes like Torrian.

Almost every day there is a new teammate getting served with child support or divorce papers. My generation of men take having babies so lightly, and that disappoints me. They talk about it in terms of how much the new baby is going to cost them and how the numbers of their babies' mamas have increased. But that's not why I'm writing. I decided I wanted to write you because I want to thank you for my gift. I love Saban, he is the perfect dog, and he protects me like you have all of my life.

I just got off the phone with Woodson, and although the first year of our relationship was challenging, I think every time we see each other and speak to each other we become more like father and son. We are so much alike in the way we look and feel about the world. We spent an entire night talking about the plight of black men and how recent incidents involving wealthy black men show us how quickly it can all be taken away. Can you believe all the trouble Michael Vick got himself into? Mom, that was my dude, and I always admired his skills on the field. I sure hope he can redeem himself and do something positive with his life. I know it would have

been tough, but I wish the Texans would have drafted me and I could see my dad and new sisters more. Still, I love being a Carolina Panther and it keeps me close to home and you. I guess what I'm trying to say you already know, but it bears repeating. I love you and I thank you for loving me. Thank you for setting the bar for my life so high. I'm sorry that there was ever a day when I doubted your love and knowing what's best for me. I always thought you wanted me to be perfect, and that was very tough to live up to. Nobody is perfect. Thanks for teaching me that one bad decision doesn't have to ruin a life well lived. That the honor comes not from living a perfect life but from living a good life, imperfections and all. I love you and I can't wait to escort you down the aisle as you start another chapter in your life with your soul mate Sylvester. I know you two will continue to make each other happy.
Your Not So Perfect Son,

Brady Jamal Bledsoe
All-Pro Running Back for the Carolina
Panthers

ABOUT THE AUTHOR

E. Lynn Harris is a nine-time *New York Times* bestselling author. His work includes the memoir, *What Becomes of the Broken-hearted,* and the novels *I Say a Little Prayer, A Love of My Own, Just as I Am, Any Way the Wind Blows, If This World Were Mine,* and the classic *Invisible Life.* Harris divides his time between Atlanta, Georgia, and Fayetteville, Arkansas, home of his beloved college football team The Razorbacks.

The employees of Thorndike Press hope you have enjoyed this Large Print book. All our Thorndike and Wheeler Large Print titles are designed for easy reading, and all our books are made to last. Other Thorndike Press Large Print books are available at your library, through selected bookstores, or directly from us.

For information about titles, please call:

(800) 223-1244

or visit our Web site at:

http://gale.cengage.com/thorndike

To share your comments, please write:

Publisher
Thorndike Press
295 Kennedy Memorial Drive
Waterville, ME 04901